The Girl Who Rode Dragons

Arthur Butt

Cover Art:
Michelle Crocker
http://mlcdesigns4you.weebly.com/

Publisher's Note:
This is a work of fiction. All names, characters, places, and
events are the work of the author's imagination.
Any resemblance to real persons, places, or events is
coincidental.

Solstice Publishing - www.solsticepublishing.com

The Girl Who Rode Dragons
Arthur Butt

Dedication
As always to Susie, my loving wife.

Chapter One

"**T**his is stupid."

The town common was packed with people, peasants from the outlying farms, merchants, and the lesser gentry, all scrambled their way for seats on the temporary bleachers set up to watch the choosing of the next dragonrider.

Jackie's sister called over her shoulder, "Nonsense, this is exciting." Her eyes shone as she picked out friends from the crowd and waved her handkerchief over her head in way of greeting. "How often is one of our own from this village selected to be a dragonrider?"

"One of four," retorted Jackie. The crowd was too noisy and she had work to do at home: collect wood for the fire, laundry she hadn't touched in a month, and start working on supper if they were to eat tonight. She groaned to herself, thinking of hauling all the clothes to the creek and wasting hours with a washing bat. Nevertheless, since Victor released all the help, the chores wouldn't get done by themselves. "And he hasn't been selected yet. He's being *presented.* Odds are the dragonet will choose a different candidate."

Victoria ignored Jackie's comment and pushed past a fat man standing in their way. "Now come along you two," she chirped. "Jackie, Thomas, let's find seats before they are all taken. It is too hot to be standing."

"You heard her, shorty." Jackie tugged on her brother's arm, drawing him behind. "Let's go."

By luck, they found three seats situated directly before the platform where four young men and a large purple egg waited. The men were between the ages of fifteen and eighteen, the egg already showing faint cracks in the middle.

Victoria angled her parasol to block out the sun's

rays, and they made themselves as comfortable as possible on the hard benches. Jackie repeated, "This is stupid. Why don't they pick a girl to be a rider?"

A deep frown showed beneath the veil over Victoria's face, and she said in a low voice, "We have been through this a hundred times. Girls cannot ride dragons. Dragons are all male. I thought you understood this."

Jackie gritted her teeth, the muscles in her shoulders tensing. Why was her sister so stupid? Victoria possessed more school learning than Jackie, more than she'd ever have now their parents were dead. How could Victoria say…? "The reason dragons are male is because they have men riders," Jackie blurted out in frustration trying to catch her sister's eye. "If a girl rode one, they'd be female." She added in defiance trying to remind Victoria she'd received instructions on the beasts too from the nuns and wasn't addled, "I learned it in school."

Victoria sighed, obviously tiring of the conversation. "If we kept you with the nuns for lessons, you would have learned this practice was stopped ages ago. Too much chance of the males breaking into fights over the females." She sat straight and faced forward. "Now hush, they are about to start the choosing."

The four candidates, one from their town of Northwood, and the other three from the surrounding domain of the barony, shuffled their feet nervously, refusing to look at the crowd. Instead, they shot weak glances at their fellow contenders, smirking, and mumbling small talk while they waited for the egg to hatch.

The egg swayed and larger cracks appeared on the surface.

Thomas bounced out of his seat and shouted, *"I see the dragon."* The rest of the people stood also, all trying to have a good view at the newest protector of the land.

Jackie didn't bother to look. What was the point? She was too short to see over the heads of the people in front of her. If she possessed a chance to one day be picked—or at least, one of the girls she knew, it would be different. She'd dreamed all her life of flying high in the sky above the clouds, soaring as if she were a bird, admired and respected by the whole kingdom. Jackie pushed the thought aside. *Let's finish this farce. I have work to do.*

"Ohhh."

The dragonet stood upright, bits of its casing scattering on the floor as it fluttered its wings trying to dry itself.

As if on cue, the four boys hunched forward, surrounding the creature, none of the candidates ever having seen a dragon this close before. Half-frightened glances shot between the youngsters, and the remarks of the candidates were drowned out by the babbling of the crowd.

The small white dragon shook off the rest of its shell, and emerged, taking a tentative step forward and tripping over the remains of its former egg. The beast righted itself, swinging the big head in a slow circle studying the new surroundings.

The four young men stepped back in awe, not sure what to expect, although each received instructions from a seasoned dragonrider beforehand in the hatching ceremony of the dragon. The wet skin of the small beast quickly dried, leathery wings fluttered again to their full extent, as the baby stretched and took a hesitant flap. The white skin at birth darkened in the sunlight to a greenish brown.

Once in command of its balance, the baby dragon switched it attention to the four who surrounded it, as if trying to determine which would be best suited to its needs. With a squawk and a flap of wings, the mind decided. The beast unerringly stalked to the legs of a candidate from Weatherhill, Jeffery the Marquis son, and bumped against him affectionately, staring upward with beady red eyes into the young man's face.

Thomas was up on the bench, jumping up and down to see. "Who's that?" he shouted in excitement to Victoria as a tall young man tossed a bloody hunk of meat to Jeffery.

"He is the senior rider," Victoria whispered, *"Johnathan."*

"Why'd he give him the meat?" Thomas asked still leaping to see better.

Victoria smiled. "Watch."

Jeffery bent over and fed the dragonet the meat. The small creature fell on the food and devoured the morsel. When finished, it glared up, waiting for more.

All Thomas said was, "Wow."

A sigh rose from the crowd with "Ohhhs" and "Awwws." Behind Jackie a few grumbles circulated because the town's candidate wasn't chosen, and on the outskirts of the square, fights broke out, as the winners of bets made their way to collects from losers. The baron's soldiers moved in before riots began.

"Are we all finished now?" Jackie snapped. She rose and dusted off the back of her tunic. "I still have wood to gather in the forest today if we're to cook and have a fire for tonight."

"Aren't you going to say hello to Fredrick," Victoria said in surprise, standing also. "I know he was not picked, but still..." She smirked at her sister, "he might make a good husband one day. Even being elected as a candidate is a great honor, you realize."

Jackie herded Thomas down along the bleachers, eager to find herself out of the mob. "Why, because he has a title?" she yelled over her shoulder to make herself hear above the noise of the crowd. "That's another thing, how come only the sons of the nobles are elected to be candidates? When was the last time a commoner was picked?"

Victoria scooted behind Jackie. "Why, it is not the case at all," she said. "There are many commoner dragonriders, maybe not lately, but in the past. Every time multiple clutches are discovered they select from the lower classes for candidates." She added smugly, "Of course the sons of nobility are always proposed though, breeding will tell, you know."

"Oh, like Victor?" Jackie replied. "By the way, where is your precious husband? Still at the tavern, I suppose? I thought he was going to meet us here. The way he talked last night I figured he would be on the platform coaching those boys."

Victoria watched her feet as she stepped off the bleachers onto the ground, her face flushing pink. She swung her parasol over her other shoulder and stammered, "He—he must have been delayed with business. You know since mother and father died he has –"

"...has to drink up all the money our parents left us?" Jackie finished sweetly, arms on hips with a shake of her head.

Those passing closest to the two sisters paused to listen. Jackie caught the baker John bending over behind her to hear better what they argued about. "Let's go Thomas." She nodded politely to the guild member and nudged her brother toward the row of carriages lined up along the lane leading out into the country. "It's time we were driving home."

The crowd dispensed, some to congratulate the new rider and to give unwanted advice, or to console the ones not chosen. The rest of the people hurried back to their shops or homes in small groups, still babbling about the dragonet and the new rider. Thomas scampered to the carriage and scrambled into the driver's seat, Victoria climbed into the back seat. Jackie assumed the driver's position, grabbed the reins, and gave them a snap.

From across the common Jackie heard her name called. Her former classmates were shepherded back to their schoolroom by the nuns. Her friends, Utta and Ebba, stood on their toes, waved. Utta cupped her hand and whispered into Ebba's ear, shooting a glance at Jackie and giggling when Jackie refused to wave back. The two girls swung around and hurried after their group. *Oh, this is marvelous. They'll spread the news I'm driving the carriage now, besides not going to classes.* Jackie squeezed the reins of the horses until her knuckles turned white and guided the carriage down the dirt road towards home.

Halfway along the road, Thomas hopped out of the carriage and ran up the lane, throwing rocks at the birds and scuffling up clouds of dust from the road. Jackie called, "Don't get your tunic all dirty." She smirked as the boy disappeared around a curve. *He will. Something else for me to clean. Better start soaking some wood ash from the fireplace in water. I'm going to need it.*

Jackie took a quick check of the sun. *Already too late to start washing. Better head straight out into the forest. I wonder how much wood I can collect before Victor returns home?* She could hear her brother-in-law complaining to no end if sufficient fuel wasn't available for his bedroom chamber tonight and tomorrow morning, let alone the snide remarks about girls who lounged around all day when they should be keeping busy.

The neighbor's carriages passed them by hurrying to the farther fiefs. Victoria waved to each with a cheery greeting, fanning herself because of the late morning heat. Jackie hunkered down in her seat and kept watching straight ahead, lost in her own thoughts.

After they reached home, Jackie unhitched the horses, hurried upstairs to change out of her good tunic, and into her ripped every day work clothes. She ran down the stairs taking two at a time and slammed out the kitchen door, passing her sister and brother as they sat at the table. As she headed to the rear of the carriage house, Victoria called out from the open doorway, "Don't be late Jaqueline, I am going to prepare supper for tonight since I've kept you out so long." The door slammed shut and she disappeared into the house.

Jackie yelled back, "I'll try not to, but don't go messing around in the kitchen without me." She hurried to fetch her cart, smirking to herself. Victoria wasn't the best of cooks and it was never a good idea to leave her alone in the kitchen. Jackie did the cooking for the family, and even when she didn't, she might as well have since it was necessary to watch her sister at all times. She wondered what Victoria would try to fix tonight. Burnt beef? Burnt fowl? Or a hastily prepared roast burnt of something else.

They should have kept Nanna cook. If Victor didn't waste so much money. He didn't mind keeping up appearances on the outside, no. The house was newly painted, bushes trimmed, garden weeded. Most of the work he could have done himself if he wasn't at the tavern all the time gossiping or gambling with is cronies. Why her parents ever agreed to let Victoria marry the lazy bum— must have been the family name. The La Montrues' were an old and distinguished line, long on heritage and title, short on gold. Jackie was sure her father thought he could make something out of Victor given the opportunity. Too bad he didn't have the chance.

By the time Jackie entered the rear of the carriage house, tears of frustration dripped down her cheeks, thinking of the injustice the last few years handed her. Victor refused to let her continue in school, according to him because, "The girl is fifteen and will be married and gone soon enough. Why waste good money on teaching her things she will never use? If her husband wants her educated, let him pay for it." Victor dismissed Nanna cook and the rest of the staff for the same reason. "The girl," *yes, the girl,* Jackie thought bitterly, "has nothing else to do. She might as well learn housework and cooking." He beamed at her as if he were doing a great service. "It will stand you in good stead, when you supervise your own people."

Yes, Sir sleep all day. What will you do when "The Girl" is gone? Who'll scrub the floor, clean the ashes out of the fireplaces, and do the wash? You? Ha.

Jackie hauled her cart out of the rear of the carriage house and delivered a good kick to the wheel. Even this—collecting firewood. She imitated Victor's deep baritone, "Why waste good money buying kindling when there is a whole forest to gather it in." She savagely grabbed the handles of the wagon, noticed with anger Victor stored more junk in piles around the walls, in her opinion garbage needing discarding, which he'd bought planning to make *art* out of. *More wasted money.*

She trudged off into the baron's woods.

The dividing line between their land and the baron's fief was Baldhill. Bald because logging denuded the top and sides, and mining destroyed the rest of the vegetation. In Jackie's mind, it acted as a clear reminder of the baron's law.

The pickings were slim in the forest as usual. If you were lucky enough to buy a permit you could cut a tree, if not, it was collect what you discovered on the ground. This was how those too poor to buy wood did it.

Slowly she collected sticks, and to her great delight, discovered a whole branch the other scavengers missed who'd swept the place clean during the early morning hours.

Past Baldhill, Jackie hit the stream separating the

baron's forest from the king's land and made a sharp right, hunting along the bank, hoping some wood drifted from the far bank onto the baron's side. She yanked out a few waterlogged branches lodged in the weeds and hurled the sticks into her cart, standing with a grimace, gazing across the swift running water. Underbrush and logs abounded, taunting her with their nearness, and yet out of reach according to the king's law. *"Ten minutes in there,"* she murmured longingly, *"and I'd be finished for the day."*

To enter the sovereign's domain without his permission was death, or worse than death from the rumors circulating around the village. If a forester caught you....

Jackie peered around. She hadn't seen anyone all morning, everyone who had the time went to the choosing. Those who didn't were already here and gone. Maybe the foresters, too? It must be close to noon. She tapped on her teeth, undecided what to do.

No, she decided. Better to leave adventures for a different time. Her cart was full anyway.

The sun was high in the sky when she arrived home and unloaded her haul outside the kitchen door. She made out the deep rumblings of Victor's voice. *Oh, great, now I have to put up with him.* Her clothes were filthy dirty, mud covered her hands and face, and her short brown hair knitted in tangles. She sighed and scrubbed at her cheek leaving a long black smudge. *If he starts in on me, I'll....*

Jackie blew a long blast from her nostrils, returned the cart to the carriage house, and stomped to the horse troth to scrub up. A quick raking of her hair with her fingers removed most of the twigs and leaves.

Okay, let's do this. Grimly Jackie squared her shoulders and marched toward the kitchen. She threw open the door, planning to sneak in as quietly as possible and make it to her bedroom to change.

"...but this property has been in our family for

generations," whined Victoria, wringing her hands in distress. "It was the first piece of land my grandfather bought. I do not see the need...."

"Oh, tosh, my dear." Victor wandered aimlessly around the kitchen, picking up plates and utensils, examining the workmanship, and placing each down again in its wrong spot. He swayed slightly. "It's ten acres. The plot has lain fallow since we have been married, you know. Never been worked, never been used, and we'll never miss it. Besides, I was offered a good price."

His wife put her hand to her mouth, stricken with indecision. Worry crossed her face as she tried to decide what to do. She swung from the fireplace where a leg of mutton roasted and said, "But the land. Father said never to sell...."

"Different times, my dear." Victor spied Jackie tiptoeing along the wall trying to make her way to the hallway stairs. "So, there you are, girl," he exclaimed, changing the subject. "How was your morning jaunt?" He smirked sourly. "Because of your tardiness, your poor sister has to cook dinner. This is your job, you know."

"I...she said," Jackie stammered, not sure if Victoria informed her husband she'd volunteered to cook tonight.

"Victor, I offered to make supper for Jaqueline," Victoria hurriedly explained, rising and placing a hand on her husband's chest. "I took the children to the choosing to see who would be our next dragonrider and we ran late. It is really no trouble. You know how much I enjoy cooking." Her lips twitched up and she said, "I remember the first time I saw you when you stood there, tall and proud, handsome too in your tunic. I knew right there, no matter if you were chosen or not, you were the one I wanted to spend the rest of my days with."

Jackie was aware Victoria really loved Victor, but

still…. A nameless rage built up inside her. *And I remember Father throwing up his hands in horror when you mentioned his name. But he caved in didn't he? He never would deny us anything, and he always found a way to provide. Wish I were more like him.*

Victor preened, mollified, but groused, "I was a handsome devil, still am, but I should have been picked, you know. It is all politics anyway."

Jackie seized the opportunity while her brother-in-law was reembracing and started cautiously backing out of the room. From the corner of her eye, she saw black smoke bellowing from the fireplace accompanied by tongues of fire. *"Victoria—your lamb."*

Victor and Victoria whirled around gasping as the flames leaped out of the fireplace, the acid smell of burning meat filling the air in waves of black smoke. Jackie snatched a pitcher of water off the table and dashed it on the fire. When this didn't stop the carnage, in fact, spreading the flames over the floor, she dumped a pail of sand on the blaze she kept for emergencies such as this.

"My roast—my beautiful roast," wailed Victoria, her mouth wide in horror. She pointed a shaking finger at the burnt lamb and whimpered, "What happened?"

Jackie stepped carefully over the mess and studied the fireplace. The drip pan was nowhere in sight. *Typical.* She knew better than to say anything, though, Victoria would never forgive herself and Jackie would hear her remonstrating in woeful tones for the next month. She played dumb, shrugged her shoulders, and tried to appear as stupid as possible. "I don't know."

Victoria continued to sob, tears streaming down her face and dripping off her nose. "I—I—wanted this to be a special dinner for the selection. No—now I have ruined it."

Her husband took her in his arms and pattered her

on the back, making soothing sounds of reassurance. "There, there, it's all right," he cooed. "This was not your fault. You should not have been cooking in the first place." He scowled at Jackie over Victoria's shoulder. "If someone wasn't frolicking in the woods all day and frittering away their time, and kept her mind on her *responsibilities,* they would have done their own job and not leave it up to everyone else."

Jackie's face tightened as her teeth ground in bitter rage. She forced herself to remain calm although her body trembled.

Victoria read the expression on her sister's face. Before Jackie exploded she said, "What is done, is done." She broke away for Victor and took a step toward the stillroom. "I will fetch a mop and clean this mess up." She smirked weakly at Victor and Jackie. "Cold supper I am afraid."

"Nonsense," Victor exclaimed. He put his hand up for Victoria to stop. "It is still early. We'll send the girl into town." He nodded to his wife and smiled. "The tavern makes a wonderful lamb and she can straighten out this kitchen when she returns, after all, she is the one who caused all the havoc." He shoved a finger at Jackie.

Jackie felt herself shrinking. *Of course, I'm the bad one. Always the bad one.*

"Make sure the cook sends along roasted potatoes, too." Victor smacked his lips. "I love their potatoes, crisp on the outside, soft inside, with gravy. Do not let him forget the gravy either." He nodded to himself. "Tell the tavern keeper to place it on my tab. I will be down later to settle up." He addressed Victoria in a hearty voice, "While we wait, my dear, let us move into the parlor. I had the bill of sale for the property all drawn up today. All you have to do is sign." Without glancing back, he maneuvered Victoria out of the kitchen.

Jackie stood rooted to the kitchen floor, mouth open in disbelief, not knowing if she should laugh or cry. Finally, she shook her head. "I wonder if the king has a position open for a whipping boy?" she muttered as she surveyed the mess on the hearth, found a basket large enough hold a leg of lamb and sides, and set off to the stable to saddle a horse.

If her parents hadn't died in the attack of the Easmen. They should've stayed at the manor house instead of deciding to take a quick trip to the coast. And then....

Her mother died there. They brought her body back in a wagon for burial. Her father lingered for a while before he too....Jackie choked at the memory of her father's last dying days, how she huddled by his side, night after night, trying to feed him soup because he was too weak to chew.

As she rode down the lane, she wondered if Victoria would consent to selling the land. Jackie hoped not. Most of their serfs ran away already, vanished to far distant fiefs if the lords would take them in, because of Victor's caustic remarks and his poor stewardship. The fief barely supported the family now. Once the land was gone, they'd have nothing.

When she reached town, the workday had ended, people bustled along the street, hurrying home. Jackie nodded to a few, older men and women whom her parents knew. Up ahead, walking out of the baker's shop, Ebba and Utta emerged carrying baskets over their arms talking animatedly to each other. Jackie slowed to a stop, eyeing the opposite side of the street, wondering if she could make it there and remain unnoticed.

"Jaqueline." One of the girls, a tall brunette, shouted her name and waved. Jackie painted a smirk on her face and rode over.

"Hi, Utta." She nodded to the shorter girl. "Ebba.

I'm so happy to see you. I've missed talking to you both." She took a quick peek at their baskets. "Buying bread?" She laughed as if she'd made a silly statement, glancing at the baker's shop. "Of course you have, why else would you be here." Jackie held up her own basket. "Well, I have to run—Victor wants lamb from the tavern." She tried to ride off.

Utta wouldn't let her go easily. "I heard he spends a great deal of time in the tavern, almost a home away from home." She winked at Ebba. "It is a *shame* he made you quit school. We miss you. Classes are not the same without your smiling face." She said to Ebba, "Isn't it true?"

The girl bobbed her head up and down in assent. "Oh, yes. We talk about you all the time. Even the nuns say how much they miss you." Ebba scanned Jackie's miserable appearance with her ripped, muddy tunic. "Why your sister's husband treats you no better than one of the peasants." She sighed and rolled her eyes, nudging Utta with her elbow. "Does he make you sleep with the pigs?" The girl sniffed cautiously. "You smell piggish." Both girls laughed.

Jackie's face burnt crimson. She glared at Ebba's ample middle and remarked, "Of course not. We always let the *porkers* sleep by themselves." She dug her heels into the horse's sides and walked off.

The tavern was not crowded. Jackie hesitated at the door, debating in her mind if she should go in the front, or walk around back and make her presences know to the cooks. She'd never been inside and decided the best thing to do was walk in, go straight to the tavern owner behind the crude bar and tell him what she wanted. *It won't be that bad. Victor comes in here all the time.*

She pushed the door open and marched in.

The interior was dark. A few men sat around a table playing cards. To her surprise, three women lounged

14

against one wall, drinking. She smiled shyly and walked to the rough-hewed bar, where a man stood watching her with interest.

"Ah, I'm Victor La Montrue's sister-in-law," she mumbled. "He sent me here for a leg of lamb." She placed her basket on the bar.

"Oh, you belong to Victor, do you?" The barkeeper nodded. "Yer in luck, got some coming out of the oven now. Be a few minutes."

Jackie breathed a sigh of relief. This was going easier than she thought. "I'll wait," she replied, looking around for a chair. "Oh, He said he wanted your roasted potatoes too."

The barkeeper nodded. "Know exactly what he wants." He scooped up her basket and disappeared into the kitchen.

"And he said to put it on his account," Jackie yelled after him. "He'll be down later to settle up."

"Hey, Missy, haven't seen you down here 'afor,'" one of the men playing cards called out. He raised a pewter tankard. "C'mon over. We'll have some fun while yer waiting."

The women drinking laughed along with the men as Jackie's face flushed pink. "Uh, no thank you," she replied, turning her back to the men. *Where is that lamb?*

The bartender returned lugging her basket. In a quick motion he took in Jackie's flushed appearance and the guffaws of the patrons. He handed the basket to Jackie and whispered, "Next time go around back and see my wife. She makes the ale and does the cooking." He winked at her.

"Thank you," Jackie breathed, grabbing her basket and hurrying out the door to the catcalls of the patrons.

Jackie leaped back on her horse, not bothering to look around. She spun her mount and saw Utta and Ebba waiting for her. "Out of my *way.*" The humiliations of the day had grown too much to accept with a foolish grin, and she wasn't about to take anymore, not from these two.

Utta ran into the street and blocked her path. "You know *Jaqueline,* with your attitude you will never find a husband," she snapped, her face wrinkling up into a snarl. "Not in this town, or any other I suspect. You should learn to be friendlier."

The statement was so ridiculous Jackie burst out in guffaws. She couldn't help herself, the mirth bubbled over, and she let it out in a loud hoot, which rolled down the street and bounced off the buildings. People on the street near the three girls halted and stared at Jackie as if she were crazy. "If the best these villages have to offer are those *boys* I saw today at the choosing, then I want none of them." She yanked savagely on the reins of her horse, causing Utta to leap out of the way or have her feet trampled. She called over her shoulder, "I hear you're friendly with everyone, Utta. You too, Ebba. Very friendly. As for me, I would prefer marrying a pig—at least they have some use—YOU CAN EAT SWINE."

Chapter Two

T he next morning Jackie rose before the sun, did her chores, finished her baking for the day, cooked breakfast, and prepared to leave to gather her firewood before she started in on the laundry. Victoria and Thomas walked downstairs.

"Food's on the table," Jackie called out from the kitchen door. "Be back in a while."

"Victoria," Thomas pleaded, "may I collect wood with Jackie? Please? I don't want to go to school today. It's too nice out." He blinked up at her without much hope.

Victoria chuckled indulgently, but shook her head. "What would I tell the nice friars at school, if you didn't show up? Wood is more important than a good education, or it is too nice for learning?" She ruffled the boy's sandy brown hair and as quickly smoothed it back in place again. "No. It is off to school you go. Jackie has her work to do and so do you."

Jackie hung on the kitchen door impatiently waiting and said to Victoria, "I may be later than usual. Wood is becoming harder to obtain every day." When her sister's eyes widened in alarm, she added, "But I'll be back in plenty of time to fix dinner. Stay away from the fireplace." She asked, although she knew the answer, "Is Victor still sleeping?"

Victoria relaxed. "Yes. He was up late last night. People came over—business, you know, and they stayed to the early morning, talking."

And drinking all the wine in the cellar. She left to fetch her cart. *There goes the land. Why does Victoria let him talk her into these things? Our parents left the fief to us, not this freeloader to fritter away a piece at a time as he pleases.*

A thunderstorm blew through the night before. A

misty white fog covered the earth. Jackie struggled to drag her cart through the muddy ruts, uttering an oath she'd heard Victor use once in a fit of anger. She entered the woods; pale wisps of cold vapor swirled around her feet as if she walked on clouds. She surveyed the scene surrounding her in disgust. "How am I going to find anything in this mess," she muttered, kicking at the musty forest loom and sending up a pile of leaves. She booted a second one and unearthed a moldy branch, so old it fell in half when she picked it up. She threw both pieces into her cart half-heartedly and trudged deeper into the forest.

Is this what it feels to be a dragonrider, she wondered as she plodded through the haze. *People say clouds are nothing more than fog floating in the sky.*

Jackie stopped and stuck her arms out like wings. Her eyes half-closed, as she tried to imagine herself flying on the back of one of the beasts, wet murkiness all around surrounding her. The dragon soared higher, Jackie squinted in her mind, and the whiteness melted away, revealing a sapphire blue sky above her head.

Jackie shook herself out of her reverie and surveyed the scene around her in dismay. *I'm being ridiculous. A stupid, silly girl who is going to spend the rest of her life collecting woods in the forest until Victor drinks the fief away and then I'll live on the street.*

By mid-morning, the fog lifted, but for all her effort, Jackie only filled a quarter of her wagon. She debated heading closer to town where she knew the baron's woodcutters worked thinning out the trees. There was always the chance of picking up stray scraps they left behind on the ground. She decided no. Last time she tried that, the Master woodcutter caught her and imparted a strict lecture on guild rules, informing her if she was caught again it was prison for her. As she scurried away in fright, though, she noticed some people surreptitiously passing coins to the man and taking away a load of bundles. When she asked around, Jackie learned this was common practice, and the women she talked to implied using money wasn't the only way to bribe the master woodcutter.

Jackie didn't have any coins, not even the pin money Victor allowed his wife for her own use on those occasions when she went shopping in town. As for the hinted bribes—the man was old, ancient, bald, and missing teeth. When he spoke to her the odor from his mouth made her want to retch. She shuddered at the thought. She wasn't about to do that so Victor would have a hot breakfast and stay warm at night. Instead, she stalked deeper into the forest dragging her cart behind her.

Might as well try the stream, she decided. *Maybe the rain last night knocked down some branches from the king's land and drifted over to the baron's side.*

When she arrived, Jackie found the reeds and sandbars swept clean by the water, made swifter by the downpour of the night before. In frustration, she took a seat on the bank, contemplating the water and the abundance of timber beyond.

Across the stream, not twenty feet from her, was more wood than she hoped to haul in a lifetime. *I've never seen a forester walking around there in my life. Who would know?*

The more she thought about it, the more reasonable the idea became. *The king doesn't use it. Cutting isn't even allowed in his forest. I would be doing him a favor, getting rid of the old underbrush so new growth would start.*

With her mind made up, Jackie sprang to her feet and grabbed the handles of her cart, splashing through the water, and scrambled up the opposite bank, hauling the wagon behind her. Maneuvering through the dense underbrush, she tugged the wagon farther into the forest until the scrub concealed the cart from view to anyone stalking the baron's land.

Once away from the tangle by the stream, the king's forest opened up park-like with wide clear spots. Jackie crept along, scanning the ground and the area beyond, in case she saw anyone walking her way. Hurrying, she tossed branches into her wagon as fast as possible, her heart thumping in her chest. After a few minutes, the cart was loaded and she eyed the wood with satisfaction. *Better start heading back before someone wanders along and I'm discovered.*

The wagon was loaded to overflowing and heavy. Jackie hadn't realized how much wood she'd piled into it. The wheels kept sinking into the soft sod every few feet causing her to stop and dig it out before resuming to the stream. "Hope I can drag this across the water without tipping over," she muttered to herself, brushing a sweaty tangle of hair out of her forehead. She staggered forward, head down, her tunic stain black under her arms and along her chest. Salty perspiration dripped and stung her eyes.

Jackie glanced up, puffing. "Where the heck is the stream, anyway?" she muttered. She dropped the handles of the cart and ran forward, casting about like a bloodhound as she took a quick search of the area, looking for landmarks she knew. The tall trunks of trees greeted her in all directions.

"Great."

She knew she couldn't be lost. She'd only walked a short distance, and no more than a few minutes. Jackie was sure of it, but everything appeared different from when she crossed the stream. Different, but all the same.

Making an ever-widening circle, and keeping the cart in sight, she searched for the tracks of the wagon as she'd entered.

Every track she saw, however, was crossed and

crossed again by earlier marks she'd made in her frantic haste to load as much wood as possible in the shortest amount of time.

A rising sense of fright clutched her chest, squeezing as it crept up into her throat. She started to panic, fear of discovery utmost in her mind. What if she couldn't find her way back out again before a forester chanced upon her. Should she run? No. What would Victor say when she returned without the cart, how to explain it? The wagon had the family crest on the side for identification in case of theft. The king would know who violated his property.

"Must keep calm," she kept repeating aloud. Jackie took a deep breath, willing her heart to slow its rapid beating. *First let's locate the sun, get a bearing—which way it's heading.* Leafy branches obscured the view of the sky.

Terror returned. In her imagination, every sound in the woods was the king's forester accompanied by a squad of soldiers marching her way with broad swords drawn to arrest her. She sat on a rotted log and hugged herself.

Dimly in her ears came the gurgle of running water. She froze, holding her breath, concentrating on where the sound originated.

The splashing of the stream echoed from beyond a screen of trees in front of her. Jackie stood with a gasp of relief and hurried forward, making long scuffmarks in the leaves to mark her way back to the cart again. Behind the trees, briar bushes and cane break formed a lower barrier. She pushed her way through, leaving scratch marks on her arms and saw the stream gurgling at her feet. With a small gasp of relief she ran back the way she'd come to retrieve her cart.

She grasped the handles and tugged.

It wouldn't budge.

"DRAT."

The wheels sank into the wet earth up to the axles under the heavy load of the wood. Jackie dropped to her knees and frantically strained to lift the cart up. It refused to move. She tugged, drawing it forward inches at a time until the left wheel stopped. She knelt again, scooped dirt away underneath the wheel hoping to dislodge whatever it was the wheel was stuck on, and hit a hard smooth surface. She kept shoveling away with her fingers, breaking her short nails, desperate to free the wagon.

The deeper she dug, the rounder and smoother the object became—and it was purple. More intrigued than frustrated now she kept scooping away dirt, restoring to a stick when the pit was deeper than her elbows. She reached the bottom. Laying on her stomach and stretching down as far as possible, she wedged her fingers under the oval object and heaved upward with all her strength. She heard a sucking noise as the object released from the wet loom and she drew her prize to the surface.

Jackie cradled the treasure reverently in her fingers. "I can't believe it," she mumbled in awe. She held a dragon egg in her hands.

Dragon eggs were rare, single eggs even rarer. The one hatched yesterday was the first one discovered in two years. By law, all eggs found belonged to the king for parceling out to his barons who did not already have a dragon to protect their baronies, and the defense of the kingdom.

Jackie's first impulse was to leap up and rush home, tell someone, anyone what she'd discovered. The king offered a large reward, she was sure of it, maybe enough so her family would not have to worry about money for years.

She paused. First everyone would want to know where she'd found the egg. It was common custom for hundreds of people to swamp the area searching for more. Jackie couldn't tell she was poaching on the king's land— no reward and prison. Maybe lie, dig a new pit on her land and tell the people that was where she'd found the egg?

No. This wouldn't work either, not if she wanted a reward. Victor would claim any money due, and drink it up, or spend the reward treating his cronies at the tavern. Besides, for years her people farmed her fief, plowing deep for planting a thousand times. No one would believe she suddenly discovered an egg in the earth.

But she wouldn't leave the egg and forget about it. Somehow, she must figure out a way to hatch the baby dragon inside.

Time was growing short. Fear of discovery reared its head again multiplied by the fact it was growing late. The time must be well past noon and she had to make it home to cook supper. Jackie sprang up, hurried to the stream, and collected a handful of river stones, which scattered along the bank from the flooding, and hustled back to the egg. She found a spot where light filtered through the tree branches, placed her prize in the middle and carefully built a nest of rocks around the oval. The hot air and sunlight would warm the baby dragon inside and the rocks would hold some of the heat during the nights. It took three more trips before she was satisfied the egg was sufficiently concealed from casual eyes and protected.

She kissed her fingers and placed the tips on the top of the purple oval. "Best I can do for you right now, baby," she murmured. "I'll see you in the morning." She strode back to her wagon, threw part of the load onto the earth, and managed to start the cart rolling. She hit the stream and made a dash for home.

For once she was glad she'd planned ahead and started soaking a smoked ham two days ago. She unloaded her pile of firewood, shoved her cart into the carriage house, and rushed into the kitchen. She breathed a sigh of relief Victoria hadn't volunteered to help and busied herself cooking. She wanted this to be a nice dinner and have Victor in a talkative mood.

By the time her brother-in-law returned home that night, Jackie had her plans well laid out in her mind. Along the way, she'd give up the idea of handing the egg over for a reward and decided to raise the baby dragon herself. Before she attempted her crazy plot, however, first she needed to learn more, and for all his faults, her brother-in-law was an expert of the history, care, and raising of dragons.

That night, Jackie set the table with extra care, even going as far as retrieving a bottle of apple brandy, hidden when it became apparent Victor would consume every drop of alcohol in the house if he could find it. As the family sat to eat, his eyes lit up when he saw the dusty bottle. He exclaimed, "My, what a feast." He glanced inquiringly over at Victoria and asked, "Is it someone's birthday? Did I forget a special occasion?"

"Why, I do not know," Victoria replied in a puzzled voice. She swung to Jackie, "What is this all about, my dear? You have us all intrigued now."

"Well—I…." Jackie chose her words carefully. "I thought since our celebration of the choosing yesterday was ruined, I could make up for it today." She studied her plate sheepishly. "I spoiled everyone's fun and Victor didn't have a chance to tell us about his selection." As protests arose from her sister, Jackie added swiftly to Victor, "Maybe you could instruct us about dragons. You know so much, and it would be *so* entertaining to hear you speak about the beasts." She watched him expectantly.

Thomas who was in the process of loading his plate glanced up and exclaimed, "Victor, did you ever *ride* a dragon?" His eyes shone with curiosity.

Victor beamed at Thomas, Jackie, and his wife. This was the kind of attention he craved and didn't receive, especially from Jackie and Thomas. He leaned back in his chair, scooped up the bottle of brandy, and uncorked it.

"Well, no, Thomas," he replied pouring himself a large snifter of the liquor. He swished the reddish fluid around and smelled the aroma. "Only those candidates who are chosen by a dragon can ride one." He sipped and helped himself to a large portion of greens and ham. "I suppose though, I do know a thing or two about dragons enough to lecture about the beasts." He sampled the meat, sipped at the brandy again, and nodded to Jackie. She smirked back happily and waited.

Thomas piped in between mouthfuls of peas, "Where do they come from, the eggs, I mean?" In way of explanation he said, "We're learning about dragons in school."

Victor took a longer sip of brandy and closed his eyes, smacking his lips. "It all began at the end of the last great age," he began speaking in a hushed voice, "before the ash fell from the sky." He opened his eyes and stared at the Jackie and Thomas, watching for their reaction. "Most of the male dragons destroyed themselves fighting over the females," he allotted Jackie a significant stare, "That is why we cannot have female dragonriders."

Jackie ignored this dig. It couldn't be true. Common sense told her dragons never would have existed in the first place if the males killed each other over females. Even the deer during rutting season didn't destroy their fellow stags, not to the point of extinction, anyway. Instead, she stared at her napkin and pretended to blush, wondering all the time why this part of the story was made up in the first place. Maybe to monopolize the use of dragons for men?

"The females," Victor continued in his deep voice

after he was sure he held everyone's attention, "produced what eggs they could, but before the eggs hatched the ash fell, covered the clutches, and so ended the last great age." He raised his hands "All the females died, and with the eggs buried, the race of dragons drew to a close."

Thomas had stopped eating, listening to Victor speak. He noticed he still balanced peas precariously on his spoon. He exclaimed, "Is this what happened, really?" and shoved the utensil in his mouth.

Victor took a larger gulp of brandy. "Yes—exactly what happened," he mimicked indulgently. "Years passed. Famine swept the country because the ash blocked the sun and made the earth cold. People starved because the grains would not grow. Invaders attacked our kingdom from the east and the west. Finally, the earth warmed again, our good king's ancestors drove out the intruders, and peace descended on our little island again."

Jackie wasn't interested in a history lesson. Besides, most of this was conjecture she'd learned while attending lessons, the nuns said so. As for peace, the Easmen still sailed from the east, attacking at will. "But what about the dragon eggs," she asked.

Victor was taking a break, shoveling ham into his mouth with the point of his knife. He chewed, swallowed, and patted his mouth with a napkin. "I am coming to this." He waved the knife at her face. "It is never wise to rush a good tale, my dear, or a good teller. Stories are meant to be savored exactly as a fine brandy." He picked up his glass and drank again, this time he wiped his mouth on his sleeve.

He noticed Victoria's glass was empty and poured her a small amount and filled his snifter as well. Her lips twitched up and she murmured, "Thank you. Do please—continue. This is so interesting."

"An egg was discovered by one of the serfs

working on the king's land. I believe they dug a well. Anyway, his Majesty, Fredrick the Great, in his wisdom hatched it and became the first dragonrider." Victor smirked and stabbed at a piece of ham.

Jackie frowned at her trencher and lifted greens to her mouth. *Well, this isn't telling me anything I didn't know before you old windbag.* "But how did he hatch the egg? What did he feed the dragonet afterwards," she asked plaintively.

Victor was busy with his glass. He glanced up, and stared at Jackie, bemused. "Hatch? Feed?" He frowned, "Why hatching is the easy part once the egg is unearthed from the cold ground, my dear young girl. Frozen, shall we say, waiting to be discovered by someone lucky enough to find one. Keep the little devil in the sun, or a warm place, and the egg will hatch. I believe, huh," he paused, thinking, and then said, "The good king Fredrick kept his in the kitchen near the fireplace." He burst out laughing. "Lucky one of the cooks didn't bake the poor thing by mistake, huh?"

Hmm....A fire—I didn't think of this. Might be difficult. Strict laws abounded about the burning of anything on both the baron's land and the king's. Someone is sure to come along and investigate the smoke, too. Go with keeping it warm in the sun and pray.

"As for feeding the dragonet," Victor continued, pouring the last of the brandy in his glass, "They eat meat." He made a biting motion with his thumb and forefinger at Thomas and said in a deep voice, *"Chomp—chomp—chomp.* Gobs and gobs of meat."

The boy shrank back with a squeak of terror and delight, his eyes wide as saucers. *"Live meat?"* he whispered in a hushed voice.

Victor waved a hand in dismissal. "Live—dead, cooked, or uncooked. As long as it is meat, they do not care." He turned to his wife. "They fed the little fellow at the choosing, correct? They usually do."

"Yes, I believe they did," she responded. Her lips twitched upward and she exclaimed, "I learned in class by the time they are six weeks old, they could swallow a small boy—the same size as you."

The smirk on Thomas's face vanished, replaced by worry. "Are you sure?"

Jackie placed her hand on the boy's shoulder. "Don't worry, shorty. By the time they're that big they eat the same thing we do—pigs," she motioned to the ham with her knife, "cattle, lambs, chickens. Victoria is teasing you." *But where am I going to find this much livestock to feed him?* This was becoming more complicated than she thought it would be. *Maybe I should sneak the egg into the village common and leave it there for someone else to find?*

A loud belch interrupted her thoughts. Victor patted his stomach and exclaimed in satisfaction, "Fine meal, Victoria—Jaqueline." He said to the table at large, "When I was a candidate, my choosing was a lot like the one yesterday." He half closed his eyes and said wishfully, "A single egg. Too bad it went to Weatherhill. If I had been selected..." Victor shook his head and sighed. "Well, even dragons make a mistake once and a while, don't they? Proved that when both rider and dragon crashed into a mountain and killed themselves. Terrible," he mused, "They never located another clutch for years afterward."

Victoria reached out and placed her hand on her husband's arm. "You would have made a great dragonrider, dear, a shame they made an error in judgement."

Thomas asked, "Is it true, dragons shoot fire from their mouths?"

Victor nodded. "At one time our legends tell us they did." He shrugged. "We have old pictures showing flames issuing from their lips, but not anymore. Perhaps they forgot how, or the tales are wrong. We'll never know unless one does it again."

"Wouldn't it be something," Thomas said, "to see a dragon flying through the air, flames shooting from his mouth."

"Yes, it would," agreed Victor. "Anyway, After Fredrick the Great discovered the first dragon, none were found until our present king located one, a single clutch again. More recently, a few were located in various parts of the kingdom. Not a one able to breathe fire though."

Victor stood. "Speaking of eggs, Jaqueline, how many times have I asked you to get rid of those bird's nests above the kitchen door eves? I am tired of stepping on their droppings." He scowled at her. "One hit me this evening all over my cloak when I stepped up to the door."

"Uh, tomorrow morning, for sure," she said to Victor. "I have to wait until they fly into the forest during the morning to feed or they'd peck me to death."

"Well, see you remember. We are not running a home for baby birds." Victor scratched his chin and straightened his tunic. "I am going down to the tavern," he announced to Victoria, "I may be late." He nodded to Jackie and Thomas, "Good night, all." He swayed toward the door.

Jackie cleaned up, taking the scraps out to the pigs and chickens. When she returned, Victoria and Thomas were upstairs, preparing for sleep. She blew out the candles and trudge up to her bedroom.

Lying in her bed that night, Jackie kept running over in her mind plans for hatching the egg, and discarding the schemes as fast. Any fire meant discovery, she was sure of it. Blankets? Nah—if the egg was warm already, but she'd put her hands on it and the shell was death cold. As she drifted off to sleep, a thought occurred to her. She would see, maybe—if it were still there when she woke in

29

the morning.

**

Jackie hurried through the woods. Halting at the stream, she threw a hasty glance upstream and down, listening carefully for any sounds out of the ordinary. Satisfied no one lurked in the forest, she plunged through the water, dragging her cart behind her. Her cairn of stones was where she left it, undisturbed as far as she could tell. She reached in and placed her palm on the shell. The egg wasn't cold, but not warm either. She raced back to her cart and snatched out a bag. Hurrying to the pile of rocks, she got busy.

A half-an-hour later, Jackie rose and wiped her hands on her pants, inspecting her handy work. From the carriage house, she'd brought bits of a mirror and a small square of glass from the rubbish Victor insisted on collecting. The shards of mirror lined the inside of the cairn, channeling the sun's rays onto the egg, while the scrape of glass, secured with clay from the stream, covered the top of the rocks, trapping the heat inside.

It wasn't perfect, Jackie admitted to herself, but the best given the time and equipment at her disposal. She scooped up her bag, threw it into her cart along with as many pieces of dead wood she could gather, and hastened back over the stream.

Every day she made it a point to hurry into the king's forest and check on her new charge resting in the makeshift incubator, and to her delight after two weeks saw the shell darkening almost to violet, and on one occasion a slight wiggle reward her probing hand when she touched the shell.

Only once did she meet any person in the king's forest. She'd finished her inspection of the egg and pulled her cart to the stream. After crossing, she heard a gruff voice behind her shout, "What are you doing here?"

Jackie froze.

The voice said, "You girl, I am speaking to you. Turn around and face me."

Jackie pivoted slowly. Across the stream stood a tall, lean man darkened by the weather, dressed in forest green, the emblem of a charging boar embroidered on his jerkin. Jackie bowed her head and studied her feet. Her boots still dripped water from crossing the stream. She gulped and tried to slip her feet under the leaves and twigs. The hem of her tunic was stained dark also. She hoped the forester didn't notice and the discoloration would blend in with the rest of the stains and dirt marks. She replied meekly, "I collect wood, sir. I am the daughter of Philip Montagain and sister-in-law of Victor La Montrue. This is the baron's land and we have permission. Have I done wrong?"

When she heard no answer, Jackie dared to glance up. The forester rubbed his chin and studied her meditatively as he ran the names through his mind.

At least Victor's done some good. The La Montrues' were big supporters of the king and their name well known to his men.

The forester replied, "Well and good girl." He glanced at her cart. "Where did you collect all the wood?"

Was there some way he could discern king's wood from baron's? Of course not. Don't panic. "Oh, I've been out collecting before the sun rose," Jackie replied quickly, waving her arm to include all of the baron's land. "Some of this," she said, trying to act as embarrassed as possible, "I dropped yesterday and must pick up again today. The rest I gleaned this morning."

The forester eyed the cart. "Make sure you stay on the baron's side of the stream," he said sternly. "You know it is against the king's law to trespass on his land, right?"

"Oh, yes. I would never do that." Relief flooded

Jackie. "The law is well known and I *always* obey the law."

"See you do." He spun, hesitated, and turned back to her with a frown. "The stream also belongs to the king." He nodded to her tunic. "If you are going to wash your clothing, do it at your home." Without another word, he walked away and disappeared into the bush.

He knows, or suspected. For a long time Jackie stood frozen, a fist choking her hammering heart as she waited for him to return, positive he would find the dragon egg and come searching for her. After fifteen minutes when she heard nothing else, she snatched up the handles of her cart and scurried home as fast as possible.

***

Jackie decided to wait a few days before venturing back into the king's forest, and confined her wood gathering activities to the baron's land as far away from the stream as possible, In case the forester lurked in the bushes watching for her return.

In the meanwhile, she put her second part of raising a baby dragon into operation—food.

While her father still lived, he'd made sure Jackie was well acquainted with both bow and blade.

"A lady must be able to defend her honor," he joked as they practiced with wooden swords. Her father made it a point to teacher her every trick he knew as if he trained a son for warfare. On her twelfth birthday, he even presented her with a rapier, showing her how to oil, clean, and sharpen the blade. The sword hung over the fireplace in her room, useless, now no one was around to practice the thrusts and parries he'd taught her. Victor never wanted to take the time or inclination to work with Jackie, and Victoria shuddered at the mention of swords, even wooden practice ones.

Her father also taught her the use of the bow and arrow, first targeting bales of hay, and later, when she was proficient, taking her out into the fields of grain they grew and hunting the geese, pheasants, and grouse pilfering the wheat. After she shot her first pheasant in mid-air, her father exclaimed, "You have become a huntress. The bird thought to eat our crops, now we shall dine on him." Nana cook roasted the fowl and presented it for Jackie's own dinner the next night.

When no rumor in the town circulated about the discovery of the egg, and no soldiers broke down her door to arrest her, Jackie deemed it safe to venture into the king's woods and check on her charge again.

At first, she had difficulty with Victor when she ran downstairs that morning carrying her bow and a quiver of bolts over her back. It was her bad luck he was awake for once having breakfast with Victoria and Thomas.

"Where do you think you are going with those?" He waved a hand at her gear. "You are supposed to be collecting wood for cooking, not out playing hunting."

"I wanted to bring them...in case," Jackie said plaintively, avoiding the urge to stare him in the face.

"In case, what?" He smirked at Victoria who sat at the kitchen table finishing a cup of tea before taking Thomas to his lessons. "Afraid of bears? You know hunting is illegal in the baron's woods. We are fortunate we're allowed to collect kindling."

Jackie threw a pleading glance in her sister's direction and murmured, "It isn't the four-legged beasts I fear," she examined the floor, "but the two-legged ones who might lurk there."

Victoria put her hand to her mouth, gasped, and shot Jackie a worried look. "Has someone bothered you?" She said to her husband, "Maybe you should accompany her into the forest, or we can buy wood. It is not necessary..."

"Nonsense," Victor replied, putting his cup down

and staring at Jackie. "Jaqueline, has anyone followed you into the forest...said anything?"

"Well, no," Jackie admitted. "I did see a forester on the king's land, and he cautioned me not to cross the stream, but still...." She left the rest of the sentence hanging, while trying to appear as scared as possible.

Victoria's eyes widened in alarm." You see," exclaimed Victoria, "What if he...."

"Stop being childish girls, you are both making too much of this," replied Victor, shaking his head while raising his hand for silence, "but if it makes you feel any safer, take the bow—but no hunting on the baron's property. Understand me? And the forester was right, I know you understand better than to trespass on the king's domain." he added sternly, "I do not want to be hauled up before the magistrate to explain why you were shooting game on our lord's land when we have a fief of our own."

Jackie nodded her head vigorously she understood, and ran out of the door as fast as she could. She wasn't planning on hunting—yet. She wanted to set a precedent for taking her bow with her, and needed to practice and sharpen her skills for when the dragon arrived.

Along the way, she trained on bushes. To her surprise while still on her property a partridge took wing in front of her as she aimed at a small tree and managed to bring it down with a lucky shot. She hid the bird in the tall grass, not wanting to have anything on her when she entered the baron's woods, where a lord's man would accuse her of poaching.

This time before entering the king's woods, she took the precaution of hiding her cart among the bushes in case anyone walked along and it was necessary for her to beat a hasty retreat. She hitched up her tunic, and carried an extra pair of shoes to change into so there would be no evidence of her wading through the water.

Summoning up as much stealth as possible, she crossed the stream and placed toe to heel, scanning each step for branches, which might snap and betray her. She saw no one, and heard nothing, except the occasional tweeting of birds and a squirrel chittering overhead in the branches.

When Jackie came in sight of the cairn, she froze. Something wasn't right. The glass she'd used to secure the top of the rocks and keep the heat in was missing, shattered on the earth as if a thousand sparkling stars all glistened on the ground. The two top rows of stones from her incubator were missing also, knocked haphazardly among the leaves.

Something had been at the cairn, she was sure of it, either a hungry animal or a nosey forester. Before she approached too close, she circled the area. A through scan of the vicinity showed no additional signs of disturbance, nor did she see tracks indicating a large beast or person passed by. Jackie gulped and tiptoed forward, pausing every now and then, surveying the forest, ready to bolt at the slightest noise.

When she reached the cairn, she knelt, and peered in, expecting to see the egg vanished.

A baby dragon gazed up at her with red eyes.

"Beep?"

Chapter Three

"Oh, you are *so cute*." Jackie smirked foolishly at the dragonet and reached an eager arm into the cairn to stroke the tiny head.

"Ouch."

Jacked jerked her hand away and sucked on a bleeding finger. *"Feed me,"* a plaintive thought floated into her mind. *"I am trapped in these rocks."* The small wings tried to spread, brushing against the side of the makeshift incubator. *"I have been here all night and all day. I am hungry."* The large red eyes in a small face stared up at her pitifully.

"Uh, yeah, sure." Jackie examined her finger. A long white rip still oozed blood, but she figured she'd survive. She stuck it in her lips again and thought. *Food? Of course, the partridge.* "I'll be right back," she promised, springing to her feet. She dashed off. "Don't go anywhere," she called back.

"I guess not," returned the glum thought. *"Hurry."*

Jackie rushed to the edge of the forest where her land and the baron's met. Frantically she hacked at the long grass with her hands, brushing it away until she located the carcass of the dead bird. She snatched the fowl up, out of breath, and sprinted back into the forest.

"Here," she puffed, face burning from the exertion of the long run. Jackie thrust the bird into the hole. "Eat."

Hungry jaws gaped and razor sharp baby teeth ripped. Mouthfuls of feathers, bone, and flesh disappeared. Within seconds, the partridge vanished with only the boney claws and beak remaining. A red tongue flicked out, first making any traces of blood vanish from the scaly body, and then licking the small mouth.

"I will rest now," the sleepy reply appeared in

Jackie's mind. *"You will feed me again?"*

To luck out and kill a stray bird on her way here was one thing, but every day? Jackie's mind raced with the logistics. *How much did this little monster eat? What had Victor said "Gobs and gobs of meat"?*

"Of course," Jackie replied in a turmoil. "Tomorrow?"

She would wake up earlier and hunt.

"This afternoon." The red eyes burned a deeper scarlet. They gazed up at Jackie. *"I need a bedtime snack. I am sooo hungry."*

Panic rippled in Jackie's stomach and worked up into the back of her neck. "Uh, I'll try," she replied. Could she sneak away from the house to hunt again? One bird was an unexpected surprise, and chances were another wouldn't come her way by accident again, certainly not morning and night or in enough quantity at one time to keep this little monster quiet. Even if she were fortunate enough to scare up anything, it would take hours she didn't have. She still must collect wood and do the rest of her chores.

"I love you." The eyes closed and the dragonet curled into a tight ball within her incubator, falling asleep at once.

Jackie hastened away, grabbing sticks and branches as she ran. She uncovered her cart, dumped her load into the bed, and clawed through the woods searching for more kindling until the wagon was full.

As she staggered home, dragging her load behind her, she ran the problem over her mind, dumping every scheme she thought up as being impractical or too difficult to execute.

In the kitchen, she busied herself preparing dinner. She hurried to the smokehouse to take a slice from a gammon of bacon to flavor the greens and spotted the remains of a roast left there from the day before. She'd meant to start a stew with the bones and meat, but events overtook her and she'd forgotten all about the meal.

She stared at the meat, scratching her chin. "Perfect, this will keep her busy, I hope," she muttered, chunks of fat hung on the ribs also. "Now all I have to do is figure out a way to excuse myself for an hour to bring it to her."

Jackie set the table early that day and yelled up the stairs to Victoria and Thomas, "It's time to eat." She ducked back into the kitchen.

Victoria stumbled down the stairs and gazed at the table, food laid out waiting. "I know it is not nearly time," she exclaimed, "why all the rush?"

"I have to go out for a while," Jackie said, moving to the door. She held up her bow and a quiver of arrows. "Fox."

"What?" Victoria's eyebrows dipped as she stared back at Jackie, confused at the seldom used word. "Excuse me, for a moment I thought you said fox."

"I did." Jackie let out a laugh of amusement at the expression on her sister's face. "I saw the tracks of a fox this morning when I was out collecting kindling," Jackie lied. "I'm going out to hunt him before it grows too dark and I can't see his tracks."

At the mention of a fox, Thomas ran into the room, saw Jackie with her bow, and exclaimed, "Are you going to shoot him?" The boy bounced up and down. "May I go along and watch? I've never seen a real fox before."

"No shorty, not this time." To her sister Jackie said, "If Mr. Fox sneaks into the henhouse, we'll have a disaster on our hands, not to mention what he'll do to our ducks and geese. One fox, and if it's a vixen with a litter of kits somewhere, it will be even worse. Imagine what would happen? They'd wipe out our flocks in a month."

Victoria nodded in growing apprehension,

38

oblivious to the fact she'd never seen a fox on the property. "Oh, dear, I never thought of it. You are right."

Jackie thrust her hand out in a squeezing motion and added in an ominous tone, "And think what they would do to Victor's prize peacocks. You know how they refuse to stay in their coops."

Victoria's eyes opened wide in alarm, and shoved her hand to her mouth, chewing on her knuckles in distress. "I dread what he would say if anything happened to one of those birds. Why…" Her lips worked wordlessly as she tried to imagine his ranting. She glanced at the kitchen table. "Is everything set here? I do not know…."

"Ready to go," Jackie assured her. She waved a finger at the bowls sitting on the side of the table. "All you have to do is place it in the trenchers. Explain to Victor when he returns home, will you, if I'm not back yet." She reached for the door, stopped as if considering something more. "This might take a couple of days, you know." Her forehead wrinkled. "Foxes hunt in the mornings and nights, unless I get lucky enough to locate his den."

"Of course." Victoria nodded as if she knew all about the habits of foxes.

Jackie ran out the door, laughing to herself. The only fox Victoria ever saw was the trim on the tunic Victor bought for her birthday one year. Nevertheless, now she planted the idea. Jackie promised herself, Mr. Fox would receive blame for many mysterious disappearances of food.

She swung by the smokehouse, gathered up the remains of the roast in a leather sack, and made it back to the cairn as the sunset.

"What took you so long?" A wide mouth opened, lined with razor sharp baby teeth. Soft eyes glared at her, half in pleading, half in anger. *"I am sooo hungry."*

"Here you go greedy glut, enjoy." Jackie dumped the bones, meat, and the dripping collected in the bottom of the sack, in front of the little dragon. With a gnashing of teeth, the dragonet fell upon its evening snack in a burst of ferocity, gulping away with the crunching of bones making Jackie wince.

Jackie watched the meat disappeared with breakneck speed. The baby definitely got bigger since the morning. *More problems.* Where would she hide the dragon after she outgrew her rocky nursery? On impulse, she reached down to stroke the scaly head, ready to jerk her hand away in case the dragon tried to nip again.

The dragon, however, still gorged itself, and paid no notice to her caress. Jackie let her fingers trail along the back of the neck and down the spine in a soft stroking motion, enjoying the feel of the soft skin underneath her fingertips.

"Oh, that feels good—don't stop."

"I think I'm going to call you Ariel," Jackie whispered. She moved from the spine to massaging the muscles of the minute wings. The dragon rewarded her with a wiggle and a low buzz.

Eyes half closed, the dragonet gazed up at her. *"Ariel? Nonsense, my name's Belinda. Why would you call me Ariel?"* Most of the roast was gone. The dragonet contented itself to an occasional nibble. She raised her head again and added, *"You may stop with the wings. They are still tender and my scales haven't hardened yet, maybe tomorrow after they've strengthened and I've received more sun. Scratch behind my ears instead."*

Jackie dutifully moved her hand back to the head, making slow circles with the balls of her fingers. "You have a name?" she asked in surprise.

"Of course," Belinda thought back. *"Don't you?"* The dragonet paused, considering the human above her. *"What is your name?"*

"Jackie."

40

"That's a boy's name." Belinda tried unfurling her wings and brushed against the stones.

"You know a lot for a baby, don't you?" replied Jackie with a smile. "My real name is Jaqueline, but I like Jackie."

"I'm a dragon, we know everything our person knows," replied Belinda with a flip of her tail, *"and if you call yourself Jackie, this is what I shall name you."*

"You don't know much then, do you?" Jackie joked, giving Belinda a light pat on the head.

The dragonet reached behind her and nipped Jackie on the finger, but not hard. More of a love bite without breaking the skin. She tried stretching her wings again. Her appendages threatened to topple the rocks and a rasping noise spread through the forest.

"Don't do that," Jackie admonished, pushing the wings back against Belinda's body. "The stones are rough. You'll hurt yourself."

"Out."

"Oh, no. I've got no place to put you."

"Why do I have to be put anywhere?" Belinda asked indignity. *"Do I embarrass you?"*

"No—no." Sheesh, this Belinda was a miniature pain in the neck. "I thought dragons knew everything," Jackie countered. "You're, uh, you're a surprise. Yes, no one is allowed to see you for a while until you are properly presented."

"Oh." Belinda yawned and curled up. *"In that case I'll wait until tomorrow. You'd better hurry up though, Jackie,"* she stretched to her full length, sending the rocks shaking. *"I'm going to need a new home soon whether the world is ready for me or not."*

The moon was rose in the night sky when Jackie made it home. An aggravated Victor waited for her.

"Where have you been?" He paced back and forth

41

in the dining hall, fuming, holding a cup, which sloshed amber liquid on the floor in a puddle trailing him.

Jackie knew she was in trouble and she'd have to do some quick thinking to talk her way out of it. Her eyes opened wide in surprise as if they were repeating a conversation already spoken. "Uh, out hunting a fox. Didn't Victoria tell you?" she stammered. "I explained everything to her."

Victor stopped his pacing, his face red. "No fox has been seen in these parts for ten years." He pointed an accusing finger at her, his lips quivering in rage. "You are lying."

Jackie placed her hands on her hips, sticking her chin out in mock indignation. "I am not," she retorted. She waved a hand toward the kitchen door. "If you don't believe me, I'll take you where I saw his tracks—scat and all." She waited in breathless silence, hoping he would back down.

"You saw scat?" He paused.

"Sure 'nuff," Jackie replied, nodding her head solemnly, "on the far side of Baldhill, I'll take you there now, let me fetch a lantern," She made as if to walk into the stillroom, "if you don't want me hunting it, fine, I won't. It's not as if I don't have enough to do around here already. I'll wait until the devil kills some of your precious peacocks, then you can pay good money for the huntsman to track it and kill the rascal," she called over her shoulder.

Victor's lips twisted down, aghast at her statement. "Forget about it. It will not be necessary," he replied dourly. He strolled to a wooden bucket he'd brought from the tavern and dipped his cup in. "But if I find out you have lied to me, girl." He tipped his head back and took a long gulp. "There will be the devil to pay. I expect to see the hide of this fox when you catch him, and do not let your hunting interfere with the rest of your duties around this house. We all have priorities and tracking foxes is at the bottom on the list."

Jackie broke out into a laugh. "I'll be sure to tell Mr. Fox how he rates and to hurry and run into sight of my bow so you can inspect his fur." She stepped away from the stillroom door and announced. "I'm going to bed. If I'm to catch the devil, I must be awake before the cock crows, but don't thank me for saving your precious little pets." Before Victor responded, she hurried up the stairs to her chamber.

Close one. Thought he'd hand me a harder time than this. Wonder if it was the idea of the money for a huntsman, or losing those stupid birds? At least everyone was on board with her coming and going at odd hours of the morning and night, now. For the time being she was free to do what she wanted.

This still didn't solve the problem of where to house Belinda, though. Jackie lay in bed, staring at the ceiling in the dark, and tried to decide the best place to hide the dragon. She couldn't be left to roam the king's land alone, this was sure, and no safe place existed in the baron's forest where the dragon wouldn't be seen.

Somewhere on their fief? She ran over in her mind the various outbuildings she might use. Many were vacant now Victor cut back on the workers and curtailed many of the activities of the farm he deemed not worth the trouble.

How about the old barn where they use to keep the milk cows? No. Big enough but too close by the manor house. The boat shed by the lake? No one went there since Victor decided keeping a family in residence harvesting fish not worth the time or money involved. The lake still contained fish and Belinda could catch as many as she wanted, and the lake itself would provide drinking water for the dragon, but Jackie discarded this idea also. The shed was hardly large enough to hold the boat and nets, and sometimes the peasants still fished in the water on occasion when they weren't busy with their plots of land. The way the dragon was sprouting up she'd outgrow the building in no time and eventually someone would spot Belinda.

In her mind, she retraced every inch of the countryside she was familiar with, but no suitable place occurred to her. In the morning, she awoke before anyone else, performed her chores in a rush, and was out of the house before dawn broke over the horizon.

Chicken for breakfast, Belinda. Jackie grabbed one of the sleeping birds from the henhouse. To make the evidence clear Mr. Fox was the culprit, she also left a trail of feathers scattered on the grass leading into the woods. *Let Victor deny a fox was running loose now.* As the sun rose above Baldhill, she halted.

She eyed the monolith of rock in a new way. *Maybe. I haven't been up there in ages.* She left her cart on the path and started a perilous climb up the slope to the top, slipping backward as the sand under her feet gave way, and clutching at small bushes not to lose her balance.

While technically on the baron's land, her ancestors claimed the mount first and harvested all the trees growing along the rocky side. But when a vein of gold was discovered the baron claimed the hill as his own, producing old maps showing the boundary lines. Her father showed equally old maps, and the dispute found its way before the king.

His Majesty decided in favor of the baron—for mineral rights, while granting her father the use of the mountain for logging. Since no more trees existed on the sloping sides, and the vein of gold played out on top after several years, the mountain stood as a barrier between the two properties ever since. No one ventured up there anymore. The place was worthless.

Jackie reached the top, puffing with her face red and sweaty as she tried to catch her breath. She confronted a dark hole, the entrance to the mineshaft dug many years ago by the baron's men. A tingle of fear ran up her spine. The place was dark, and in her imagination, everything from bats to bandits lurked within its black maw. The tales of the nuns of caves being the entrance to the underworld sped through her mind. Steeling herself, she crept inside the opening and stared about in the dim light.

"Roomy," she muttered. The rising sun illuminated the inside for a few feet, enough for her to estimate the dimensions of the shaft. Her fear forgotten, she stepped forward until darkness obscured the farthest reaches of the tunnel. *High ceiling, too.* Jackie backed up and stared out the mine entrance. The tops of trees stretched out as far as she could see. The opening faced away from the town, no one would notice the arrivals or goings of Belinda when she started to fly. She nodded to herself in satisfaction. *Little baby dragon, I think we've found you your new home. I hope you enjoy dark caves.* With a whoop, she raced back down the mountainside, sliding on her backside when the slope grew too great and hurried into the woods.

"Well, it's about time." Belinda grew during the night again. Rocks scattered on the leaves in all directions from her impatient waiting. *"Did you fetch me breakfast?"*

"Yes, and more," Jackie exclaimed, reaching into the cairn and hauling the dragonet up in her arms. She cuddled Belinda and cooed to calm the baby when the dragnet struggled to jump down. "Oh, gosh, you weigh a ton." Belinda approached the size and weight of Thomas. Jackie inhaled deeply and nuzzled the youngster. A clean, fresh odor reminding her of cloves emitted from the dragon's skin.

"Stop doing that, it tickles," tittered Belinda.

A tender smile crossed over Jackie's face. "I make no promises, but for now, off we go to your new home."

"Food, I am so hungry," the dragon whined looking up at Jackie with pleading eyes and jaws open, as the girl tramped through the woods.

"You can eat on the way," replied Jackie, depositing Belinda in the cart. "Think of it as a picnic."

The dragon tore into the chicken. Jackie picked up sticks, building a nest for her and weaving a mat out of vines into a loose mesh to pile up on top of the dragon in case anyone should wander by and peek inside her wagon.

"Good morning to ye."

Jackie froze. Walking her way was an old woman, the wife of the lord who owned the fief next to hers. Under her arm was a bundle of sticks. The woman waved and hobbled to Jackie.

"Lady de Quincy, what a surprise." Jackie hastily drew her screen of vines over Belinda's head. "What are you doing out so early?" She peered at the sticks under the woman's arm. "Collecting wood? Why, whatever for? You have servants for that."

"Beep?"

"It was a beautiful morning and I decided to take a walk," Lady de Quincy replied. She shook the bundles of sticks under her arm. "As long as I was out I decided to collect wood too." She wagged her head. "What with the price of kindling these days..." She squinted her eyes at Jackie's cart. "I see you are doing the same thing."

"Beep?"

Nosy old woman. Mother always said the same thing, too. Wish Belinda would shut up. "It was nice talking to you Lady de Quincy, but I have to go now. I...."

"What is that noise?" The old woman stared around, centering on Jackie's cart. "Do you have something alive in there?" She tried to peer in.

"Oh, no. Must have been a bird." Jackie pointed up into the trees. "There he goes now, do you see it?"

Jackie's heart hammered in her chest. *Let me go, you old biddy.*

The old woman stared up. "I do not see…?"

"Well, gotta go. Hope I see you again. Bye." Jackie grabbed the handles of her cart and scurried off, leaving a confused Lady de Quincy gawking at her. As Jackie hurried away, she heard the woman mutter, "What an impertinent little girl. Nothing good will ever come of her."

***

When they arrived at Baldhill Jackie surveyed the long slope ahead of her. It was tough enough climbing up the mountain by herself, but carrying Belinda? "Think you can make it to the top on you own," she asked the dragon who peered over the edge of the wagon at the mountainside in curiosity.

"Sleepy."

"Oh, you." Little eyes blinked at Jackie. Belinda lay down on the bottom on the cart with a sigh and curled into a ball, her eyelids fluttering closed.

"I know you're still awake," Jackie chided. "Don't try to fool me."

Belinda snored softly.

Glowering at the sleeping dragonet, Jackie bent over with a groan and scooped up the baby in her arms. Struggling for more than an hour, sliding backward at every fourth step, and making rude comments about lazy dragons, which Belinda either didn't hear or chose to ignore, she reached the top soaked in perspiration and covered in dirt.

"Here," Jackie huffed as she and Belinda entered the mine, "your new home." She laid the dragon on the rock floor. "Don't thank me, or anything."

Belinda chose to ignore this too. Instead, she roused herself, uncurled, and sniffed at the rocks on the floor. She reached out her neck and nibbled on one. *"Yum,*

47

tasty. I will enjoy living here," she commented, biting the rock again. She swallowed a small piece.

"Don't do that, you'll hurt yourself," Jackie scolded. *Babies, they'll put anything in their mouths.* When Thomas was a younger, he'd almost choked to death on a small wooden ball. Her father's quick thinking saved him. She tried shoving a finger between Belinda's teeth to scoop the stone out. The dragonet locked her lips tight.

"Stop it, you're hurting me," Belinda backed up and hissed. *"I know what I can and cannot eat."*

"You eat rocks?"

"I don't know," Belinda said, perplexed, *"but these smell—urp."* She belched and a small tongue of flame shot from her mouth. *"Oh, this is better."* She waddled into a corner against a wall and curled up again. *"I will sleep now,"* she announced. *"Wake me when dinner is served."* She closed her eyes and draped her tail over her snout.

Jackie stared at the sleeping dragon in amazement. *This is worse than waiting on Victor and Victoria hand and foot. I wonder if real dragonriders have to put up with this?*

Jackie walked away from Belinda and returned to the stones the dragon was interested in. She picked up the rock and examined it. The crystal possessed a silvery sheen and was blurred at the edges as if her eyes weren't focusing correctly. More of the strange rocks scattered on the floor, cast-offs by the miners who'd dug the shaft searching for gold ore.

Jackie shrugged. The dragonet felt the stones wouldn't hurt her, and perhaps dragons were like birds that ate small pebbles to help their stomachs digest food. Jackie checked on her sleeping charge, saw no ill effects, and hurried down the hill to hunt for more wood.

Chapter Four

B y the time Belinda was a month old, she'd gained her full length, but was still skinny from the growth spurts she'd gone through. To Jackie's relief, however, the dragon hunted for herself at night and Jackie's duties as chief procurer of food for the dragon halted.

Jackie's absences from the manor house in the mornings and late night were custom now. As long as her chores were completed and the family's meals arrived on time, she wasn't hounded. Occasionally Victor would ask, "How is the fox hunting coming?" to which Jackie would shake her head and mumble a reply. She began using phrases as "Foxy little critter," or "Furry tailed vixen" to describe her frustration in tracking down the animal. She guaranteed Victor, however, it was a matter of time before she caught the animal. "After all," she said, "who is smarter? Me or a fox?"

Depending on the mood he was in, she'd receive a laugh, or a snarled remark about the intelligence of young girls.

To be on the safe side, on occasion, she still took a chicken, or goose to the dragon as a treat, sprinkling feathers by the handful as she walked into the woods.

On the morning she decided to ride Belinda, Jackie dressed in her warmest fur-lined tunic, riding cloak, leather gloves, and carried with her a pair of men's trousers she retailored from an old pair of her father's meant for Thomas when he grew taller. To add extra protection she wrapped a muffler around her neck and chin, and jammed a wool cap on her head to keep her hair from flying in her face. She sauntered into the mine, her bow over her back along with her quiver of arrows. Setting her bundle of clothing down she announced, "Well, are we ready to go flying?"

Belinda was sleeping. At the sound of Jackie's voice, she raised her head and stared at the young woman in surprise. *"We? I didn't know you could fly."* She stretched her long neck out and surveyed Jackie's quiver and tunic. *"I don't see any wings. Are they hidden beneath the wrappings you have on?"*

"Not me, silly," Jackie scolded, smiling. "I sit on your back." Before the startled dragon responded, she clambered up onto Belinda between her wings and wrapped her arms around the long neck. "Like this."

"Are you sure?" The sinuous neck swung back and Belinda gazed into Jackie's eyes. *"This is the most ridiculous thing I've ever..."*

"Oh, yeah." Jackie nodded vigorously, even though the dragon still appeared dubious. She patted Belinda on the side. "This is how it's supposed to be done. I'm a dragonrider and you're my dragon. Do you know of any different way I can ride you?"

Jackie already smuggled harnesses, straps, and ropes Victor would not miss out of the carriage house, waiting a few days between each thefts before she snuck more up to the mine.

Jackie vaulted off the dragon's back and dragged her tackle beside Belinda. "Let me strap this stuff around you...."

"Are you crazy?" Belinda shifted away, a worried snort issuing from her nostrils.

"Well, we don't want me falling off, do we?" Jackie replied reasonably. She patted Belinda on the head and rubbed behind her ears, putting the harnesses and saddle on the dragon. Belinda kept shifting, watching Jackie as the girl climbed over and under her body. "Now hold still," Jackie said, as she tightened belts under Belinda's stomach, "this is hard enough without you wiggling around."

"Silly, girl," Belinda taunted. *"Well...."* She stood motionless as Jackie threw more straps over her back, and crawled under her belly again, fastening each tight. *"Hey, you're tickling me,"* she tittered with her head between her legs, squirming as Jackie ran a finger under a loop to catch a loose end of rope. *"Stop it."*

Jackie finished lashing her gear on the dragon. She wrapped a rope around her waist in case she needed it. "All done," she exclaimed stepping back to admire her handy-work. "There now, as beautiful as a picture, fit for a dragonrider." She scrambled onto Belinda. "Ready to fly?" She held on tight.

"If you say so," Belinda replied. She surveyed herself in dismay, sniffing at her bindings. *"I feel stupid. Are you sure...?"*

"YES."

Belinda waddled to the edge of the mine opening. *"Here we go."*

The dragon threw herself into the air with a flapping of wings, and sailed out over the forest treetops. Jackie held on tightly, afraid if she loosened her grip, she'd plummet into the woods below. The wind whipped in her face and her cheeks stung. Belinda angled upward as if aiming for the sun and the world shrank behind the two.

"Where are we going?" Jackie shouted above the roar of the air to make herself heard.

Belinda twisted her head back. *"How should I know? You're the dragonrider, right? You tell me."*

"Uh, yeah. Of course." Jackie racked her brain. Where did she want to go now the whole world was hers? A mischievous smirk crossed her face. "Let's buzz the town." Her clothes bundled her completely. No one would possibly recognize her, and she wanted to see the expressions on the townspeople's faces. Maybe Ebba or

Utta were walking the street and she would wave to give the two a thrill.

Belinda rotated in mid-air and made a long dive toward the village, occasionally unfurling her wings to slow their rate of descent. Below, men, women, and children stopped in the road and pointed or gestured in greeting as Jackie and Belinda sailed up the main street heading east.

"Again?"

"No," Jackie decided. She didn't want to cause anyone a heart attack. "Keep going straight. Let's see the ocean."

With mighty flaps, the dragon regained altitude and soared toward the rising sun. Within minutes, the town of Barnard's cove rose into view, nestled between high cliffs on one side and sitting on a wide bay. An invisible hand gripped Jackie's throat. This was the place the Easmen attacked her parents. This is where her mother died.

Jackie discovered guiding Belinda wasn't as hard as she'd thought. Besides talking directly to her, the dragon was sensitive to her every movement. Jackie banked her body to the right and after a moment's hesitation, the dragon swooped in the direction she wanted. Jackie hunched forward. Belinda paused, and then angled down. She made it a point to observe dragonriders the next time she saw any to see if this was how they did it, or if the understanding was something between her and her dragon alone.

The townspeople of Barnard's Cove rushed out of their homes gawking as the dragon flew over. Sailors in the broad bay stood in their boats to have a better look. When one of the skiffs tipped over because the occupants all rushed to one side to view her Jackie realized they'd overstayed their welcome.

"Do you want me to fly low?" The thought drifted to back.

"No."

Belinda kept flying over the ocean. Below, small whitecaps on the greyish-green water marched toward the land. The tangy smell of salt water filled her nose. Farther out to her left, ten dots sped to the shore.

"Do you see those?" Jackie yelled, gesturing. "What are they?"

"Ships."

"Well, yeah, I figured as much. I mean whose?" Jackie shaded her eyes against the glare reflecting off the ocean. "They don't appear to be fishing boats," she said at last. "Let's fly closer and see what's happening."

Belinda banked, angling lower until the water was a hundred feet below. The vessels rushed toward them.

"Oh, no." the first of the ships swept beneath Belinda. In each, thirty men bent to the oars rowing. "They're Easmen this is an invasion fleet."

The last time the devils from across the sea attacked this far south, they'd driven inland for miles, burning and stealing everything in their path. First small raids sailing from the east, and then larger ones assaulted the shores of Micia in waves. They hadn't plundered the land for two years, not since the assault killing her mother. Now they were back.

"Oh, my gosh, what do we do?" moaned Jackie.

"Do? Why should we do anything," the thought echoed in her mind. *"They are not bothering us."* Belinda paused, considering Jackie's statement, and thought, *"You woke me too early this morning. I suppose we could catch breakfast in the ocean. I'm hungry."*

"You don't understand," Jackie screamed. She waved one hand over her head and shoved a finger back to shore. "They're going to murder everyone in Barnard's

Cove."

"*Oh.*" A shrug traveled through Belinda's body.

"We have to warn the town," Jackie gasped. "Fly back."

As Belinda banked, arrows zipped from the boats, leaping upward. None flew close. When the bolts dropped on the ships, Belinda's sole comment was, "*Not nice, are they?*"

"No, they're not—*hurry.*"

Villagers still lined the beach watching the flying dragon as Jackie stormed back. Belinda made a flurrying halt and landed along the shore while spraying sand in all directions. At the last minute, Jackie jerked her muffler higher on her face under her nose until only her blue eyes showed. She ripped off the ropes binding her and vaulted off Belinda's back shouting, "EASMEN." She pointed a shaky hand out to the sea. "*They sail in ten ships. Hurry— warn everyone. Save yourselves.*"

The men and women crowded around her with blank stares trying to figure out what Jackie meant. She screamed again, "EASMEN. OUT THERE. RUN."

A jabber of speech arose as the danger they faced sank in. The townsfolk fled in all directions. Jackie watched the people run with a twisting in the pit of her stomach. *What do I do now?*

The king bequeathed a dragon to the baron who controlled this part of his kingdom. Should she take Belinda and try to locate the rider? The dragon probably stationed at the noble's castle, but her notion of where this lay was hazy at best, somewhere to the west and north, she thought. It would take hours of fruitless searching to try to locate the place if she able to find it at all.

No. The people of Barnard's Cove would know better than she did and would dispatch a rider on horseback. Unless....

She hoped the townspeople didn't take her presence as a sign they were protected and didn't send anyone. She had no idea what to do or how to fight the invaders.

Even if the people did send a messenger, it would still take time to arrive at the castle, locate the rider if he weren't there, and bring him back. The Easmen would attack at any minute. *There wasn't time to wait.*

The boats were drawing close. She saw the masts plainly far out on the ocean as they rose over the horizon.

"What am I going to do?" she paced in a small circle, scuffing up sand as she kept muttering to herself. Jackie tried to remember the stories of how the dragonriders fought. Victor always prattled on, but she'd long ago stopped listening to his stories when it became clear girls would never ride a dragon. Something about tooth and nail, the memory drifted back. They attacked with gleaming teeth and razor sharp claws, ripping apart their assailants while the riders used swords. That was it. She carried her bow, too, if necessary. At the least, she could keep the Easmen occupied and slow the raiders long enough for a real dragonrider to appear and handle the situation.

Jackie unslung the bow and snatched a handful of arrows out of the quiver. She swiveled to Belinda and shouted, "Okay, Belinda, we have business.... What are you doing?"

Fishermen strung a long line of their morning's catch between two poles on a rope, drying in the sun. The dragon smelled the free breakfast and was busy ripping the fish off the cord and devouring each morsel whole. Belinda glanced up from her meal. *"What? I told you I was...."* She saw the look on Jackie's face, flipped her tail high in dismissal, and returned to gobbling seafood.

"This is no time for snacks," snapped Jackie,

scampering onto the dragon's back, "and those aren't yours anyway. Leave the fishermen's catch alone and let's move. We have work to take care of."

Belinda looked up from her breakfast again, annoyed. *"Work? I am a dragon. I do not work. This is for lesser beings."*

Jackie kicked the dragon in the ribs with her heels.

"Oh, all right," the dragon made a grumbling answer. Belinda threw a sad glance at the rest of the fish. *"Where to this time?"*

"Back out to sea," Jackie said grimly. She belted on a single strap across her waist. *Hope this will be enough. Don't have time.* She clutched her bow in one hand, arrows lodged between her fingers.

Belinda took three steps and hurled into the air, flapping her wings, and sped aloft.

As they approached the first of the ships, Jackie clenched her legs tight around the dragon and notched a bolt. "Steady now," she cautioned Belinda, "don't shake me off." She took careful aim at the tiller man and let fire.

The arrow missed, but the helmsman ducked, releasing the rudder. The ship swung to port, losing speed as the rowers stopped their strokes. The sailors scrambled for their weapons and a hail of spears flew upward, some, shot from throwing strings, barely missing Belinda. She threw a haughty glanced at the boat. *"They keep hurling twigs in my direction. I do not think they like me."*

The rest of the ships separated and veered out of the way of the first, but kept rowing for the shore, aided by their square sails pushing the fleet forward. Jackie replied dourly, "I guess not, and I don't believe they'll appreciate us any more once we finish with their boats." She notched a bolt. "Let's swing around and try it again."

Jackie released two more arrows at different vessels. This time arrows flew back at her, close enough to make Jackie flinch. Belinda braked, swooped upward to avoid a bolt. Jackie felt herself slipping and clutched at the dragon's neck, dropping the arrows she held, to fall harmlessly on the men below.

"Hey, be careful, will yah," Jackie yelled as Belinda straightened out her flight again. "You almost lost me."

"Hold on tighter next time," the dragon retorted calmly. *"I am not responsible for unsecured baggage."*

Jackie muttered an inappropriate word under her breath and reached back to grab more arrows from her quiver.

It was empty.

"Oh, shoot." The rest had fallen out. "What are we going to do now?"

"Your problem," came the clipped reply.

"Our problem, you mean," Jackie yelled, frustrated, unable to leave the townspeople to their own defense and with no weapons to battle the Easmen. "Now we have to go down there and fight. I hope your talons are sharp." She loosened the small hatchet at her waist she used for chopping wood, her features locked in grim determination.

Belinda stopped abruptly, hovering in mid-air, resembling a hummingbird. *"I did not come here to fight,"* she declared, considering, *"unless,"* the dragon swung her head to face Jackie, *"I am allowed to eat what I kill?"* She watched Jackie with hunger, her red eyes glowing in anticipation of the meal she'd been denied on the beach.

Jackie's mouth bent in a show of horror. "Most certainly not. Why—the mere thought, it's disgusting."

"Then I'm not going," Belinda thought returned with a bob of her head. She added primly, *"Besides, I am quite neat when I eat."* She started a slow flap back to the shore trailing the fleet.

"But you must fight," Jackie pleaded as she watched the long ships row away from her toward the beach. "Otherwise all those people in Barnard's Cove will be killed, the town destroyed, not to mention the rest of villages the Easmen will attack."

Belinda fell silent in contemplation. Finally, she exclaimed, *"Oh, if it'll make you happy—here. Let's get this over with. We've wasted half the morning with this nonsense."*

She flew after the fleet, passing over the ships.

"Where are you going?" Jackie craned her neck, watching the ships retreat behind her. "The Easmen are back that-a-way."

"Foolish human. You'll see."

Belinda tipped her right wing, sweeping in a wide circle, and started back toward the boats, angling downward. *Next time, I do a loop-the-loop,"* the dragon cautioned Jackie, *"so you'd better learn how to hold tight if we're going to do this often."* She flew at the Easmen low, hardly higher than their masts.

Jackie gasped. *"Watch out."*

Belinda released a blast of flame, which washed over the first ship setting the sail on fire. The warriors on the deck leaped overboard, screaming in panic, their heavy tunics ablaze.

Jackie watched in disbelief as the sailors evacuated their ship, her eyes wide in amazement. "How did you...?"

The dragon flew on, spewing fire until the entire fleet blazed. As black smoke curled to the sky, she banked, flapped hard, and set her nose on the shoreline.

An empty, sandy beach awaited her. Back sweeping, the dragon made a skidding landing in the exact spot on the shore where they'd first started. With a grunt of satisfaction, she shuffled to the line of dried fish still hanging on the line. She pulled another one off, tossed it in the air, catching the tidbit in her wide maw and swallowing with a satisfied grunt. *"Yummy. Now, if you don't mind, let me finish my snack, please."*

Jackie was still gazing out to sea in shock at the plumes of smoke swirling upward into the sky. "Belinda, how did you—how did you do what you did?" She gasped, scrambling off the dragon's back and falling onto the beach in her haste to rush to the dragon's head. She sprang up, brushing sand off her jacket. "The fire...where...?"

"Fire? Oh, you mean this?" Belinda swallowed a fish and blew a short blast of flame. *"Those delicious rocks in the cave. They make me burp."*

"The rocks?" Jackie remembered the silvery stones she'd seen Belinda nibbling on the first day in the mine shaft, and the tiny tongue of flame shooting out of her mouth. "Have you been able to do it all this time?" She asked still unsure if the dragon meant the rock caused the flame or some innate ability of Belinda.

"I hadn't thought about it, until you insisted we fight, but now you reminded me, of course, once I tasted those stones. Blowing fire makes it hard to fly afterward." Jackie heard the equivalent of a mental laugh. *"But I'm not flying right now, am I?"* Her long neck lifted and she glanced over Jackie's shoulder, inland. *"Someone's coming this way."*

Jackie heard a clatter of wings behind her. She whirled around, startled, as a dragon landed on the beach beside her.

A young man, two or three years older than Jackie, jumped off his mount and stormed up to her waving his hands in aggravation. "What goes on here? Who are you?"

Jackie adjusted the muffler up her face until only her eyes showed. *He's angry. Why is he angry with me? I haven't done anything.* Jackie hesitated and then replied, "I'm a dragonrider." She gestured to Belinda who was busy surveying the other beast with interest. The audacity of his attitude got the better of her and she snapped, "Who do you think I am?"

"Why, I…"

The aggravation she'd felt for so many years boiled up inside her. Even when it was obvious what happened she was still in the wrong. She pointed out to sea where the black smoke curled to the sky. "Are you the one who's supposed to be protecting this coast? A fine watcher you are," she scoffed. "I'm doing your job for you. An Easmen fleet was about to land and attack the town."

The man stared from Jackie to the ocean with his mouth open. His attitude changed from one of belligerence to mystification. "I received a report of ships attacking. Why are they ablaze? What magic is this?"

Jackie strode over to Belinda, who was still studying the male dragon intently, and patted her on the wing. "We used fire on the ships."

The rider delivered her a startled look. He turned to his dragon and a silent communication passed between the two. Even more puzzled now the boy gazed out to sea again at the smoke.

Belinda's head swung to Jackie. *"We used fire? I didn't see any flames shooting out of your mouth."*

Jackie ignored this and surveyed the tall boy standing in front of her, bewildered, taking in the dark eyes and the beginning of a black beard curling off his chin. "What's your name?"

"Richard." The dragonrider measured the rider before him staring back with piercing blue eyes and a stocky body covered from head to toe in heavy clothing. "I've never seen you before. You are not one of the riders from Mercia. Where'd you come from?"

Oops. I didn't think I'd have to make up a story. I can't tell him I'm from a barony around here. He'd know right away I was lying. "Uh, North Umbrea," She muttered. "Yeah—flew here for some fun and excitement. You should be glad I did." She made a resolution to concoct a bunch of stories for the future and have one handy in case another rider quizzed her again. She was glad she'd taken the precaution to bundle herself up. What would this boy think if he realized she was a girl?

To direct the conversation away from herself, she said, "Don't you think we'd better go check the Easmen fleet? I won't guarantee I stopped all of it."

Richard's eyes opened wide and he nodded agreement. "You are right." He strode back to his dragon. With faint embarrassment in his voice he said, "You need not accompany me, if you do not wish too. I am able to handle everything from here without your help." With this, he leaped onto his mount and the dragon sprang into the air, flapping out to sea.

"Why those..." Jackie exclaimed. She threw her hands on her hips and glared at the two flying away. She said to Belinda, "Of course they don't need our help. We've done all the work for them. They didn't even say thank you. Of all the ungrateful snobs. I wonder if they're all the same?"

"Niohoggr was nice," remarked Belinda with a sigh, *"and he did say goodbye."*

"Niohoggr? Who's he?"

"The dragon with what's-his-name. The human you were speaking too."

Jackie issued a deep sigh. "Forget about it." She scrambled atop Belinda. "Let's follow and see what they do. Maybe we'll pick up some pointers how real dragonriders operate."

When they arrived at the scene of the battle,

Richard was flying around in a wide circle. Below, the remains of the ships smothered. The boats not set aflame in Belinda's attack caught fire from those already burning, which drifted into their way or ignited by flying embers from the blazing sails. The Easmen, some clinging to charred pieces of wood, the rest swimming, floated shoreward with the incoming tide, lost flotsam adrift on the waves.

Richard spotted the two and his mount zipped to Jackie, back sweeping at the last second and hovered close. The rider cupped his hands. "You and your dragon have done well," He called grudgingly. "Nothing is left for me to do here. I and the villagers will wait until these," he nodded to the drifting men below, "wash ashore and they will be dealt with." He paused, thinking. At length, he shouted, "You never told me your name, or what your dragon is called."

"Jackie," she yelled back. "You may call me Jack if you will." She reached over and patted Belinda on the neck. "And this is Belinda, mightiest of all dragons."

Richard drew his head back, puzzled. "Belinda? This is a female name. No female dragons exist."

To cover her mistake Jackie yelled, "And dragons do not breathe fire, either, do they rider?" She checked the sun. It was high in the sky. She realized it was late. She'd only meant to be gone for an hour. Wood still needed to be collected and the supper started before Victor returned home and began complaining. "Now I must be away, dragonrider," she called out with a wave of her hand. "I leave the invaders to you."

Bafflement showed on Richard's face at her sudden need for departure, but he nodded. Jackie whispered to Belinda, "Let's make ourselves scarce before Mr. Snoopy asks more questions. I've run out of lies for now."

As they flew home over pastures and farms, Jackie

spotted a large expanse of forest with a clearing in the middle abutting a river. No one was about.

"Belinda, land there, will you?"

"More fighting? I don't fight trees, you know."

"Don't act clever. Put your tail down in the empty space."

This was an old logging camp. Jackie didn't know if it were on the king's land, some baron's, or a fief she wasn't familiar with. It didn't matter, the area contained what she needed. Dried branches and trimmings from the logs lay scattered all around. She unwrapped the rope from her waist and got busy gathering up the scraps.

A half an hour later she was finished, three bundles of wood tied and secured around Belinda.

"Is this necessary?" The dragon moaned nudging the sticks with her nose and surveying the load critically. *"Some retribution for the remark I made about trees? I feel so stupid."*

"Yes, it is," Jackie teased with a swift kiss on the dragon's neck, "and be gentle when you're flying." She checked her handy work and hoped the wood didn't fall loose in the air. "If we lose this lumber we'll have to search and collect more. Let's scat before someone wanders along and catches us."

After they flew back to the mine and Jackie tucked her wood into her cart she said to Belinda, "I'll be back tonight, okay? But I gotta run, honey, I'm awful late."

Belinda released a large yawn, resting her head on her forepaws with her tail curled over her nose. *"Don't bother. I'm stuffed with those delicious fish, exhausted from flying all over the kingdom, and the sea air has made me sleepy. I'll see you tomorrow."*

"You're sure?"

"Uh-huh," the drowsy reply seeped into Jackie's mind. A languid quiver ran down the length of the dragon's

body and Belinda's eyes flickered closed. *"And Niohoggr was nice."*

Chapter Five

W hen Jackie woke in the morning, she was surprised to discover Victor, Victoria, and Thomas awake before her and assembled in the dining hall. As she wandered downstairs rubbing her eyes and entered the room, Victor paced around in a tight circle, arms behind his back, his long body bent in thought as his black hair framed his face.

"What's everyone doing up so early?" Jackie yawned. Something important must have happened. Victor had drawn his prized rug from beneath his chair and spread it out to walk on. This only happened at the most important of family crises.

Victoria placed a finger to her lips and motioned her sister to sit and be quiet while her husband spoke.

"...remarkable," Victor said. "A strange rider from a kingdom no one has ever heard of saves one of our towns from the Easmen and disappears almost like a ghost rider."

Jackie became alert. To hide her excitement she poured herself a mug of sage tea and drew out a chair next to Thomas.

Victor glanced up to make sure all eyes were upon him. "It was even said his dragon breathed fire and gulped down the Easmen barbarians in a single bite."

Thomas issued a low exclamation of awe, his eyes growing as big and round as walnuts. "Wow," he breathed. "A whole Easmen?"

Victor nodded soberly. "This is what I was told at the tavern by a farmer who heard it from a fisherman who was there."

A whole Easmen warrior? I remember some fish disappearing but.... Jackie made a face. Drunken talk from drunken men, she decided, but there might be a gem of true in what they talked about, and his informant got the mystery rider correct and the dragon breathing fire. She smiled at Victor with the proper amount of awe and asked, "And no one knows who this ghost rider is? Sh—uh, he appeared out of thin air?"

Victor shrugged and moved to the window, peering upward into the sky as if anticipating a squad of fire breathing beasts to descend on the manor house at any moment. "It was late when word arrived at the tavern...garbled report...unknown rider fighting an invasion force of Easmen. Then Richard from Lord Steben's Barony joined forces with him, but the fighting was already finished." He smirked importantly. "I expect to be called to our baron's side any time now to discuss what must be done about this new rider. Ghost or not, fire breathing dragon or not, the fact remains a strange rider has entered our kingdom from an unknown country. This could well be the start of an invasion by an enemy we know nothing about."

Jackie frowned. "Why must anything be done?" she said, blinking in astonishment. "This sounds as if he did Baron Steben and the rider Richard a favor."

Victor glared at her in amazement and lifted his hands in the air. "Why girl, don't you understand what all this means? Were you not listening to what I said?" He spoke in slow words as if he talked to a simpleton. "Unknown riders flying into our kingdom—from someplace we have never heard of? ON DRAGONS— WHICH SPEW FIRE?" He paused to let his words sink in. "I am sure no matter who this rider is, he is not dropping in on distant countries because he is bored and has nothing better to do. I know our riders do not, and I am sure the baron does not think so, nor do I. No matter what his motives are, I am positive they are not in our best interests." He glared at Jackie as if to say he wouldn't tolerate any more stupid questions from a female.

Jackie knew the look, understood what it meant, however she was unable to stop herself. "But—but...." Jackie sputtered. She didn't believe what she was hearing. She took a gulp of tea to clear her throat and said, "What you're saying is preposterous. How would anyone think this was part of an attack? You said the rider *saved* one of our towns. How can you believe he was attacking us?"

Victor's scowled deepened. He wasn't use to having Jackie criticize his remarks. "Eliminate the competition maybe? Perhaps this new rider thought the Easmen fleet was part of our navy and made a mistake, and then tried to cover up his true intentions later by telling the townspeople he was saving the village?" Victor shrugged. "I can think of a hundred different reasons for him to do what he did, and none of his motives good." He picked up his tea, downed the contents in one gulp, made a face at the cup, and declared, "I am returning to the tavern for *intelligent* conversation. If a messenger from the baron arrives, tell him I am there." With a self-important swirl of his cape, he stalked out of the hall.

After her brother-in-law left, Jackie said to Victoria, "This is stupid. Even the drunks at the tavern wouldn't accept his drivel as possible. You don't believe this nonsense, do you?"

"Hush, Jaqueline." Victoria's eyes narrowed. "I am sure Victor understands these matters better than I do— or you. Besides, it is always better to err on the side of caution." She surveyed the scattered mugs on the table. "Let's clean this mess up and start breakfast. Uh, do you need help?"

Jackie made little circles on the table with her mug. "No, of course not."

"Fine." Her sister stood and waved Thomas along.

"Back upstairs with you and get dressed for school. I expect there will be excitement in plenty in the village today. I may even join Victor at the tavern for a moment to hear the latest news."

As she gathered the dishes together and started breakfast, Jackie kept going over in her mind what this all meant. *What happens next time I go up on Belinda? Will archers shoot at us from every hamlet? Will the dragonriders attack me on sight? I can't fly to the village or into the baron's castle and explain to the people they've made a mistaken—they'd arrest me on general principles because I'm a woman. What am I going to do?*

For the next few days, Jackie kept a low profile, only visiting the mine to see Belinda on her excursions to gather wood in the forest. To her relief the dragon's ravenous appetite abate once she'd reached her full growth and she didn't stray from the mine, content to sun herself at the entrance or sleep.

To Jackie's chagrin, a messenger from the baron did arrive for Victor summoning him to the castle. From what she learned on her brief trips into the village the baron mustered anyone who knew anything about dragons or dragon lore to plot out a strategy of defense in case an attack occurred. Each night Victor returned home, dropping hints of what this council discussed, or with a broad smirk and a wink of the eye tantalizing the family with plans until Victoria, Thomas, and Jackie begged him to say what happened during the day.

As Jackie stepped out of the kitchen one morning to conduct her morning fuel hunt, she was surprised to see a dragon flying over their fief. The rider spotted her staring up and dove down for a landing, scattering dust, chickens, and leaves. Jackie hopped backward out of the way, stumbling in the process before righting herself. The tall figure of Richard leaped from his mount and strode up to her, taking in manor and outbuildings at a single glance.

"Good morning," he said politely, "I am Richard de la Fey. I hope I didn't startle you. I sometimes forget people are not use to having dragons land in their yard."

Jackie glanced down and studied her feet. *Does he recognize me? Does he know who I am?* She replied in a low voice, afraid to look up, "No sir. I am Jaqueline Montagain, and you didn't frighten me, but we have never had a dragonrider visit our poor holding before, and Jeffery of Weatherhill protects our baron's lands. What do you here, if I may ask?"

"The king has commanded all dragonriders to sweep his kingdom," Richard bent low trying to see her face, "searching for a strange dragon not of our realm. You have heard the news?"

"Oh, yes," she glanced up, nodded, and stared at her boots again. "My brother-in-law, Victor La Montrue, sits on the baron's council to advise our lord on what might occur."

"Good." Richard surveyed the sky carefully. "Then you know what I speak of. Have you seen any dragons in the sky, perhaps a boy not of your village wandering about?" He measured her up and down. "About your height, I imagine."

Jackie tried to stand smaller, the thumping in her chest slowing as she relaxed. *He doesn't recognize me. He's seeking a man.* "No. Nothing sir. In fact yours is the first dragon I've ever seen close up, besides in the air, of course." She peered around Richard, studying his mount. The dragon was busy sniffing the breeze. "How do you stay on? Are they hard to ride?" *He has a single saddle like a horse, not the ropes and straps I used on Belinda. Do we have a saddle I can steal?*

Richard chuckled and beamed down into her eyes. "Not hard at all. It takes practice, but once a dragon and rider learn each desire's, it is as if they are bonded together." He stopped and his lips broadened. "Do you want to take a ride?"

Jackie gasped. "Me? Is it allowed?" Her heart leaped, racing in her chest. Caution took over. The rider didn't recognize her, but what about the dragon?

Richard released a deep guffaw. "Of course, if I say you are, and Niohoggr agrees to it." He swung to his mount. "What think you, old friend? Want to give this pretty girl a ride?"

Jackie heard no reply, but Richard nodded. "Niohoggr says yes. You smell good. Well?"

Before she answered, he sprang onto the dragon's back and extended his hand to her. With growing excitement, Jackie grasped his outreached fingers and Richard hauled her up into the saddle behind him. "Put your arms around my waist and hang on tight," he commanded.

With a leap, the dragon launched himself into the air. Wind rushed through Jackie's hair as the mighty creature streaked upward with powerful flaps of wings. The beast leveled off and started a long glide, then banked making a grand circle around the manor and fief.

"How are you doing back there," Richard yelled to Jackie over the howl of the air.

"Great." When she rode Belinda, she was too nervous to enjoy the flight. Now she gazed about, taking in the landscape below as it drifted past, and the sensation of floating in the sky. She gazed at her fief, never having seen it from this angle before. "How do you tell him where you want to go?" she screamed back.

"Once you have ridden a dragon for a while, he'll learn your movements. Watch." Richard leaned forward and Niohoggr sped up with a few flaps of his wings. Next Richard bent to the right and the dragon immediately followed, dipping into a turn. "See?"

This confirmed what she was beginning to learn with Belinda. *Practice is all we need. We have the basics. Must learn this if we are to become a true dragonrider and her mount.* She wiggled in her seat. The saddle was tight and secure. *Much better than the way I'd rigged Belinda. Why didn't I think of this before?*

They continued to sail. Jackie snuggled closer to Richard, laying her cheek against his muscular back while she enjoyed the sights, and the warmth of his body. The odor of sweat and leather from his jacket mingled with the scent of cloves from the dragon.

"I have yet to search this section," Richard yelled to make himself heard over the howling of the wind. He pointed to the left toward the baron's forest where Jackie's fief met the woods. "We'll take a ride and survey it together." The dragon swung.

Before Jackie and Richard, jutting into the air, sat Baldhill.

Jackie's insides convulsed in panic. *What if Belinda sees us? What if she takes flight?* She called back to Richard, "Your wasting your time. I walk this forest everyday searching for wood. If anything lurked, I would have noticed it. But…" She tugged urgently at the back of his jacket, "fly back toward the manor house. If someone wanted to hide a dragon I might know where it is."

Richard's attention flipped from Baldhill to Jackie. "Where?" The dragon swung sharply and started to Jackie's home.

"Keep going," Jackie yelled, relief surging through her as the mountain shrunk into the distance. A moment later she said, "Do you see it—on the left…the building and water? Land there."

They swooped down between boathouse and lake. Jackie waved an arm at the dilapidated structure. "I know it's little, but if a person wished to hide a dragon this would be the place. We stopped fishing when my brother-in-law deemed it a waste of time. No one works here anymore." She nodded to the lake. "Here is water to drink and fish to eat for rider and dragon also."

Richard dismounted and eyed the small building dubiously. "You are right, too small," he declared, walking to the door and peaking inside. He studied the muddy earth searching for tracks. "No one has been here in a long time." He glanced at Jackie. "You say this is not used anymore?"

Jackie shook her head. "No. Victor... he thought it...."

"Not a wise choice, I think." Richard strolled to the water and stood on the shore, taking in a lungful of air. "I enjoy fishing," he murmured, picking up a pebble and tossing it as far as he could. "Would your brother-in-law mind if I returned here one day to fish and relax?" His eyes shifted to a rowboat turned over and resting on the shore. "Maybe you would take me out and show me the best places to toss in a line. It would be nice to drift along with a beautiful girl at my side." He threw her a grin.

Jackie's face flushed pink. She spun and pretended to study the water. "Of—of course," she stammered. "This is the least I can do for a dragonrider who protects us, and I am sure Victor would have no objections." She wanted to add, "I'll be waiting," and then put her hand over her mouth.

Her uneasiness didn't go undetected by Richard, who chuckled and glanced at the sky, saying, "I have kept you too long, Lady Jaqueline, and it grows late. I will take you to your home and be on my way."

A few moments later, Richard deposited her on the front lawn. Before he few off she said, "Thank you for the ride, it was fun." She studied his face. She'd noticed without noticing black marks under his eyes. She wondered if it was from riding or for some purpose she was unaware of. "Why are your cheeks black? Did you ride through fire flying here?"

"This?" He rubbed a finger lightly beneath his eye and drew away a black tip. "This is soot. Dragonriders put it under our eyes to cut down the glare from the sun when we fly." He smirked. "I do not know if it does any good, but we all do it."

"Oh." She would file this away for later use. "Again, thank you for the ride, I had a wonderful time."

Richard nodded. "Thank *you* for the information—and your company. I will make sure to keep an eye on the lake, and if you will, take note of any strangers passing by." He waved and flew away.

Jackie watched him go with mixed feelings. She didn't want him nosing around where he would sight Belinda, but she hoped he'd return to see her again, or go fishing. The thought kept circulating in her mind what it would be like, both of them flying together on their dragons in the sky.

***

"Okay, you. We gotta practice." Jackie vaulted on Belinda's back. "You remember the moves?"

"Of course," the huffed reply buzzed in her head. *"I am a dragon. I remember everything."*

For the past week, Jackie spent hours a day with Belinda in the mine practicing body commands. She'd discarded the series of straps and ropes she used to secure herself onto Belinda's back. Instead, the binding were replaced with an old saddle she discovered in the barn, modified with a wider belly strap to accommodate the dragon's broader girth. An additional belt looped around her waist, in case her feet loosened from the stirrups while Belinda made one of her bizarre twists.

Two days after her meeting with Richard she

73

observed a dark shape flying high over her fief from the safety of the shaft opening, but it never reappeared again. Victor brought rumor the dragonriders continually scanned the kingdom searching for the phantom rider, besides keeping watch on the coast awaiting an attack by the Easmen. Jackie thought it was best to wait a few more days to be on the safe side, before attempting her silent commands in the air. Now she was all set, she hoped.

In addition to bow and quiver of arrows she habitually carried now, Jackie also smuggled her sword out of the house to the mine and wore it while practicing, noting Richard armed himself in the same manner. She bundled up tight in her warmest clothes, scarf around her neck, and wool cap on her head. She'd also scrapped soot off the bottom of one of the cooking pots, mixed it with pig's fat, making a black salve and saving it in a clay jar. She dipped her forefinger in and underscored each of her eyes. *There, now I look the perfect dragonrider.*

Jackie scrambled on Belinda's back. "Are we ready?"

"I've been ready, slowpoke."

"Okay." Jackie gulped. "Here we GO." She leaned forward.

Belinda leaped out of the mouth of the mine and sped into the air, gaining speed and height rapidly with thrusts of her wings. Once they were high enough for the trees to appear as bushes, Jackie leaned back and the dragon stopped beating her wings and soared.

"Perfect," yelled Jackie with a broad smirk spreading across her face.

"Of course." Belinda swung her head to regard Jackie and answered smugly, *"What else did you expect?"*

Jackie ran through every maneuver she'd seen Richard and Niohoggr perform. Even sitting in the saddle felt safe once she grew accustomed to the lack of security the ropes provided, binding her to Belinda's broad back. By the time she deemed they'd practiced everything as well as she possible, Jackie discovered herself far out over the ocean.

"More dragons ahead."

"I see 'em," Jackie replied. Winged specks darted downward to the sea, while more dashed upward into the clouds. "There's a battle going on."

She shifted and Belinda mimicked her movements.

As they flew closer, a flotilla of ships leaped into view on the water. Some flew the lion crest of her Micia kingdom. The vast majority carried the sinister eagle, the emblem of the Easmen. The two forces battled—the lion was losing.

From the sky, the dragonriders darted down, slashing masts with massive tails while cruel jaws and talons ripped the enemy warriors to ribbons. They would leap upward again, gaining height, twist to dive bomb another ship, but the sheer volume of enemy boats made it impossible to stem the tide of invasion. Two of the king's vessels trailed smoke while dragons and riders streamed blood from dozens of wounds.

Jackie drew her scarf tighter around her face to protect her from the acid smoke rising from the burning ships. She yelled, "We have to help our people. Let's go." She leaned forward and put Belinda into a dive.

As Jackie joined the fight plunging downward, she passed a startled Richard swooping upward on Niohoggr, both dragon and rider streaked red in sword wounds. Jackie and Richard's eyes locked, his with surprise, hers narrowed in determination.

Faintly the cries of battle rang in Jackie's ears, the moans of the wounded and dying echoing from below. Even fainter, the shouts of the dragonriders spread as they called back and forth in confusion about Jackie's sudden presence. She ignored everything and concentrated on the destruction beneath her, an avenging angel swooping on the unwary. "Let's show those boys what a real dragonrider does," she whispered in Belinda's ear.

Jackie drew her sword.

Chapter Six

The flagship of the Easmen fleet lay before her. Belinda screeched, talons extended, as she flashed down, snapping off the mast of the ship with a claw. Rowers scattered as she released a blast of fire, which swept across the deck in a rolling wave. Both sails and ship ignited, warriors caught in the blaze screamed and jumped overboard in terror as their clothing burned. Jackie swung her sword as they skimmed along the deck when one sailor leaped at her in a desperate attempt to rip her off the back of the dragon. Her sword connected with a THUMP and the man tumbled away.

Belinda lunged upward, beating her wings to gain height for another dive.

"This is kinda fun," the dragon announced with a savage chuckle as she leveled off.

"Yeah, fun." Jackie glanced down. Easmen blood splattered her right leg. "Let's hope the fun doesn't attack our way."

Jackie circled above the locked ships, seeking additional targets. Four longboats broke away from the main battle and rowed toward shore. Jackie pointed the tip of her sword at the fleeing vessels. "They're next."

Belinda flew in low, the crest of the waves missing her belly by feet. This time her wings clipped the mast of two ships as she flashed between the boats, snapping the wood and showering the sailors with splinters as if they were spears intended to pierce the flesh.

The rest of the ships behind the lead two saw the dragon approaching. In desperation, the helmsmen leaned on their tillers trying to evade her rushing onslaught without success. Belinda blew a blast of fury over the boats and they exploded into flame. Jackie breathed with satisfaction, *"This is five for us."*

During the fight, they'd drifted apart from the rest of the battle. As the two increased altitude, Jackie scanned the ocean to see how the balance of the melee progressed.

The enemy fleet stopped dead in the water. The tide of battle turned with the Easmen ships trying in vain to swing about and flee home. Those few remaining who chose to stay and fight engaged with the ships of the king in a riot of confusion. The escaping vessels were easy meat for the dragonriders, picking out individual targets and harrying the boats.

One ship, larger than the rest, fought in raging combat with a dragonrider. Instead of the usual swoop and dive attack the riders employed, this time dragon and rider landed on the deck of the embattled boat struggling furiously with the crew. Jackie drifted closer to see why.

The rider stood guarding his mount while the dragon snapped at the attacks, also ripping at ropes with a clawed forefoot, trying to free a wing tangled in the rigging of the mast keeping the creature bound to the ship.

Belinda made a hissing noise deep within her throat. *"Fouled himself, the fool. He is trapped now."*

"His rider refuses to leave him," Jackie replied. As they sailed closer she exclaimed, "Those are Richard and Niohoggr, We have to help them escape or they'll be killed."

Belinda's thoughts raged in Jackie's brain. *"Stupid—stupid. How dumb can you get?"* She dropped into a long fall, but slowed as she approached the ship. *"There's no place to land,"* she complained in aggravation gliding in a tight arc around the vessel.

"Yes there is," Jackie yelled back, training her sword at a spot as they zipped past, "on the stern—by the rudder."

Belinda braked, went vertical, twisting her body as she shot upward. Jackie felt herself slipping down from the dragon's back and as suddenly slamming forward. Belinda plunged again. With a clattering of wings, she made a skidding landing on the stern of the boat.

At once, two of the sailors broke off their attack on Richard and started toward Jackie with murderous shrieks and swords lifted over their heads. She heard the hissing that preceded Belinda belching fire and screamed, "No. You'll hit Richard too." She leaped off the dragon's back, swinging her sword, and engaged the two warriors with a flurry of clashing blades.

One Easmen swung at her head. Jackie bent low and the edge missed her scalp by inches. She jabbed back, slicing into his calf muscle. The sailor howled and fell over grasping his leg, tripping his companion as the warrior rushed forward.

Jackie sprang up again, leaping headlong at the sailor. The point of her weapon caught the man in the chest. He bellowed in pain, clutching at the sword in agony as he toppled to his knees. Jackie yanked her blade back and vaulted over the bodies, struggling to Richard through the jumble of rigging tangling the deck. Belinda waddled behind with gaping jaws protecting her back from any more assaults.

"Watch out."

Niohoggr was tearing at the ropes trapping him. Richard pivoted around as a sailor attempted to pierce the dragon in the eye. The rider swung his sword, connecting, but failed to see a warrior spring at him from the far side of the ship. At Jackie's shout, Richard leaped backward and stumbled over his first opponent.

Without hesitation, Jackie heaved herself on the warrior, wrapping one arm around the sailor's neck and locking the crook of her elbow against his windpipe. The Easmen bent forward, trying to throw her off while tearing at her forearms with his fingers. Jackie clamped her legs around his waist and rode him as if she were astride a bucking horse. A gurgling noise arose from his throat and the man fell to his knees, hands clutching at her arm.

Faint screams echoed in Jackie's ears. She realized she was the one producing the shrieks.

The sailor stretched prone on the deck, motionless. Jackie staggered to her feet in a crouch prepared for more fighting.

"It is you."

Richard dispatched an attacking sailor and stared at her again. "What are you doing here?"

Jackie drew herself erect. "What does it look like? Helping you—again." Her eyes darted to the deck of the ship. Dead bodies littered the surface, the rest of the sailors bolting over the side of the boat. For the moment, they were free of danger.

The frantic struggles of Niohoggr, however, coupled with the combined weight of both dragons, caused the waves to slosh over the gunwale of the longboat. The ship was taking on water and sinking fast. "We gotta escape out of here."

"No." Richard glanced over his shoulder. If anything, the rigging tangled Niohoggr more than ever. "If my dragon drowns, I will drown with him," he declared stoutly, taking a stance as if to say no one would deny him the right.

Jackie made a face. "Dumb," she hissed back. Water covered her ankles lapping at her calves. It was a matter of minutes before the longboat would disappear forever, dragging the dragon and rider down with it. She studied the ropes carefully. Even hacking away with their swords, the beast would not be free in time.

"Are we ready to leave now, or is there some reason to go swimming?" Belinda sniffed at the water. *"I sense fish below us. If we are to stay I am catching*

something to eat for breakfast."

"Belinda, do you know…?" She pleaded with her dragon, hoping the beast discerned a solution as she tugged helplessly at the ropes.

"Oh, is this why we aren't leaving. You three are the most incompetent…. Take the foolish human and climb on my back before we all drown."

Jackie reached out and snatched Richard's arm. "Quick, mount on Belinda. She has an idea." She dragged the startled rider toward her mount.

"But…" Richard yanked back refusing to flee his dragon's side.

"NO TIME." Jackie seized the fringe of his collar and shook him. "Get up behind me—*now.*" She leaped up on Belinda, dragging Richard to the dragon's side and hauled him behind her.

"We all set now?" Belinda swung her head from the two riders to the dragon before her. *"This won't take but a moment."* Flame blazed from Belinda's mouth, washing over Niohoggr.

"Stop it, you are killing him," gasped Richard. He pounded on the dragon's back trying to gain her attention.

The fire stopped. Black ashes swept away in the water, the ropes binding the male dragon burnt completely off. Belinda leaped into the air as the water splashed around her stomach and flicked her tail in arrogance at the male dragon. *"Enough, but not too much,"* she thought at Jackie with a lofty sniff. *"Make sure he stays behind me and doesn't get lost."*

Jackie swung around and checked Niohoggr. His neck and tail angled straight out as he beat upward. "Don't worry, he is," she replied proudly. "You've got one frightened dragon on your tail."

As Belinda flapped into the air, the male dragon continued to match her wingbeat for wingbeat until they hovered high above the battle. Richard surveyed Niohoggr in admiration. "Not a burn mark on him," he exclaimed, shouting over Jackie's shoulder to Belinda, "Thank you."

Below, the battle ended. The remains of the Easmen fleet fled back over the horizon. The king's ships picked up survivors of the fight, friend or foe, while the dragonriders acted as spotters.

Belinda labored, taking two wing strokes to Niohoggr's one. Jackie whispered in the dragon's ear, "What's the matter, girlfriend, we weight too much for you? Did you get hurt in the fight?" Jackie hadn't seen the dragon take any injuries in the melee, and no gashes showed on the scaly sides, but her attention was directed elsewhere.

"I am fine, but I feel so heavy," the dragon wheezed, gulping air. *"I don't know…"* she gasped, *"I'm all funny inside."*

Jackie yelled to Richard, "Is there someplace close to set down around here? Belinda isn't feeling well. I don't know what's wrong with her."

"Yes." Richard shouted to Niohoggr, "Take the dragon to the island. You know the way."

The male dragon assumed the lead, banked, heading shoreward but to the east also. A small island rose on the horizon, stunted trees standing guard in the middle of the barren landscape.

"We use this place as a resting spot and rendezvous point when we are on patrol over this part of the ocean," Richard explained to Jackie. "The balance of the squad should be arriving after they have finished with the navy."

"So heavy," whimpered Belinda. Her wings faltered and she dropped with a lurch before regaining her beat. Niohoggr's long neck twisted back and he regarded her with concern. He slowed and dropped until Belinda

82

flew directly above him. Then he rose again until she rested on his broad back.

The island grew larger. When they reached within a mile of land, the male dragon disengaged himself from Belinda and she swept in making a rough landing in the sand. Jackie and Richard leaped off the dragon's back and Jackie rushed to Belinda's head.

"Are you all right, honey? Does it hurt someplace?" Jackie felt Belinda all over searching for wounds.

"Feeling better," she admitted. Belinda stared at Niohoggr. *"He says I lost the air from my body using the flame. It will return in a minute, and I'll be fine."*

"Air?" Jackie glanced from Belinda to the male dragon and back again. "You talk to him? What's this air all about?"

"Of course. We are both dragons, aren't we?" Her nose pointed to Richard. *"You speak to this human, right?"*

Richard watched this one-sided conversation in confusion. He asked, "What's she saying?" He stepped close and stroked her side. "Everything all right now?"

"She's saying something about her air," Jackie replied, perplexed. She took a deep breath. "Maybe the air we breathe?"

Richard paused and listened. "Niohoggr says dragons have special bladders filled with air which makes their kind light. They mix it with...." he frowned. "I do not understand the word, a rock they chew apparently, producing fire. She used up all her "air," now she must recharge." The boy nodded in relief. "She will be fine in a minute."

The silvery rock in the mine—of course, but why didn't the rest of the dragons eat it?

Richard studied Belinda speculatively and his eyes

shifted to Jackie. "The question is, where did she find this magic stone? This is the first I have heard of it. The rest of our dragons could be breathing fire as well."

Jackie fidgeted and shrugged. "Uh, I don't know. Have you asked your dragon why he doesn't locate some himself and eat it?" If she told Richard about the mine, he'd realize her true identity. She was a girl—they'd take Belinda away from her.

"Niohoggr says there is none to be found." Richard rubbed his cheek. "This is something I must discuss with the rest of the riders. Want a marvelous discovery if our dragons breathed fire."

Richard stared at the dragon a minute longer and dropped onto the beach, saying in disgust, "It never fails." He threw a shell into the surf, his eyes flashing. "I do not know how it is in you kingdom, but here the fates stand in our way preventing us from reaching our full potential of protectors for the realm." He reached into the sand for another shell.

Jackie took a seat next to him hugging her knees. "I'm not sure what you mean. How so? Except for your dragon's breathing fire what skills don't you have?"

"It's not talent," Richard denied. "The dragons even without fire are fine. It is the people ruling us. The barons keep us too close to their own fiefs for us to do much good protecting the land," he explained sourly. He waved back to the mainland. "It took the direct order of the king for us to join to prevent this attack."

"Well, at least you did prevent it," Jackie replied.

"Yes, but we can do much more. Now if we had this stone the dragons speak of..." Richard sighed. "I do not know if this would be for the better or worse."

Jackie studied Richard's face, saw the slumping of his shoulders in defeat. "How could it be worse?" she asked. "Wouldn't the barons feel more secure? I know I would if fire-breathing dragons protected this land. They should let you roam more freely."

"Perhaps," Richard agreed, reluctantly, "or maybe they would feel more threatened by our power and disband us, king's orders or not. He might even command it himself."

Jackie hadn't thought about it this way. "Politics and veiled acts of intrigue are way beyond me," she admitted. Jackie gave a small laugh, still watching Richard's expression. "Perhaps I am too naïve to see what is beyond a person's statements."

"I also," agreed Richard, "and I was brought up in a household of half-truths and secrets." He scrubbed at his forehead. "I met a girl a few days ago." He laughed. "Quite alluring she was too—asked her to go fishing." He broke out into a loud deriding laugh. "Afterward I realized how much of a bore I must have acted, speaking the way I did. She must think me…" He hesitated and said in a low voice, "Sometimes I wish I was never chosen as a rider, and go fishing with beautiful girls all the time."

Underneath her scarf, Jackie's cheeks burnt hot. *He thinks I'm attractive? The scullery maid? The wood collector? I thought he was being polite, not a bore at all.*

Dots in the sky grew into dragons and riders as they appeared closer. Each made a swooping landing shooting sand and water in all directions until the whole squad assembled on the beach.

"Richard." A tall, blond-haired boy scrambled through the sand and grabbed the rider, pounding him on his back. "I thought you were a goner for a moment when I saw you stuck on that ship." The rest of the riders crowded around the two. The young man swung and bowed to Jackie. "And we have you to thank, sir. I was sure we'd lost this yeasty pile of dough to the Easmen raiders." He smirked with a sly wink. "It took me a year to train this one. I do not want to go through the problems of breaking in a new student."

The balance of the riders released a chorus of chortles. Richard laughed along with the rest while flushing pink and said to Jackie, "Johnathan was my mentor when I first became a rider, taught me everything I know, except how to unstick my dragon from a fallen rigging."

The sun was well up, beating down on the group and reflecting off the sand. In her heavy clothes, Jackie felt sweat trickling down her back and sides, ticking and itching as it seeped through her undershirt and stained her tunic dark. The other riders sweated also, stripping off their heavy riding cloaks and tunics with sighs of "This is better," and "Feel the breeze."

"You are going to roast if you do not shed your cap and cloak," advised Richard to Jackie as he saw her wilting under the heat.

"Uh, no, it's okay," stammered Jackie as perspiration dripped down her face. "I'm fine the way I am."

Richard waved to the trees in the center of the Isle. "At least sit up here in the shade. I want the rest of the riders to hear about this magic stone your Belinda eats." He strolled to the biggest tree set in the middle of the small island, waving his hand for Jackie to join him. The balance of the riders lounged there already, talking excitedly about the battle. When they saw Jackie and Richard approaching, and Jackie still wearing her heavy clothes they shout for her to make herself comfortable.

Jackie began taking off her riding cloak and froze. She knew she was not big on top, but her bodice clung to her from the sweat, even though she also wore a tunic, the cut made it plain she was female. "I'm okay," she called to the riders, avoiding their eyes and scowling at the sun instead. To Richard she said, "It's getting late. I gotta go."

"Wait." Richard ran after her. "You cannot leave yet. Everyone wants to know you and hear your story." He reached out an arm and placed his hand on her cloak.

Jackie spun, her eyes narrowing to mere slits. "Take your hands off me." She shook herself loose, fingers going to the hilt of her sword. She had to take this from Victor, but this *boy* held no authority over her. "If you want to know about me then know this, I arrive and depart as I please and no one will tell me different."

The rest of the riders fell silent, listening intently to the conversation. Richard drew back, shocked. "I did not mean... We are all—" His shoulder slumped as he read the expression in Jackie's eyes. "I meant to say we are all interested in you. The first time we met your dragon wore straps and ropes—so different from our gear. Now you use a saddle but with a belt to keep you secure." He stopped, mulling over the enigma she presented. "You appear out of nowhere. You vanish..." His voice trailed off. "You are welcome to join us any time you wish," he ended lamely.

Jackie relaxed, realizing she'd overreacted. She said quickly, "I'll find you again, don't worry, and we will have a long talk then." She snapped her fingers. "Maybe I can discover what Belinda chews and bring a sample back. How does this sound?"

"It would be great."

Looking up at the sun, she knew even at the pace Belinda would set she was in trouble back home. "Let me go. I'll meet you back here tomorrow morning as the sun rises."

Jackie hurried to Belinda. The male dragons crowded around her. "Oh, out of the way, you brutes." She kicked one in the tail and received a surprised grunt in return as the beast lumbered out of her path. "Back—back, I say." She pushed her way through the dragons until she was at her dragon's side.

"They were being friendly," complained Belinda. *"No need to twist your trousers out of joint."* Jackie swore she hear a dragonish giggle echo in her mind.

"Don't worry about my trousers, fresh, and you're too young to have boyfriend dragons," Jackie scolded. She leaped on Belinda's back. "Maybe when you're older."

"You're no fun," the sullen retort floated to her. The dragon swung her head to stare Jackie in the eye. *"Just because you aren't interested in Niohoggr's rider doesn't mean I...."*

"Oh, shut up and start flying." She darted a quick look over her back at the riders watching her from the trees. She whispered, *"You don't know what you're talking about."* In a louder voice she said, "Are you filled with plenty of air now? Sounds as if you're full of it."

Belinda gave a small spring testing her buoyance. *"Yes,"* she grumped. She shot a sideways glance at the male dragons. *"See yah later."*

All the way back to the mine, Jackie mulled over in her head the things Richard talked about.

So, it wasn't fun and games being a dragonrider. In a way his life was as bad as hers, always wishing to do great things and not allowed to. At least all she must put up with were Victor's snide remarks, not the political intrigue Richard hinted at. Tomorrow she would take a piece of the silver rock and present the stone to Richard. There must be more places in the kingdom where it was available. Baldhill couldn't be the sole mine. They would search. If necessary, she would hunt with the riders until Richard and his friends had a plentiful supply. How was dragons breathing fire be a bad thing.

Did he really think I was beautiful?

Chapter Seven

J ackie woke and hurried to the mine. Overhead the moon sank beneath the forest tops and false dawn crept across the horizon. Belinda still slept, coiled into a tight ball with her eyes showing between the loops of her tail and forelegs. She woke with a start and a short snort of flame as Jackie stumbled through the entrance in the dark.

"Go away," she mumbled. *"I'm still tired from yesterday, and had to hunt last night."* She yawned deeply, and her head rose to regard Jackie with annoyance. Her red eyes glowed above her tail in the darkness, half closed. *"What happened to the good old days when you use to bring me my breakfast?"*

"You grew up and became fat and lazy," Jackie retorted, "but maybe tomorrow," she hedged, "a snack if you promise to be good. Today we have too much to do." Early on, she'd smuggled candles out of the house, using the tapers to explore the back reaches of the mine tunnel. She hadn't noticed any of the silver rock strewn on the shaft floor, but then again, she didn't search for any either being more interested in seeing how far the passageway extended. This time as she lite a candle, she made a careful examination of the walls and rubble scattered on the floor.

To Jackie's delight, she discovered small crystals of the stone mixed in with the common stone, and as she wandered deeper into the shaft, a few more spots where it jutted from the walls as the tunnel twisted and turned, tracing the vanished vein of gold. She filled her pockets with as many as would fit and ran back to Belinda.

"Is this what you've been chewing on?" Jackie held out a piece of rock. "The stone making you breathe fire?"

Belinda uncurled enough to sniff at the stone

89

curiously. Her eyes opened wide in delight. *"Yummy. This is better than breakfast. I used everything up in my stomach yesterday. You are forgiven for not fetching me food."* Her black tongue flicked out and the rock disappeared into her gullet.

Jackie snatched her hand back but it was too late. The dragon nuzzled her arm for more. "Hey, I was going to save this piece." Her lips bent up. "I suppose you deserve some too, though. You did well yesterday. Here…." She handed the dragon a few more morsels, which vanished as quickly as the first did, and dumped the rest into a carrying bag. "Now we have to take another ride."

"Too early," moaned Belinda, and wrapped her tail over her face again, neck slumping back down onto the floor.

A mischievous expression flashed across Jackie's face. She bent close to the dragon and whispered in an exposed ear, "We have to meet Richard and Niohoggr at the island again. Who knows, maybe the rest of the riders will be there too, with their dragons. It would be a shame if all those *boy* dragons didn't get to see you again, wouldn't it?"

Belinda's eyes snapped open. *"Oh, all right, if you insist. I guess I should let the males bask in my magnificence."* She stood, stretched to her full length with a wiggle, and sauntered to the entrance of the mine. *"Hop on."*

Jackie chuckled to herself, drawing her riding cloak tightly about her, and wrapping the scarf around her mouth. With a grunt, she hauled herself onto the back of the waiting dragon. "You remember the way?"

"No fighting this time?" Belinda countered. *"It seems as though every time we fly together we end up in a battle. No fun."*

Jackie crossed her fingers. "No combat—I

promise." She added to herself, *I hope not.*

Richard waited on the island when they landed, sitting under the same tree as the previous day as if he'd never left. Belinda skidded to a halt in the soft sand and a serpentine neck popped out of the ocean—Niohoggr. Jackie startled and yelled to Richard in surprise as the boy sauntered up, "Dragon's swim?"

He laughed. "Of course. In fact, they love it. Good at it too. Niohoggr says it's the same as flying underwater." He added, "Your dragon never swum before?"

Niohoggr watched Belinda, head sticking up like a tree from the ocean. He made a twisting motion with his neck, snout pointing to the deeper reaches of the water.

Jackie did a quick take from Niohoggr, to Belinda and back to Richard. "Ah, yeah. Sure, but we don't live near the ocean, so the dragons never have a chance. I didn't know they all did it."

Belinda swung her head to Jackie, *"Would you mind...? Niohoggr says there are delicious fish waiting to be caught and I haven't had my breakfast yet."*

"Oh, go ahead," Jackie replied with a wave of her hand, "have fun and fill your belly if you want to. Don't drown or get lost." The dragon waddled off, sliding into the surf in Niohoggr's direction. The two dragon heads disappearing from view under the waves.

"The rest of the riders aren't coming?" Jackie scanned the small island. "I thought they were eager to..."

"Oh, they will be here," Richard assured her as they strolled back up to the tree, "but first they must do fly-overs of their baron's territory." Richard checked the ocean where a red sun rose. "This doesn't start until now, when they can see what is happening below. Afterwards they report to the master-of-arms. When all this is finished, they are free for the day, unless their barons have a mission of importance, or a message needing delivery in a hurry. Then they must sort of," he groped for the word, "sneak away."

"Huh?" Jackie stuck her lip out and her eyes narrowed. "They're dragonriders. You said their duties are finished. Why must they sneak anywhere?"

Richard sprawled out under the tree, and patted the sand next to him, still searching the ocean. Jackie sat next to him, wrapped her arms around her knees with a quizzical expression.

"Let me explain the politics of this kingdom to you," Richard began. "Riders are both feared and loved. The barons and king love us because we add protection to their land and provide rapid communication in case of danger."

"Of course," Jackie replied as if his answer were obvious. "This is what riders do. Why would anyone fear you for doing what you're supposed to do?"

"They also worry about us…"

"But why?"

Richard stared at her. "Imagine what would happen if the riders united under one baron or, worse yet, united together against the king and barons."

Jackie's eyes widened in alarm. "It would mean civil war at the least," she said slowly in dawning comprehension.

"Right." Richard nodded enthusiastically and spread his hands wide in the air. "This is why the king is not allowed to have all the riders under his direct control. The nobles fear an iron hand would rule the land, and they would have no recourse. This is also why the king makes sure only one dragon is allotted per barony. Both king and nobles wish to keep the power divided equally among them so no one has the upper hand." Richard added hastily with a sense of loyalty to the kingdom, "This was agreed upon in council after the king united the various chiefdoms of this island under one rule. The system has worked well up to now."

"Now?" Jackie shook her head, still not understanding. "What has changed?"

Richard sighed and stretched his long body on the sand, making himself comfortable against the tree with his hands behind his head. "Us, the dragonriders. You must remember, when the council agreed to the division of dragons among the barons, they did not know how many would be discovered, or if any would be located at all. In the last few years, many eggs have turned up. Both King and nobles fear the growing power of my kind."

"I guess you riders aren't allowed to assemble often?" Jackie said.

"Only in emergencies, as you saw yesterday," Richard replied with a sharpness making Jackie study his face. He noticed Jackie's expression and added with a shy smirk, "Or when we have a reason to steal away. The lords fear us gathering. They think we plot and plan against their rule."

Jackie never thought of these things before. Up until now, the manor house encompassed her world, the duties Victor laid on her, and the slow destruction of her parent's fief. Remarks as politics and, a majority of nobles nominated for riders, now began to make sense. *Keep it in the family. The loyal will be loyal.* A thought struck her. "Why were you able to slip away without having your whereabouts questioned?"

"Well," Richard started, blushing, "My uncle is steward to my baron."

"He is?"

"Yes, and also the brother of the baron. My father is brother also, and supervises the estates of my uncle."

Jackie drew back from him in awe and exclaimed, "You're like a noble, right?"

"Yes, but the point being, they trust me not to start

any rebellions," Richard hurried to explain. "This morning I was able to make a quick survey of the barony and excuse myself without questions asked. The rest..." he grimaced, "are not as lucky. If our dragons learn the secret of fire, it may well be, I will have problems excusing myself also."

Belinda and Niohoggr stomped out of the ocean, spraying water and sand in all directions as they frolicked up the beach to the tree and shook themselves.

"Oh, you," Jackie sputtered as she and Richard covered their heads and faces. She wiped a glob of mud from her riding cloak. "Over there, both of you." She waved a finger at a stretch of beach well away from her and Richard. "Don't return until you are dry." The two dragons waddled off with flicks of their tails.

Jackie brushed at her clothes. "You would think they'd have enough sense." Her hand hit the purse on her tunic. "Oh, speaking of fire, I forgot. Here." She tugged off the pouch around her neck and dug into the interior, producing a handful of the silver stones. "This is what Belinda's been chewing on to produce fire."

Richard accepted the rocks gingerly, holding each up to the light and examining the crystals from all sides. "Shiny," he murmured, "blurry at the edges." His fingers tightened around the small rocks. His eyes lit up with excitement. "Where did you find these? Are there more?"

"Uh, far to the north," Jackie lied quickly. "I traveled all night back to my land, and no. I uncovered no more. If any are to be discovered within easy reach it must be here in Micia or not at all."

Richard looked past the stones in his hand and raised an arm, gesturing out to sea. "The rest arrive. Perhaps one of the riders knows if any of these rocks can be located."

Within minutes, all the young men landed and huddled around Richard and Jackie as the rider held up the crystals for all to see. He passed each around and the stones made a circle as every rider examined the objects as intently as Richard had done.

"I think this is called lambda," Johnathan exclaimed. The tall boy held the rock up to the light. "I remember my cousin showing me a piece once. He was a miner on Baron Holdorff's fief." He scanned the faces around him, picking out a short, ginger-haired boy. "You ride his barony, James. Have you ever seen crystals the same as this before?" He passed the rock over to James again for closer examination.

Maybe." The boy squinted his eyes in inspection, and gazed off into space while he balanced the lambda in his hand. "I think I saw something like this on patrol last time I landed, but I only stayed a minute. Have'ta take a trip up to the mines and ask around." He said to Jackie, "May I hold onto this?"

"Sure." She reached into her purse and hauled out the rest of the stones. "There should be enough for everyone to have a piece to show around."

One of the riders asked, "What do we do if we find more. Won't the people who mine...."

Jackie shrugged her shoulders. "Take it. If people wanted this stuff, you would have heard about it long ago, right? They won't know the difference."

James glanced at Richard. "Do you thing we are allowed to? Isn't it the same as stealing?"

Before Richard replied, Jackie said to the riders, "You're dragonriders, aren't you? Who's gonna tell you no? Whoever is throwing these rocks away won't care. They'll be glad to get rid of the waste. Besides, this is for you dragons. They've been waiting their whole lives for the chance to belch fire." *These boys are so timid—can't take any action on their own. The barons must hammer obedience into their brains every day.*

"True...."

"...he's right."

"Imagine our dragon's flaming."

"It's all settled then," Jackie exclaimed. She clapped her hands together. "First one to discover more of the Lambda wins a prize."

The riders stared back at her, trying to figure out what she meant. Richard's lips twitched upward and he said, "And what would this prize be, Jack?"

"Why a fire breathing dragon, of course, dummy." She laughed. "Isn't this what it's all about?"

***

After the dragonriders flapped off on their mission, Jackie and Richard were alone again. "Why aren't you leaving with the rest," Jackie asked. She signaled to Belinda who'd wandered into the water again to play with Niohoggr. "Out you go," she yelled to the dragon in amusement as the two leaped out of the ocean to plunge back in again with roars of joy. "Time to get dry."

Richard stood and said, "I had thought to ask you to accompany me on my search since you are a stranger in this land. Perhaps show you some of our kingdom as long as we are doing it, and I still wish to hear your story. I know nothing about you or this land you live in."

Jackie hesitated. The idea was tempting. To see the countryside, yes, but more, she wanted to be with Richard. She found him fascinating. His life must be so different from hers. The time was growing late, however, and she still had chores to perform at the manor. "I can't. I have things which must be done...maybe tomorrow," she evaded.

He laughed and shook his head. "These must be important matters. Where do you stay at night? You cannot be flying back to your kingdom, if it is that far away no one has ever heard of it."

He's probing. Mustn't touch close to the truth. "I have friends," she replied as she tried to concoct a lie as she spoke. "Not powerful ones as you have, but they provide me with a crust of bread and a place for Belinda and me to sleep. They arrived here many years ago seeking a new life. I repay the people by helping as best I am able to." She watched him to see if he believed her fabrication.

Richard rubbed his chin and nodded. "So be it, man of mystery, but one day I will force the full story out of you." He put two fingers to his lips and blew a long, shrill whistle, waving to Niohoggr he wished to leave. He vaulted onto the dragon's back. "Same time tomorrow?"

"I'm—I'm not sure," Jackie stammered. "I'll try."

Long after Richard disappeared into the distance, Jackie gazed at the sky wishing she could tell Richard, or tell anyone for that matter, the truth. *So unfair. I'm flying as well as those boys, and fight even better. I'll show the whole kingdom one day.*

With renewed determination, she squared her shoulders. "Belinda, time to go."

When they returned to the mine, Jackie changed into her girl clothes. "I'll be back tonight," she promised, Belinda. "I'll see if I can bring you a snack."

"Don't bother," a languid reply floated into her mind. *"Niohoggr and I caught a school of delicious fish, big ones they were too—very tasty. I'm stuffed."* Belinda released a yawn and tucked her snout under her tail.

"Laziest dragon I've ever seen," Jackie muttered as she climbed down to her cart. "Wish I had the luxury of loafing whenever I wanted to."

The sun was well up in the sky, supper waited for her to start, she'd never done the laundry, and a dozen more chores still remained for her. Jackie scooped up as much wood as possible while wishing more hours existed in each day, and trudged back to the manor. She shot venomous glances at the ruts in the path, which cause her to weave back and forth, wasting more time as the grooves caught a wheel and refusing to let go until Jackie stopped to tug with all her might. She kept slogging forward, head down, trying to make up for lost time from the morning gathering with the riders.

When the wheels became stuck for the third time, Jackie swung around with a resigned sigh, determined if the cart handed her a hard time again, she'd kick the wagon to death to teach it a lesson. She heaved, her sweaty, muddy hands slipped off the handles, and she fell backward with a grunt.

"It appears I have appeared at the right moment."

"Oh." Jackie's head snapped around in panic, searching for the source of the voice. Richard strode toward her, a faint smile crossing his lips as he saw the shock on her face.

"How did you get....What are you doing here?" she gasped, getting her arms under her and struggling to stand erect. She brushed at her hair trying to smooth it down and only succeeded in tangling the strands more over her eyes. Without thinking, she scrubbed at her face to clear her vision, leaving a long muddy streak across her cheek matching one on the opposite side. *Oh, no, I'm a filthy wreck.* In desperation, she lifted her arms to twist her hair behind in a knot. Her own odor rose about her and assaulted her nose, the smell of old sweat, moldy wood, and the scent of chicken manure, which clung to her clothes from feeding the fowl in the morning, overwhelmed her. *I stink like an old goat.* Vertigo hit her from standing erect fast, and she tottered, knees weak.

"Do not act so startled, Jaqueline." Richard held her waist to steady her. "I told you I would be back." His eyes laughed at her flustered appearance, "You look as if you have seen a shade returned from the dead to take you with him."

"We—You...." Jackie took a deep breath. "I thought you were on the hunt for this mysterious dragonrider," she blurted out at last. "Have you finished your mission?" She had herself under control once more, but kept her distance in case the wind changed directions.

"Yes, but now I have taken up a different quest." Richard reached into the bag hanging around his waist and extracted a piece of lambda. "Here," he thrust the crystal rock into her hands, "take this and examine it. Have you ever seen a stone as this before?"

Jackie accepted the rock tentatively and held it up to the light. "No, not in these parts," she said at last, handing the stone back. "Is it important?"

Richard dropped the stone back into his sack. "Very." He scanned the area, his eyes resting on Baldhill. "A worker of the mines in my Lord's barony said there is an old gold mine here. This dwells in mines. When I learned I hastened here to search." He swung a hand toward the hill. "Is it up there?"

I mustn't let him go up on Baldhill. "Uh, yes, but don't bother," she hastened to say. "I've gone up there dozens of time myself, searching for bits of gold, or anything unusual of value the miners left behind while they dug." She touched his pouch. "I would have noticed a crystal as this if any existed. I don't know if it's worth anything, but it looks interesting."

"Another dead end," he muttered sourly and kicked at the mud with a dirty boot. "I take it you did not find any gold either."

Jackie ran her hand over her filthy clothes and snickered bitterly. "What do you think?" She scraped off muck from her tunic and flicked it at the cart mired in the rut. "Does this appear as if I have nuggets of gold in my purse?"

Richard released a loud laugh. "I guess not." He sauntered over to the cart, grasped the handles, and heaved, releasing the wheels from the sodden pothole with a loud squishing moan. "Here, I will help you drag your treasures to your home," he said, lugging the cart behind him. "I must go back this way anyway to fetch my dragon."

Jackie walked beside him, taking two steps to his one. "This is better than I hoped for," she tittered as he puffed along, "but here I thought you'd returned to go fishing."

He grunted out a laugh along with her, stopping to wipe sweat from his forehead. "Not today, lass." He noted the bow strung over her back. "You hunt on the baron's lands?" he asked, surprised. "Are you allowed?"

"Oh, no. I don't hunt there," Jackie assured him. "On our fief only. Fox trouble." She took an imaginary arrow from her quiver and placed it in an imaginary bow, pretending to take aim at the animal. "*Zip.* I'll catch the chicken thief yet, and when I do…" She released the bolt with a chuckle, "someone wears a fur wrap."

"This is something else I must place on my list after I have found what I'm searching for," Richard said in admiration. "Fox hunting along with fishing."

Richard yanked the cart and started again. "How did you find me, anyway," Jackie asked as the manor came into view. "I am sure you didn't arrive here specifically to see me."

"Stumbling upon you was an added bonus," he said shyly, with a sidelong look, "but when the baron's fief was mentioned I did think of you," he admitted, "and I knew you were familiar with the area, and your help might save me hours of searching. Your sister told me you had gone to fetch firewood and were returning any minute so I waited. Do you mind?"

"Not at all," Jackie replied. She bit her lip. She

wasn't use to wordplay with a man, and the subtle give and take put her off balance. She tried to remain casual and added, "I'm having my cart pulled for free, best thing that's happened all day."

Richard dragged the wagon to the kitchen steps and dropped the handles with a sigh. "I must go, duty calls, but if you have any information of what I want tell your baron to send a messenger to me and I will return." He waved to Niohoggr. "In any case, I want to revisit once more, simply to fish and relax."

"Or hunt foxes?" Jackie said with a fast smile.

Richard's brown eyes bored into hers. "Perhaps to hunt foxes, too." He spun on his heel and walked away.

Jackie watched him leave with a fluttering in her stomach. She unloaded her wood in a daze and hurried into the kitchen to start supper. Victoria sat at the kitchen table chewing on her fingernails. She rose as Jackie entered, her face threatening to split in joy.

"You shoot high," she said with a note of approval in her voice.

"Victoria." Jackie bustled around the kitchen, starting a fire and organizing food, not daring to look her sister in the eye. "He needed help, that's all. Doesn't Victor always say to help dragonriders when we are asked?"

"Uh-huh," Victoria's lips broadened into a wide smirk, "especially when he is Richard De La Fey, nephew of a baron and grandson of the king."

Jackie halted what she was doing and froze. "He is the grandson of the king?" *He never told me. Why didn't he mention it?*

"Oh, you did not know?" Victoria replied, paying no attention to Jackie's expression. "Play your cards right and you may one day be a baroness, or a duchess," she suggested.

Jackie thought about herself living in a castle,

wearing long skirts trimmed in fur, and covered in jewels. *It only happens in tales the traveling minstrels sing about when they pass through the town,* she reminded herself. "Right." She waved a hand in dismissal to her sister, and hooked a thumb at herself in her raggedy clothes. "This sow's ear will one day be royalty, but he's nice anyway. *He did return to see me, though.*

Chapter Eight

After this, Jackie noticed a profound change in attitude toward her by Victor. The following day, before she snuck out of the house, she discovered him waiting in the kitchen for her, a benign expression on his face.

"Forget about collecting wood from now on," he exclaimed, crossing his legs and lounging back in the chair. "From now on we will buy kindling from the woodcutter."

"Huh?" Jackie edged over to the fireplace, not sure what Victor was up to, or perhaps the drink talked and he was in one of his playful moods.

Victor flicked his hand as if swatting a fly. "I keep forgetting, you are fifteen years old, a woman ready for marriage. You should not be doing children's work anymore. When I go into the village this morning, I shall notify the woodcutter. What do you think of a weekly delivery?"

"Uh, sure," Jackie replied, amazed in this switch of outlook, while wondering at the same time what extra work would replace her daily excursions for kindling. "Do you know how much…?"

"Tut-tut. I am sure the cutter knows how much wood a household uses in a week, and I shall negotiate a fair price. Think nothing more of it." He peered at her. "You can devote yourself to your music, or knitting now. Victoria is always sewing something or another…"

"I'll start my baking then," Jackie touched her bow, "and afterwards, I was going to hunt the fox, if you don't mind."

"Never mind him." Victor scowled in distaste. "You should not be traipsing about in the woods as if you were a common wench. You must learn to act the woman of gentle birth." He studied her as if seeing Jackie for the first time. "Your skin is burnt from the sun. Highborn women are fair of face. Maybe Victoria has a veil you can wear."

A veil? Jackie began to have an inkling of what was going on. She replied, "Richard, the dragonrider who was here yesterday, said he would return to help me hunt the fox. If I am not out there...." She slumped and took a step back to the stillroom where she kept the flour.

Victor bolted upright. "Oh, you misunderstood me. Fox hunting is fine—for sport. Go ahead. In fact here," he reached into his purse and extracted a handful of copper coins, laying the money on the table, "run into town and buy bread. It is always wise for a lady of the house to know prices so her steward does not steal from her lord."

Jackie stared at the coins. This was the first time Victor trusted her with money—and no more baking? She must still be asleep in bed. "I don't know what to say. I'll—I'll do my best."

"Do not let me keep you any longer." Victor paused remembering something. "Oh, if you see this dragonrider, give him my regards. You might mention I was once selected as a candidate, work into his good graces, if you know what I mean, let him know you associate with the right people."

Jackie understood what he meant. With her new freedom staring her in the face, she saddled a horse and rode into town. *If this keeps up, Victor will have me riding sidesaddle.*

To her disgust, she met Utta and Ebba as they walked to school. The two girls started giggling.

"Look who it is." Ebba exclaimed in mock surprise, "Are you starting back to school again? I didn't know they taught pig herding in class?" Both girls broke out into laughs.

Jackie held her temper. She had more important

tasks to accomplish today than trading nasty remarks with these two. She replied, "Buying bread from the baker. Hope you have a good day."

Utta chirped in with, "My, aren't we the lady. You should have been here yesterday. A dragonrider was in our sky. He would have stopped to see you if you'd been here."

They saw Richard flying out to our fief. Jackie couldn't resist herself. She replied, "He did, but he didn't stay long, so we didn't go flying. Maybe later." She granted the girls a smirk, leaving the two standing in the middle of the street with their mouths open and rode away before they thought up a retort.

After the baker, she darted to the house to drop off her plunder of baked goods and hurried to the mine. Belinda snored and barely opened her eyes as Jackie donned her riding clothes and dabbed on black makeup under her eyes.

She buckled on her sword. "Time to start moving," Jackie announced, prodding the dragon in the ribs with two fingers. "Busy day today."

Belinda arched her back with a ripple running up her spine. *"Island again?"*

"Uh-huh. Let's see if any of the riders have located lambda."

The squad of dragonriders awaited her as Jackie landed, two in deep conversation while the rest listened. As Jackie sauntered up to the group, Richard said to Johnathan, "You are wrong. Our first loyalty is, and always should be, to our baron and king. It is their job to protect the people and we should also."

"But you do not understand." Johnathan's fists balled in frustration. "The great lords care nothing for the people. Never have. As far as they are concerned we are no more than cattle," he said. "My father is a smith. If it were not for the fact a large clutch was found I never would have been chosen as a rider." He eyed Richard. "You know the rich and nobles are selected as candidates. Nominations for rider should be open to all who show ability, not the privileged."

"I agree with you," Richard replied, "but still…"

"Still what?" Johnathan paced within the small circle of riders. "If the nobles hold all the power to themselves, and the king refuses to do anything, they are both wrong. At least we, as dragonriders, know what is fair and wise." He searched the faces around him, seeing nods of agreement from many. "If the authority does not originate from the top, it must be imposed from the bottom."

Johnathan pounded his fist in his palm, swinging to each man in turn, his eyes shining with a strange light. "This is the chance we have been waiting for," he declared. "We have the ability to right the wrongs we have observed the common people suffer for so long—the social injustice, inequality. Why we could even force the guilds to open their doors to whoever wishes to join, instead of the skills and knowledge being a closed secret passed down from father to son."

"Softly, my friend. Sounds good," Richard agreed, "in theory. We all know these things exist, but to draw all the power to ourselves and impose *our* rules on everyone? We would be no better than the nobility and guild masters you wish to replace."

The faces of the riders locked in avid consideration to the debate, Jackie becoming aware this was a discussion the two riders hashed over many times before. She said, "What's the matter. Did I miss something?"

Johnathan was not wholly successful in hiding his annoyance with Richard as he said, "No, not really. We were mulling out plans what to do after our dragons breathe fire."

Excitement surged through Jackie. She said, "You have unearthed a source of the lambda in this land?"

A shadow fell across Richard's face. "Not yet." He placed both hands on his knees and said to Johnathan, "Perhaps we are storing grain before the harvest, huh?" To Jackie he said, "Not all riders have presented themselves yet. We may not even find out today. Making excuses for gathering as this are hard on a daily basis. Some of the riders cannot think up a pretense to return here for a day or two."

Richard jerked and snapped to attention. "Look, a rider approaches now."

A dragon circled overhead, four heavy bags hanging from the saddle. The rider landed, leaped off his beast to fall flat on his face into the sand in his haste to reach the group. He scrambled up again and yelled, "I have it." James ran to the rest of the riders hooking a shaky finger over his back at the sacks. "Lambda, as much as anyone wishes for."

Jackie leaped back to avoid being trampled as the riders stampeded to the dragon, and then trailed along as the men hauled the sacks up the beach and spilled the contents onto the sand. Four mounds of stone glistened in the sun, some chunks as large as Jackie's fist.

"Wow." She gazed in astonishment at the shiny piles. She said to James, "Where did you collect all of this?"

"Next to a gold mine," James exclaimed, elated. "The miners separate the lambda from the gold ore before they ship it to the smelters, and..." He stared at the rest as if he didn't believe what he said, "leave it there. When I asked one of the miners if I could take some, he shrugged and said, "Take all you want." He smirked. "So I did. There must be ten wagon weights of stone lying about outside the mine opening."

The rest of the riders were busy calling their mounts and feeding the beasts bits of stone by hand. The dragons consumed the rocks with grunts of delight until all remaining were a few small fragments of shiny dust mixed in with the sand.

One dragon raised his head to the sky and bellowed, flame shooting into the air, a fiery shaft of light blazing in the heavens. Another took up the call, and then two more, until a column of incandescent fury stood reaching the clouds.

The cold air flowing over the ocean was sucked into the void left by the hot air rising. Wind devils sprang up along with waterspouts, circling the island and threatening to sweep sand, trees, and riders away. In panic, Jackie grabbed Richard's sleeve and shouted over the rush of air, "You have to make your mounts stop or we'll all be killed."

Richard stood gazing at the dragons in awe. He shook himself out of his trance and screamed to the rest of the riders, "Calm your mounts, otherwise we perish." He dashed to Niohoggr's side, shielding his face from the heat with his left hand, while stroking the dragon's neck with the right, whispering words of quiet up to the ears of the aroused beast.

The balance of the riders copied his example and soon the dragons settled down except for an occasional short wisp of flame leaking out of a nostril.

"If they are to flame, I think it would be a better choice if we did it in the air," Johnathan stated with a laugh to his friends. He saluted the rest, leaped on his dragon, and directed it toward the open ocean. The beast spread its wings, took three steps, jumped, and landed in the waves.

"What...?" Johnathan stared about him in chagrin, and abruptly dove into the surf, floundering back to shore listening to the jeers of his fellow riders. "What happened?" he gasped, pushing water out of his eyes, and swiping the wet sand off his riding cloak with a scowl. His dragon threw him a reproving glance and waddled to shore with him.

"The air in his body," Jackie cupped her hands and shouted back to make herself heard above the laughter. She chuckled with the rest at the expression on Johnathan's face. "Lambda somehow ignites it and causes the fire. He used it all up in flaming and now he can't rise again until he produces more."

The rest of the riders were having the same trouble. After two futile attempts to rise his dragon, James asked Jackie, "How long must we wait?" Disgruntled riders craned their necks to hear her reply.

Jackie thought back to how long it was before Belinda was her old self. "Not long," she replied. "The dragons will know when they are ready and tell you." Silence erupted as the riders conferred with their mounts. Jackie said to all of them, "But this must be kept in mind when you go into battle. Short bursts and not too many at any one time, or you will find yourselves with a disabled dragon unable to rise or breath fire." She heard Belinda in her mind. "*Rookies.*"

Johnathan took his riding cloak off, shook it, and draped the garment over his arm while surveying the rest of his clothes in dismay. "This will give us time to decide what we do next," he declared. His eyes swung to Richard. "What say you to the plan I proposed earlier? Have you thought over what I said?"

Richard's jaw muscles tightened. He took a step toward Johnathan. "I told you once. There is a right way and a wrong way of going about these things and...."

Johnathan's face flushed and his eyes narrowed as he tried to keep his temper in check. "And yours is the wrong way," he snapped. "The nobles will never listen to us without being forced too and...."

This Johnathan is too eager. Reminds me of Victor, never planning ahead. His dragon's had fire for five minutes and already he thinks he has all the answers. Jackie spat on the sand. "Stupid, both of you." She stepped between the two men before their argument turned ugly. "Hold on. Don't you think we should worry about external threats to this kingdom before we attempt any kind of changes here at home?"

This got their attention. Richard shifted his gaze from Johnathan to Jackie. The rest of the riders stopped talking and stared at her with questioning looks. "What do you mean?" Johnathan sputtered.

Jackie spun to the ocean, fist clenched, a finger pointing east. "There lies our first enemy, the barbarians who invade us—or have you forgotten the battle you so recently fought? You want to change things here, throw this realm into turmoil for years? First, make sure you are secure from invasion, otherwise you shall be overrun and none of your plans will come to pass."

Johnathan and Richard spun to the ocean as if expecting to see an invasion fleet on the horizon sailing their way.

"True," Richard muttered. He nodded to Jackie and said to Johnathan, "Again, we rush in where we should think."

Johnathan scrubbed at his face. "You are right, Jack. Thank you for you wise council." He gave a mirthless laugh. "I have never thought this far into the future. All of this has occurred so sudden. You appear to have a better grasp of what lies ahead than I do. How should we handle the Easmen? Any thoughts?"

Johnathan's question took Jackie by surprise. She possessed no idea, and hadn't given it anymore thought than Richard or Johnathan did. "I—uh…" She paused then asked, "Is it even possible to reach the Easmen on a dragon? How far is their homeland? I have no idea."

One of the riders piped in with, "The merchants who sail to their land said it takes three days with a good wind to your back to reach the far shore."

"Maybe half of this for a dragon," murmured Richard, "depending on how the breeze blows."

"Is a trip this far too long for a dragon flight," Jackie wondered aloud. "I have never flown over the sea and…"

Richard asked, "How is it you do not know how long a dragon stays aloft for? You said you flew from a far kingdom. Land or sea, it makes no difference."

Oops. I'd better think of something quick. "Ah, flying here we made short stops, resting on islands as we traveled. I was in no hurry, and didn't want to over tax my dragon." She watched Richard to see if he would believe her tale.

Apparently he and the rest of the riders did. Johnathan nodded. "I would do the same given the chance, not for the dragon, but for myself. Dragons will glide on the air currents to rest their wings as a hawk would do," he assured her with a laugh. "Make sure *you* do not fall asleep though, and slip off the dragon's back. It would be a rude awaking."

"I have tied myself down," volunteered James, "on long flights and taken a nap."

"The strap on your saddle will come in handy," agreed Richard.

"This is well," said Johnathan, "but we all cannot go. Even with our dragons breathing fire, what good would it do? We still could not defeat the whole Easmen nation, nor will the lords allow it." His lips twisted down in a scowl. "As it is, they keep us on a short leash as one uses on a rabid cur."

A few "ayes" echoed around the group.

The sun rose well up over the island, as did Jackie's temper. *How tentative these men act. They're dragonriders.* "The point is we know *nothing* about *the Easmen*," she retorted. "Are they one people? A group— clan? A breakaway tribe outlawed by their people and making raids without the permission of their lords? Perhaps there is dissension among the ranks we can exploit. We'll never know until we go see." She placed her hands on her hips and declared, "It isn't necessary for all of us to go— two should be enough to scout out their territory and learn whatever there is to learn." She caught each by eye. "Who will volunteer?"

The shuffling of feet and blank stares at the sand answered her. She glared at each with contempt.

"I will."

Richard raised his hand in the air. "Do not fault these riders," he said to Jackie, reading her expression. "Three or four day's absence would set their barons into a frenzy of rage. I will think of some excuse."

She admired his bravery and wondered what explanation he would give. Even though he was a noble, and the grandson of the king, still he was the junior of his kin, and subject to their whims.

Jackie watched the rest. When no one else spoke up, she said in aggravation, "You mustn't venture out alone. You'll need someone to guard your back. I will go also. I need no excuse." *Yeah, right. Me and my big mouth. How will I explain this to Victor and Victoria?*

"It is settled." Richard's voice was stern, but filled with underlining excitement for the trip ahead. "I will meet you here tomorrow as the sun rises," he said to Jackie. He stared at Niohoggr as a silent communication passed between the two. "The dragons are ready to fly," he announced and bowed to the company at large, presenting an extra one to Jackie. "And to you, sir, I will see you on the morrow."

***

"This should do it." It was Jackie's second trip to the mine, hauling everything she thought she would need for a three-day trip. Belinda surveyed the two packs curiously and sniffed at each. *"You creatures need a lot to survive, don't you?"*

"Food, weapons, clothes. No, not much, and I won't need half of what I'm bringing. All of this is to be on the safe side." She cringed inwardly. *Now for the hard part.* Somehow she would have to tell a convincing enough story to be believed so she wasn't missed for three days. She threw back her shoulders and braced herself, marching to the house.

To her relief Victor wasn't home yet. With any luck he wouldn't return until late at night and Victoria couldn't tell him until the morning when Jackie was (she hoped) already far gone.

As the family sat for dinner at night Jackie casually said, "The dragonrider, Richard, has invited me to the baron's castle for a few days."

Instead of the argument Jackie thought she'd receive, Victoria's mouth dropped and she hastily wiped her lips. "Oh, this is wonderful. I cannot wait to tell Victor. He will be excited." She rose, sat, unsure what to do. "When will Richard be here to pick you up? Is he sending a carriage? Coming himself on his dragon?" She thought for a minute. "Oh dear, I should go with you as a chaperone, too. What would the neighbors think, him whisking you away? It would be most improper..."

"Oh, no," Jackie said, putting her hand to her mouth, "you needn't worry. He is arriving before dawn and picking me up with his dragon."

"Well, I must speak to him then," her sister replied primly as she nibbled on a piece of bread. She pulled her soup closer to her and studied the broth, thinking. "Seems odd, though," she said at last, glancing up at Jackie. "I realize he is a dragonrider, but he is a noble also and…"

"You shouldn't bother," Jackie exclaimed quickly as she began running out of excuses. She took a spoonful of soup and mumbled, "Besides, I'm not meeting him here. He is to pick me up at the edge of the forest."

"What?" Victoria dropped her spoon in her tureen, splattering the hot liquid all over herself. She dabbed at her dress with the edge of the tablecloth, shaking her head. "I must have heard you wrong. What did you say?"

"We thought it best," Jackie replied desperately trying to make the story sound as reasonable as possible. "With all the noise of the dragon landing, you know, the dogs barking and everything, chickens squawking. We didn't want to disturb, you, Victor and Thomas while you were sleeping."

Victoria reached for her goblet and took a long sip of wine, studying her sister over the rim of the cup. "The baron *does* know about you staying at his castle?"

Jackie blushed and examined her food. "Of course he does. What are you thinking, Victoria? It's—you see, Richard has to patrol as the sun rises. He's to drop me off at the castle, and do his duty while I get settled into chambers. In fact, the baron suggested it himself," Jackie lied again. "Everything is being arranged today."

"Humph." Victoria placed her goblet down and pretended to rearrange the silverware on the table. "Remember, Jaqueline, people do not buy the cow if they receive the milk for free." Jackie's mouth dropped. "You are a proper young lady of gentle birth from a good home. Act as if you are."

"Victoria." Jackie's face burnt red with mortification.

Thomas, who listened to this exchange with fascination asked, "Is Jaqueline going to the castle to buy a cow?"

"Hush, Thomas," Victoria replied.

***

"Are we all set?"

Jackie scanned her dragon. She'd taken every precaution she knew of, her packs secured on Belinda's back, she bound herself in ropes in case she dozed, with her saddle strap cinched around her waist. She waved back to Richard, "Good here. Ready whenever you are."

Richard's Niohoggr carried similar luggage, and the rider himself strapped securely to the dragon's back. His voice filled with anxiety as he issued Jackie last minute instructions. "Remember, keep together and do not act childish. This will be a boring trip and we don't want any accidents because of foolishness, right?"

Jackie saluted with palm out. "Are you making speeches, or are we flying?" she yelled. Exhilaration and apprehension filled her, not only for the danger of confronting an enemy, but she noted with chagrin, this was the first time she'd ever been away from home. "Let's start moving, Belinda," she told her dragon, "we've got a long trip and we're wasting time."

The dragon spread her wings, and with a hop, soared into the air, Niohoggr flapping hard to catch up. The two dragons gained height, discovered air currents traveling east, and glided lazily on the breeze below the clouds. Underneath, the waves of the ocean appeared as tiny ripples on a blue chalkboard, stretching to the horizon with no end.

As the sun set, Jackie choked down a meal of dried rations with a few swallows of water from her canteen. "How you doing?" she called out to Belinda.

"Easy flying. Boring," replied the dragon with a yawn.

"With any luck, we'll be there tomorrow," Jackie promised the dragon. "I'm going to sleep. Don't let me fall off."

Jackie heard a soft chuckle echo in her mind. *"Not a chance."*

She awoke the next morning with a start, made a swipe at the horn of the saddle, before recalling where she was. A red sun shone in her face as it crested the horizon, the wind whipping her face. After a few calming breaths she muttered with a yawn, "Morning, Belinda." Jackie stretched her arms and wiggled in her seat. "How are you— *Whoa.*"

The dragon fell into a steep dive, almost vertical, toward the ocean. Jackie flailed wildly for the straps holding her as the force of the dive forced her backward. At the last moment, before they hit the water, Belinda leveled out. She touched the ocean and soared upward into the sky again.

"What was this all about?" Jackie gasped, clutching at her ropes with one hand while jamming her woolen cap down on her head with the other.

"Breakfast," returned the humorous thought. Belinda swung her head until she stared into Jackie's eyes. Clutched between her teeth was a fish as long as Jackie's arm. *I haven't eaten since day before yesterday, and I'm hungry. Do you want some? I'll share. There's still plenty down below."*

The thought of eating raw fish made Jackie's stomach feel queasy. "No thank you, and next time...."

The dragon blinked at her. *"Suit yourself, but don't complain later,"* and the fish disappeared as Belinda looked away.

"...next time, *warn a girl,* when you're going to

116

do something like this. I almost peed in my pants."

A dragonish snicker drifted to her. *"Sissy."*

Jackie glanced around for Richard. Behind, traveling a hundred yard to her rear, Niohoggr tracked their movements. When Richard saw her searching, the dragon sped up until the two beasts flew wing to wing.

"We will be there soon." Richard waved a hand at the barely visible horizon. "What do you think, skim along the coast searching for an invasion fleet?"

"Are you kidding?" Jackie called back, "and announce there are dragonriders in their sky scouting their homeland? We land the dragons on a suitable spot and search by foot inland."

The shore grew in their sight, tall ragged cliffs with deep in-cuts. Far below Jackie spied tiny specks on the water, fishing boats, and silently prayed the sailors wouldn't look up and notice their passing. As they reached the coastline, cracks and crevice appeared in the cliffs, perfect roosts to hide Belinda and Niohoggr until they returned.

"Jack." Richard jabbed a finger farther into the interior. "Smoke."

"Land at the top of the cliff," Jackie said to Belinda. The dragon spiraled down with Niohoggr close on her tail and roosted behind a boulder. She leaped off and met Richard who hurried to her over the rough ground.

"This is the smoke from chimneys. A town must be close by."

"Well, at least we know which way to go." Jackie unloaded one of the packs from Belinda and slung it over her back. Richard hurried to retrieve his. "You two," Jackie ordered the dragons, "find yourselves a cave and stay hidden, okay? We'll be back in a day with any luck, but no one must see you in the meantime."

The two dragons snorted their agreement and

117

disappeared over the side of the cliff. Jackie said to Richard, "We'd better start walking. We have a long hike ahead of us."

It took almost an hour of scrambling over rocks and pushing through thick under-bush and trees, but they made it to a ridge overlooking a fair-sized town set on the banks of an inlet.

"Maybe we should scout around the edges," suggested Richard in a low voice. "I don't see anything appearing to be a warship. All these vessels are loaded for trading." Boats lined up on the shore, some tied to docks, the vast majority covered with skins to protect their cargo. "Perhaps they have more vessels moored out of sight." He frowned. "This would be easier if we could walk in and ask."

Jackie grimaced and shrugged. "Why don't we, I mean, walk in and ask?" she replied. "Who would care?"

"Are you crazy?" Richard said, aghast. "They would arrest us for sure."

"Not necessarily, if we pretend we wanted to sign up with a raiding party," Jackie said. "The Easmen must enlist mercenaries from nearby tribes, or at least take on warriors from surrounding towns. They don't know everyone in the region by sight."

Richard rubbed his chin and licked his lips. Jackie stood and hitched her pack higher up on her shoulders. Without glancing back to see if he followed, she trudged down off the ridge toward the village.

Chapter Nine

"Who should we ask?" the townspeople hurried past Jackie and Richard, paying no attention to the two strangers as they strode about their tasks, entering and exiting half-timbered buildings to conduct their daily business.

The two riders wandered along the main street of the village keeping a low profile. Jackie watched a group of sailors making their way to the docks. She nudged Richard with her elbow and muttered, "Let's trail this bunch, not too close, but near enough that we look as though we belong to their party."

They fell in to the rear of the group, swaggering along with the rest, until they reached the water. The seamen clambered onto a ship and began preparing the boat to depart. Jackie and Richard strolled along the shore, searching for someone not too occupied to talk to them.

She spied a lone man working on the beach, a carpenter busy with an adz, patiently shaping a keel for a ship. Jackie sauntered to him and grunted, "Know of anyone enlisting for a raid?"

The carpenter glanced up wiping sweat from his forehead, and straightened with a groan. "Who handed you an idea like this son?" He cocked his head and scanned Jackie and Richard. "No one here's gone raiding for over a year."

"Oh, ah..."

Richard stepped forward. "We have traveled from down south. Stories circulated warriors go out seeking fame from these ports, and riches abounded for those brave enough to reach and take what they wish, but no one named a town." He gave a savage wink to the carpenter. "We traveled here to throw our lot in with these adventures, but I see we have reached the wrong village. Forgive us for disturbing you." He snatched Jackie by the arm and jerked her away.

"Not so fast." The carpenter placed his adz down next to him. "If it's adventure and fighting you seek, about two miles up the coast at the village of Izar they raid, but I do not know if they plan any now." He asked with a penetrating gaze, "Any news of more fighting in the south?"

"No." Richard said in a neutral tone. "Not any more than usual, this is." He tried to edge away.

"Those Fanks." The man spit. "They've got the whole country stirred up—homeless people fleeing north invading our lands." He stopped as if he realized the two before him were from the south. "Not that I'm saying anything against you, mind yah, but the rest of 'em." He spat again and picked up his tool. "Heard tell the prince is collecting an army to march against those devils, my son is talking about joining. If yah don't find a raiding party to attach to, he'll enlist yah."

Jackie squeaked, "Thanks," and they hurried away.

"What was this all about?" Richard whispered to Jackie looking back when they reached the edge of the town. A well-worn path paralleled the water.

"Dunno." She studied the position of the sun. "Fighting somewhere, I guess—none of our concern. Let's push on to this Izar. Guy said it was two miles down the coast."

"You sure?" Richard glanced at the sky also. "Do you think we have time? It's growing late."

Jackie started walking. "Let's go, if we hurry we'll make it there and back before it grows dark. We still don't know who's making the raids, or if they plan more."

The path curved around an outcropping of boulders into dense pine forest. As they passed the rocks, a party of armed men on horseback emerged from the trees. Upon sighting Jackie and Richard, the riders pounded down on the two.

Jackie froze, debating whether to run or draw her sword. Before she made up her mind, the lead horseman shouted, "Halt. Make no move or you shall be cut down." Arrows trained at their chests with murderous intent.

Richard shoved his arms in the air. "We travel in peace."

Jackie put her hands up over her head. "We mean no harm. We seek employment in the village of Izar."

The riders encircled them, cutting off any attempt of retreat. The first horseman leaped off his mount, pushing his purple riding cloak back over his shoulders to reveal chainmail armor embroidered with the emblem of an eagle. "I am Prince Sevorson," he declared, "Regent of this province. I say who moves about in this country and where they go." He rested a hand on the hilt of his long sword; the other touched the haft of a throwing axe in his belt. The men who didn't carry bows lifted spears. The prince's pale blue eyes surveyed first Richard, and then Jackie, from head to toe. "I see by your dress you are foreigners. Tell me your story."

This one we cannot fool as we did with the carpenter. A lie, but one not too complicated. "The Fanks destroyed our village in the south," Jackie replied, "and we have journeyed here traveling from town to town seeking our fortune. We were told raiders sail to the lands of the west fetching back treasure, and sought to join a party."

Prince Sevorson stroked his beard in silent contemplation of their story. He finally exclaimed, "You will be happy to know I raise an army to fight against the Fanks. You are now enlisted." His men leveled their spears and closed in around Jackie and Richard.

"But..."

"Gladly," Richard boomed. "We would enjoy nothing better than having revenge." He bobbed his head up and down, lowering his arms. "Tell us where your camp is and we shall meet you there."

A chorus of chuckles broke out from the warriors. The prince smiled maliciously at Richard. "Aye, I am sure you will find us. You may accompany my party now to guarantee you will not lose your way." He remounted his horse and waved for the two to follow.

The rest of his troop fell in behind Richard and Jackie. They had no choice but to walk along.

"What are we going to do?" Jackie whispered to Richard.

"I do not know," he murmured back out of the side of his mouth. *"Play along and wait for a chance to escape. I don't see we have much choice."*

They marched inland, traveling a winding road through the forest until they reached a wide meadow ringed with guards. Along the way, more parties of warriors met the prince, most herding men on foot as the noble's party did.

In the field, hundreds of men milled about sharpening weapons or cooking. Two warriors with spears ran up and the prince ordered, "Take these conscripts and place both with the rest." To Jackie and Richard he said, "Prepare yourselves. We march into battle tomorrow."

The guards collected Jackie, Richard and the rest of the prisoners and led the captives to a separate portion of the camp. The men held there markedly different from the Easmen warriors. None wore armor, and carried rusty swords or axes more suited to chopping wood than fighting in a battle.

Jackie glanced around the stockade fence surrounding the area in dismay. "I don't think this place will be easy to escape from." Besides the guards around the whole perimeter of the camp, more sentries encircled their little portion.

Richard tracked her gaze. His lips compressed into a thin line as he ran his fingers through his hair. "The prince said we march tomorrow. Maybe along the way, or as the battle starts, we can desert." He didn't sound convinced. "Let's find someplace to bed down for the night. Maybe luck smiles and our dragons fly to our rescue."

"You're assuming dragons reckon time the same as we do." Jackie jammed her fists into her belt and trudged off to an unoccupied portion of their enclosure, dropping to the grass with a sigh. "Knowing Belinda, she went to sleep and won't wake up for a week."

Richard slumped next to her. "You are right. By the time Niohoggr realizes we haven't returned we may be a moldy pile of bones lying on the ground."

***

While it was still dark, a guard aroused the conscripts with yells of *"Up you go. MARCH.* The prince wishes to address you."

Jackie and Richard fumbled erect, their sleeping blankets clutched around their shoulders against the cold morning air as their breath made white clouds of smoke in front of their noses. They plodded with the rest of the prisoners out of their compound to where Prince Sevorson waited on a coal black stallion with the balance of his warriors.

"You are all refugees from the south," he called out. "The Fanks have stolen your lands and destroyed your homes, murdered your children and raped your women. Today we march in war against those fiends and you will reap your revenge against the men who have wronged you. If you die in battle, know the gods praise your valor, and you will feast in their halls as honored guests."

A few "Ayes" rang out from the crowd. An old man clutching a wood axe waved his weapon over his head and yelled, "When we are done with the Fanks we will feast on their flesh and leave the scraps to the ravens and the crows. The gods will have to wait for us to attend their banquet."

The prince broke out into a laugh, nodding. "This is the spirit. I am sure you will. These devils have destroyed the trade between our lands. In order to survive my people venture out to the sea raiding distant lands for their survival. Perhaps this is the time to finish this chaos and resume our normal lives." He glanced along their ranks. "May the gods be with you."

The prince allowed the conscripts to go back and collect their belongings. Serving women entered the compound passing out coarse black bread along with strong beer wishing each prisoner luck in the battle. When the camp was packed, the guards entered and herded the group away.

This isn't happening. Jackie searched in the predawn darkness for a break in their guard's attention to make a dash for freedom as they sloshed through mud puddles marching toward the battlefront. *No chance of escape.* Riders flanked the column on either side. The Easmen trooped behind. All the conscripts could do was walk forward and hope for the best.

Richard muttered a prayer to himself. Jackie said, "I'm sorry I talked you into this. I never thought we'd be captured."

"Not your fault," The boy replied. He slapped Jackie on the back. "You didn't persuade me to do anything, my friend. I volunteered, remember? My only regret is I didn't say goodbye to the lass I told you about. I have thought much of her lately."

Even in this desperate moment, Jackie's heart

124

quickened. *He's been thinking of me?* "Richard, I want to tell you...."

"Spread out, *single file*." Their column emerged from the forest onto a yellow plain of grass. Before Jackie, a dark row of warriors waited on the opposite side of the field. Easmen riders sped along, urging the conscripts left and right to form a battle line. The warriors to their rear did the same in even ranks.

The men they faced held wooden shields, the pictures of boars, bears, or large staring eyes painted on their fronts. In their right fists, they clenched throwing axes and started a rhythmic beating on their shields, screaming and chanting and hurling curses at the Easmen.

From behind each line, horns blew, signaling the beginning of the battle.

Jackie drew her sword. Richard did likewise. "Our one hope of survival is to hack our way through their ranks and make a run for it," croaked Jackie. Terror mixed with excitement clenched at her shoulders, moving up into the base of her neck.

"I know," replied Richard. "You guard my back and I'll guard yours."

The field grew silent.

A single horn blew.

"Charge."

Both sides surged toward each other with howls, brandishing their weapons over their heads. Before the lines merged, the Fanks heaved their axes. The weapons flew end over end, making a hissing sound as they cut through the air to impact with muffled thuds against bodies or shields. Those axes missing their targets bounced on the ground, clipping legs and bringing more charging conscripts to earth. Jackie dodged an axe, which narrowly missed her head, slamming into the man behind her.

The two armies merged. A sword thrust at Jackie's

belly, poking out from behind a shield with a lion painted on the front. She knocked the blade aside, squatted, and made a sweeping cut across the warrior's calves. He howled in pain, lowering his shield to protect his lower body. Jackie made a thrust through his chest and dashed on.

Richard was pushed up tight against a Fank warrior, so close they couldn't stab each other. Their swords clashed overhead. Jackie leaped, catching the warrior on his side and spinning him around. Richard lunged forward with his weapon, stabbing the man under the shoulder blade.

"Good one," Jackie shouted. She sidestepped a thrust to her chest and snatched up a fallen shield.

"Thank you," Richard called back. A Fankish warrior stormed at him with blade high. Richard rushed the man, placing a shoulder into his shield before the blade descended. The man stumbled backward, tripped and fell on the earth.

Jackie took the time to glance around the field. The battle was sweeping past their position, the Easmen pushed back by the superior numbers of the Fanks. The enemy surrounded the riders on three sides.

A bugle erupted from behind the Easmen line. Prince Sevorson led a determined counter-attack with his cavalry, driving forward through the enemy middle. Fankish soldiers buzzed around his squad, black bees determined to drag the riders down. Jackie's view of the horsemen chopped off as the fighting encircled her and Richard.

The prince's counterattack forced the enemy back. At the same time, the Fankish commander committed his reserves and a seesaw collision of men erupted in the middle of the field around Jackie and Richard, each side trying to swing the tide of battle in their favor.

The balance of Fanks swept into the Easmen

cavalry, ripping riders from their saddles, forcing the few remaining Easmen foot soldiers to fall back or face slaughter.

Jackie and Richard retreated with the rest of the warriors, the two pushed rearward until they stood against the horses. Jackie dodged swords on one side, flashing hooves on the other.

Fankish soldiers swarmed over their position, jerking the few remaining riders from their mounts.

A warrior stumbled into Jackie, paused in his swing as he scanned her and pivoted back to the attacking Fanks. It was the prince, bleeding from a half dozen cuts along his body. Richard closed in from the side and the three fought shoulder-to-shoulder in silence for their lives.

Jackie caught a chop at her midsection with the shield, twisting to catch a cut aimed at the prince's groin. Her foot slipped on the out-flung hand of a dead Fankish warrior and she tumbled to the earth. The dark shadow of a warrior loomed over her, a Fankish soldier with sword raised in a death stroke.

The prince sprang in front of her, catching the blade on the down swing with his own in a shower of sparks. He slashed sideways and the attacker fell away. Sevorson groped behind him, grabbing Jackie by one sleeve, yanking her to her feet with a grunt. "I cannot lose you now, lad," he yelled, his lips bent in a savage snarl. "The wheel of death has yet to spin against us."

"Behind you, Prince." Richard cut at an attacker, sending the man spinning away in death. The rest of Sevorson's riders either vanished, dead, or brushed away in the battle. The circle of Fanks tightened.

"Duck."

Jackie grabbed the prince and the three fell to the earth as gouts of flames washed above their heads. More balls of fire in short bursts peppered the grass around their bodies, igniting Fanks and driving the rest of their attackers back.

A dark silhouette passed over Jackie's head and hammering wingbeats filled her ears as Belinda landed next to her. *"Well, here you are,"* the dragon huffed, *"I've been waiting all day in a cold, wet cave and..."*

"Sorry." Jackie vaulted onto the dragon's back. Niohoggr stood by, blazing fire at Fank warriors who froze in fear at the beast. Grass and bush ignited, along with the dead and dying scattered on the field. Smoke belched into the air as flames ignited the dry vegetation and fires spread in every direction.

Prince Sevorson halted in terror, gawking at the dragons as if he stood before the gates of hell. Fire licked around his boots, singing the hairy exterior and transforming the threads into ash.

Oh, heck. I can't leave him here. He saved my life. Jackie reached out a hand to the man. "Hurry up and hop on, Prince. It's time to go."

Sevorson stared into her eyes with his mouth hanging open and clasped her arm. Jackie jerked him up behind her. Richard already mounted on Niohoggr eager to escape the battle. He shot her a thumbs up sign and the two dragons leaped into the air.

Both battling armies stopped their fighting, watching the dragons in wonder, their lust for fighting disappearing at the arrival of the winged monsters. As the beasts rose into the sky, panic broke out.

The Easmen fled back into the woods with moans rising in their throats. Groups stood at the edge, staring in disbelief at the two soaring beasts. The Fanks scattered in the opposite direction, casting terrified glances over their shoulders as the wildfires burnt all around their ranks.

The lust for battle and adrenalin rush Jackie felt from fighting still surged through her. She shouted to

Belinda, "Let's hand these carrion eaters one last taste of what they'll receive if they ever mess with us again."

"May I save a few to eat?" Belinda replied, hopefully. *"You know I haven't eaten all day, and it was a long flight searching for..."*

"Burn 'em, but don't eat them," Jackie said. "We don't have time for snacking."

"Waste of good food, if you asked me," the grumbled thought floated back.

Belinda swept low over the fleeing warriors, the wind of her passing knocking Fanks off their feet. A few short blasts of flame set the grass in front of the warriors on fire, trapping the retreating men between two blazes.

"Good enough," Jackie said. A tight grip on her shoulders guaranteed her she still had her passenger. *What to do with this one, now?* She wondered. Niohoggr and Richard circled above Jackie, waiting on her lead.

"Back to the cliffs," she decided and ordered Belinda. Jackie waved over her head toward the ocean. Richard nodded he understood and the two dragons dipped wings, sweeping into a sharp arc toward the water leaving the blackened battlefield behind.

The smell of the sea and rocky crags rose before the dragons. Belinda's wings swept backward and she settled on a salt covered boulder overlooking the ocean. Niohoggr made a fluttering landing next to her.

"All right, Prince," Jackie called over her shoulder, "this is where you get off."

Prince Sevorson scrambled from Belinda's back. "Wh—who are you two?" he gasped. His eyes darted in terror from Jackie to Richard, the dragons, and back again.

"We are the dragonriders of Mercia," Jackie announced in a grave tone. "Now you have sampled a brief taste of our power, I trust your people will trouble our shores no more with your plundering," she stared him in the eye and she saw a glimmer of understanding, "or we will be forced to return to this kingdom with a hundred of our comrades to ravish your land."

The prince blanched. "Most assuredly," he croaked out. "We would not raid at all if it were not for the Fanks cutting off our trade in the south. Perhaps now, with this defeat...." he left the sentence hanging.

Richard called out, "Today the Fanks have seen our power also." He gestured to the rising smoke clouding the sky. "Make it known to your enemy if we are forced to return, our wrath shall fall equally on all, not only on Easmen, but on the Fanks as well. I think you will find your foes more than willing to arrive at some peaceful agreement between the two of you. If you won't, both of you deserve the wrath we will set upon you."

Prince Sevorson twisted his beard in thought, the breeze from the turbulent sea whipping his long blonde hair around his face. "When I return to my people, I shall send messengers along the coast to my kin," he promised, "informing each of what has happened here today, and what you have said." He broke out into a laugh, "and I will send a herald to the Fanks, also. They saw you rescue me. They know we have spoken and I speak for you also." In a softer tone he added, "I thank thee for saving my life. If there is ever a way to repay you, I will."

Jackie glared down her nose at the prince. "I hope you don't speak those words rashly. One day I may hold you to your promise."

Sevorson bowed low and touched the tips of his fingers to his forehead. "My word is my bond."

"We of Mercia hold honor above all else," Jackie replied." She glared sternly at him. "Remember," Jackie released a barking laugh. "Sometimes our wrath is tempered by mercy, too, Prince, but do not rely on this. Curb your people, otherwise you will not find us gentle."

She whispered in Belinda's ear, *"Show him a taste of what you'll do next time we come."*

"I sure will, making me starve and wait all night." The dragon drew back her neck, pointed her head to the sky, and released a shaft of flame. Niohoggr did the same. The air shimmered around the two from the heat. The prince leaped back in terror and fell on his knees.

"See you remember this Prince Sevorson," Jackie shouted over the roar of the dragons. "Next time it will be you and yours." She waved a finger inland. "Now go, and do not forget what we said."

The prince scurried away, throwing terrified glances over his shoulder as if he thought Jackie and Richard would change their minds and burn him to cinders. After Sevorson disappeared over a ridge, Jackie exclaimed, "We'd better make tracks. We should have been home today. Everyone will think we've been killed."

They arrived at the island late the next day at dusk. An impatient James paced back and forth on the sand, throwing nervous glances to the sky until he saw the two flying low under the clouds. The rider waved his hands frantically over his head leaping up and down and rushed to their sides as they landed.

"Thank goodness you're all right," he exclaimed as they dismounted. "When you did not return we thought the Easmen took you captive or you crashed into the sea."

"No such luck," Richard answered with a laugh. "The Easmen tried, the Fanks tried." He wacked Jackie on the back, doubling her over. "Remember those seagulls dive bombing us for our supper last night? They tried, too."

When James failed to laugh along with him, Richard asked, "What is the matter? Has something happened...? The Easmen attacked again while we were away?" He balled his right fist and smashed it into his left hand. "We extracted a promise from the Easmen prince he would conduct no more attacks. If he...."

"NO," James shouted in Richard's face. The rider stared back at him, aghast, and James looked down, scuffing at the sand with his boot and studying the mark he left. "When we thought you were not returning, Johnathan and a few of his closest friends decided to secure the mines at Nicos with the lambda for our own use."

"What?" Richard grabbed James' shoulder and shook him. "Why, we cannot do that—it is stealing. Those mines are not ours."

James' face clouded up as if he were about to cry. "This is not the end. The baron sent soldiers to take back his mine. A fight occurred. All the soldiers were killed."

"NO." Richard stared at James in horror and swung to Jackie. "We must go to Johnathan," he whispered in desperation, "stop this madness before it spreads any farther."

The rider broke out in tears. "It is too late. I tried, others tried, but he wouldn't listen. Johnathan has declared he rules now; the kingdom of Mercia is his, and the time of the dragonriders has arrived."

Richard put his hand to his mouth, horrified, and cursed under his breath.

Jackie whispered, *"This means civil war."*

Chapter Ten

"**W**hat did the rest say? They are not going along with this? No one tried to stop him?"

"I told you—*we tried,* but events were chaotic... he had numbers on his side."

"How many? Who?" Richard rasped as if he still refused to believe what happened.

"Maybe half," admitted James shamefully. "It happened quick. Johnathan must have plotted this in his mind for years, and convinced his closest friends to go along with him." The rider spread his hands. "The rest of us were at our baron's fiefs. By the time we gathered, we didn't know what to do, and then it was over and too late."

"I must seek him out, convince Johnathan to stop this nonsense now," Richard said in an expressionless voice. He marched back to his dragon.

James reached out and grabbed his tunic. "Wait, I must tell you the rest, and perhaps you will not be so quick to confront Johnathan," he said. "Johnathan has promised the peasants and the riders the lands of the nobles if they follow him. He issued this by proclamation throughout the realm. Most of the serfs scoffed, but enough rallied to his cause to take the outlying areas of three baronies, and he has raised a small army from their ranks at his back. The last I heard another fief of a lord fell to this mob, the noble's house ransacked and set on fire. I do not know how far the rebellion has spread, but if the uprising continues the revolt will set the whole kingdom aflame."

Richard stared stony-faced at the rider and turned back to Niohoggr.

"Wait, I will go with you." Jackie sprang to his side. "You should not do this thing by yourself."

Richard leaped astride Niohoggr. "Thank you, but your help is not necessary. I am sure once I talk to

Johnathan we can straighten all this out. Besides," he gestured to the setting sun, shooting pink ribbons on the horizon, "the hour grows late, and the people whom you live with must be worried about you."

He's right. Only the gods know what Victoria was thinking, or what trouble she was in with Victor. The last thing I need is Victor showing up at the Baron's castle and the lord or his steward not knowing what he was talking about, or who I am. The thought made her cringe in alarm.

"All right," Jackie agreed, "but keep me informed. I will meet you here tomorrow morning; if one of us doesn't make it, we'll gather the day after. Okay?"

Richard nodded impatiently. "As you will, but let me go. The sooner I put an end to this nonsense, the quicker events will return to normal." With this Niohoggr leaped into the sky and flew off.

Jackie said to James, worried, "Go with him. I have a bad feeling. Everything may not go as easily as Richard believes it will."

"I think you're right," James replied, mounting his dragon. "He did not see the expression on Johnathan's face as he declared the dragonriders supreme in the land." The boy shivered. "His eyes held madness."

Jackie flew over the town. In days past, people would stop and stare, some waving if they spied a dragon in the sky. This time the citizens scattered and ran, cries of alarm rising at the sight of Belinda.

News of the rebellion has spread here already." Jackie fought the urge to land and tell everyone things would be all right. *I wonder what Johnathan has done to make the people frightened. Have the rebel dragonriders struck this barony with their insanity?*

After Jackie and Belinda returned to the mine, Jackie changed into her girl clothing and cautioned Belinda, "Don't roam tonight. Some of the dragonriders are causing problems and people could shoot at you. No one knows what's happening but I want you to stay safe, and I will need you on a moment's notice if there's trouble."

The dragon was busy nuzzling around in the mineshaft, sniffing out chunks of lambda, chewing and swallowing greedily. *"After I have my stomach settled, I'm for a long sleep,"* the dragon exclaimed, eyes fluttering. She released a deep yawn. *"You've kept me flying for a week and I need my beauty sleep."*

***

"Thank goodness you are home," exclaimed Victoria as Jackie opened the kitchen door and peeked inside. Jackie groaned to herself. Stacks of unwashed dishes piled everywhere. Half-finished trenchers of food jammed to one side of the table along with crusty mugs. Victoria slumped in a chair, dividing her attention between Jackie and a blackened pot hanging in the hearth threatening to boil over.

Jackie hurried to the fireplace and swung the pot off the fire, sweeping old ash onto the floor, and surveyed the kitchen and dining hall in dismay. "What in the world happened here?"

"Oh, everything has been chaotic since you left." Victoria raised her trembling hands and dropped both back in her lap, a long angry burn mark showed on one forearm. "The dragonriders have gone mad. You never returned and we thought they killed you when they attacked the castle...."

"Baron de la Fey's castle was attacked?" Jackie gasped, pushing crumbs from a chair onto the floor and sitting opposite her sister.

"Why yes." Victoria stared at her for the first time and swatted at a strand of hair hanging in front of her face. "How do you not know? You *were* there."

"Ah..." Jackie calculated the days. "It must have

happened after we left," she explained quickly, but I'm sure you have heard wrong." Before Victoria protested, Jackie continued, "Richard decided to take me on a tour of the kingdom via dragon and we just returned." She hugged herself. "It was wonderful—from the mountains of the north to the ocean. You should see how the people appear when you see them...."

"Yes, yes. I suppose you are right," Victoria snapped, "but I did not mistake what was said. Victor heard it firsthand at the tavern. Do you realize what is happening now?"

"Now?" Jackie thought of what lies to use. "You said the dragon riders are...."

Victoria answered her own question before Jackie replied. "Whether you enjoy it or not, Victor is nobility—and I am also—which makes you and Thomas nobles too. And the dragonriders are attacking the nobles—we might be next."

"But Victor's not really..."

"The La Montrue's are big supporters of the barons and king. They have a title." Victoria scrubbed at her smudged face. "Everyone knows this." She gazed around the kitchen as if realizing for the first time what a mess it was. "I do not know what to do. I cannot think."

Jackie stood and hugged her sister. "Don't worry. What does Victor say?" She began picking up trenchers and cups. Someone brought water in from the well. Jackie dumped the dishes into a tub and started washing.

"Oh, Victor," Victoria issued a weak smirk. "Sometimes he acts as a child. He says the same thing as you—not to worry."

Jackie nodded. "Well, for once he's right. I'm sure this dragonrider thing is a big mistake, even if Victor did hear something at the tavern." She wagged a finger at her sister. "You know how stories race around the common room, especially after a couple tankards of ale." Victoria reluctantly nodded in agreement. "I bet the next rumor will say nothing happened and all this will be resolved in a few days." Jackie waved a soapy hand toward the steps leading upstairs. "Why don't you go and get cleaned up and put on some fresh clothing," she suggested. "I'll finish here and start supper." She sauntered over to the stew Victoria was cooking and sniffed. The mess smelt burnt, but maybe salvageable. "Oh, this smells wonderful. A few tweaks and we'll eat. I'll call you when it's ready."

As Jackie cleaned, she wondered if Johnathan would go as far as attacking the lesser nobility also. If true, who could be next? *Is Victoria right? Her family in danger? Where would Johnathan stop, or would he stop at all?*

Oh, quit it. I'll turn myself into a complete nervous wreck the same as Victoria.

As she fell asleep that night, the worry wouldn't go away. Jackie lay in the dark, tossing from side to side, the images of flaming dragons descending on castles and manors alike, ruined farmhouses on fire, flashing through her mind.

The visions wouldn't stop, and sleep refused to arrive. She leaped up, dressed, and hurried through the darkness to the mine. Belinda was still fast asleep. Jackie shook the sleeping dragon awake. When Belinda didn't stir Jackie swore softly and kicked the dragon in the tail "C'mon, lazybones—time to rise and fly."

"Huh?" Belinda's eyes opened a crack. *"It's still dark out. Go away. You said no flying tonight."*

"I changed my mind," Jackie replied as she threw on her riding clothes. She put her hair up and stuck her cap over her head. "Besides, it's not night anymore—it's morning."

"Oh, all right. Of all the..." The dragon uncurled

herself, and stood stretching, tiny flickers of flame issuing from her mouth. Jackie tossed the saddle on the dragon's back and cinched it tight, and then finished readying herself. *"Where to?"* Belinda asked glumly.

Jackie stopped midway in fastening on her sword belt. Where was she going? No one would be at the island yet; it was too early—if James or Richard showed at all today. His uncle's castle? Not if he was tracking down Johnathan—and if he'd found the traitor...?

He could be so many places. She knew her own little piece of her world, but the rest of the kingdom? The location of the mines at Nicos she knew, her father took her there once on a trip. Johnathan might still be there, and that was where Richard would head as well, if Johnathan hadn't left, she amended blankly.

"We fly to the king's castle," she said at last. No matter what happened Richard was sure to report to the king. The problem was, she wasn't sure how to get there. No matter, she'd figure the way out. She knew in general the location. "Did you chew enough lambda in case you need to flame?"

"The yummy rock? Plenty," Belinda assured Jackie. *"It's sleep I need, but it doesn't appear as if I'll have any."* She waddled to the mine entrance. *"Hop aboard."* The dragon swung her head from one side of the mine entrance to the other. *"Which way?"*

Jackie knew the king's castle sat somewhere in the northeast along the high road. She studied the dark sky and located the guiding star. "This way." She gestured to the right where the main highway stretched. The road would take her there and it touched on all the major centers of commerce, although it was the slower way. *Follow the lights of the towns until dawn breaks.* "Keep the lights in sight," Jackie yelled to Belinda as they flew through the sky. "You see the glows, right?"

"Of course," Belinda replied smugly. *"Dragons have good night vision. How do you think we hunt in the dark?"*

They passed over the town, a few lights shone from the nunnery windows, and the outdoor stoves of the baker's glowing red, marked their way, and then it was dark again. Jackie felt as though she rode through a featureless tunnel, the only thing alive the glistening stars and the yellow moon above her. More fires appeared on the ground and vanished with a wingbeat from Belinda.

The stars disappeared and Jackie realized she made out rivers and trees below, clothed in morning mist.

"What was that?" At first, she thought a shaft of sunshine streaked across the sky from the rising sun. The light repeated again, joined by more. "That's dragon fire."

"I sense Niohoggr flying toward us," Belinda added. She shifted her flight path until she flew toward the bolts of flame. *"More trail behind."*

Four dots appeared, growing larger, making loops, and diving as they pursued the one in front, which zigzagged in an attempt to throw the attackers off its tail. More fire belched and the lone speck dodged, went into a loop and dove behind the lead attacker, bathing it with flame before zipping off again.

"It's Richard on Niohoggr—the riders are trying to kill him," shouted Jackie, pounding on Belinda's neck. "We have to help." She racked her brain. They hadn't been sighted yet. With any luck, they might take the riders by surprise. "Gain altitude," she ordered Belinda.

"I can do that." The dragon pointed her nose up and beat her wings, rising into the sky high above the warring dragons. Jackie waited until the dots were directly beneath her.

"Okay, now *dive*. Let's blast 'em with some fire of our own and take the pressure off Richard."

Belinda drew her wings in and flashed downward, a dart aimed at the rear of the formation. As they closed the gap, she extended her wings slightly, changing her headlong dash into a fast glide. Fire erupted from her mouth as she passed over the heads of each dragon.

The unexpected attack caused the riders to bank in confusion. Belinda dipped a wing and veered to the left as the lead dragon jerked upward, narrowly avoiding a mid-air collision. *"Ha, missed me,"* Belinda exclaimed soaring upward again.

The dragonriders, realizing they were under attack, urged their mounts to take up pursuit, but their response was slow, the dragons sluggish as they labored to catch up to Belinda.

Ahead, Niohoggr and Richard opened a wide gap. Richard glanced back, saw Jackie, and shouted in his dragon's ear. Niohoggr started banking.

"Keep going—keep going," Jackie screamed at the top of her lungs, swinging her arm wildly over her head. Richard's eyes opened wide. He nodded, and his dragon continued on its flight.

A short trickle of flame passed over Jackie's head and flicked out. Belinda dipped left, and then right. *"Watch this,"* she cooed. The dragon backswept her wings, stopping dead in the air in the path of the pursuing beast. The dragon chasing her fluttered in panic, passing over her in disarray as it avoided a midair collision. The dragon clipped wings with one of its fellows who'd flown back to attack Jackie, and both beasts spiraled downward.

"What's the matter with those two?" Jackie yelled at Belinda, who was speeding up again. "They weren't hurt badly, were they?"

"Too much fire. They've used up their air—can't stay aloft right," Belinda chortled. She swung her neck back to regard Jackie with scarlet glowing eyes, a

140

dragonish grin on her lips. *"Rookies."*

The two dragons in pursuit slowed also, falling farther behind as their strength eddied, finally swinging to check on their companions who rested in a clearing with disgust. Niohoggr slowed also, the large beast huffing in exertion. As Jackie flew abreast of Richard, the dragon's sides heaved in and out with each breath, and frothy lather ran off his sides.

"Is he all right?" Jackie called over to Richard with concern.

Richard stroked his mount on the neck and patted the dragon. "He's fine. Have to take it slow, that's all," The rider yelled back. "Where did you come from?"

"Searching for you." Jackie did a fast check of their trail to confirm no rebel riders shadowed the dragons. "I saw what happened." She hooked a thumb over her shoulder. "I take it you didn't convince Johnathan to see it your way?" Richard frowned, spat, but made no comment. Jackie asked, "What are you going to do now?"

"Now?" The boy shook his head. "I do not know. I dare not return to my baron or the king. This would bring instant attack by Johnathan and his fellows if I did." He shrugged. "I guess Niohoggr and I will hide in the forest until I decide on a plan."

Jackie pictured the two of them cuddled among the trees in the cold and wet. *No time for secrets anymore. Better start collecting a new pack of lies.* "Follow me." She waved a hand in the direction of Baldhill and her manor house. "I'll take you to a safe place." She shouted to Belinda, "Back to the mine, we have people coming for supper."

The dragon beat her wings and hurried for home with Richard and his dragon trailing in her wake. Jackie worried when they swept over the town, fearing the people would see the two beasts and which way they flew, but at first sight of the two winging monsters, the streets emptied. *Hiding in fear,* Jackie guessed. *They don't know if an attack is coming.*

To be on the safe side, though, she made the dragon fly east and swing sharply south toward her home. Belinda swept low over the Baron's forest and made a neat landing on the ledge outside the mine entrance. A second later Niohoggr settled down beside her.

"I know this place." Richard leaped off his dragon and surveyed the green landscape below. Jackie walked over to stand next to him as the two dragons waddled inside the mine. Jackie noticed Belinda's head was close to Niohoggr's and wondered if the two were having the same conversation she and Richard were about to have.

"Is this where you have hidden all the time?" Richard asked Jackie. "I thought you said…"

"It's a long story," Jackie replied rapidly, taking him by one arm and leading him into the mine. "What's more important now is your story. What happened back there? Did you meet Johnathan? "

Richard sat inside the entrance where he scanned the sky for possible danger, making himself comfortable against the rocky wall. He picked up a piece of stone and hurled it over the edge. Jackie settled next to him. Faintly the smell of burnt wool waft from his clothes. His heavy riding cloak singed black in a dozen places.

"Johnathan tricked me," he said at last. "I found him at the Nicos mines. He welcomed me with open arms, and fool that I am, I believed him when he said everything I heard was a misunderstanding." He chuckled with a hiss of derisiveness at the end of the sentence for his stupidity. "As soon as they separated me from Niohoggr, my former friends fell on me." Richard grabbed another stone, the muscles in his jaw bunching in anger as he remembered the fight. "They were my companions—brother riders. I have known each since my choosing. How dare they...?" He hurled the stone at the opposite wall of the entrance. It shattered into a hundred shreds. "They did not even let me talk."

"How did you escape?" Jackie studied his hands. Red blisters from dragon fire marked his arms as far as she could see.

"Niohoggr," he answered. "He heard the scuffling as I fought the rebels, sensed my rage and despair. The other dragons did not try to stop him. He entered the mine, bellowing rage and blowing fire." Richard's lips rose as he recalled the anger of his dragon. His mouth drooped into sadness again. "The rest of the riders scattered. I vaulted on Niohoggr's back and off we went." He shrugged and picked up a third chunk of rock and dropped it, his wrath sated for the moment. "The rest you know."

"I see." Jackie studied her hands, and then raised her eyes, vision intent on his face. "What now?"

Richard shook his head. "I do not know. There are thirty riders, not counting the king, of course." He smirked. "His dragon is old. I do not think it has risen for flight a score of years in the last twenty. Of the thirty riders, twenty have sided with Johnathan. I did not see the other nine, but I guess they wait to see what Johnathan does before they decide to unite with him or not. As long as he controls the mines and lambda, they cannot do much, can they?" He sighed wearily and searched for another stone to throw. Finding none within easy reach, he shrugged. "I guess we wait until the last minute when Johnathan decides to kill us." He threw back his head and laughed. "Unless we are luck and he hurls us in a dungeon." He cleared his throat. "I jest. We will flee for our lives. Maybe the Easmen will take us in, or your kingdom. What choice do we have?"

Jackie stared him in the eye.

"We fight."

Chapter Eleven

"**H**ow?" Richard glared back at her, disbelief and amusement written on his face. "We are outnumbered, no lambda to feed the dragons for fire. Who knows how the common people will...."

"We have lambda," Jackie replied grimly. She stuck out a shaky finger to the mineshaft. "In there, all we need."

Richard leaped to his feet. "Are you sure? I was told none existed here. I talked to a girl...."

"She lied."

Richard stomped into the opening, glaring at the walls as he walked. "Show me," he ordered.

"Wait." Jackie strode to her bags of supplies, rummaged through, found a candle and lit it. Belinda and Niohoggr curled together in a corner, fast asleep. She whispered, "This way," and took Richard's hand, guiding him deeper into the shaft where a pile of shinny rocks scattered on the floor. Jackie waved her hand. "Lambda. All we desire for our dragons."

Richard picked up a rock, examined the crystal, and swore under his breath. "The lying little trollop. I thought she was nice." He squeezed the stone in his fingers. "Wait until I get my hands on her."

He will hate me now forever.

"It wasn't her fault." Jackie sought desperately to think up an excuse, knowing she dug herself deeper into a hole with each one she told. "I forced her to say this. You see, umm..." She grasped for some plausible explanation, "at first I didn't know what people lived in this kingdom, and was afraid to divulge the secret, fearing if I took you into my confidence the exact problems we face now would happen. Later I didn't want you to know where I was, but I knew there must be more lambda in this kingdom if you searched hard enough for it, and saw the need for you to possess the stone's magic for your dragons. I never dreamed Johnathan would turn into a rebel."

Richard kept his gaze steady on Jackie. He said with bitter resentment in his voice, "And why should this girl, Jacqueline, lie for you? Are you two lovers?"

"What?"

Oh, gosh, I gotta remember, he thinks I am a man. What to tell him now? Jackie pretended to count the stones scattered at their feet while she thought up a believable story. "Uh…of course not." She gave a small laugh. "She is my cousin."

"Your cousin?"

"You mustn't tell," Jackie hurried on as if she were divulging a great secret. "Even her sister and Victor La Montrue do not know I am here. I did not learn we were related either until the death of my aunt and uncle, and overheard my father speaking about it. I, err, became curious, yes. This is why I flew to this kingdom you call Mercia. I met Jaqueline and told her the story and swore her to secrecy."

Richard studied her face and nodded. "Yes, I see the resemblance now you mention it, those blue eyes. I always thought I saw something familiar about you two, but why the secret?"

Jackie stammered, "Uh, it's a family disgrace. I'd rather not say." She dropped her head. *Please don't question me further. I've run out of lies.* Jackie took a deep breath and dusted off her hands. "Back to our original problem. You said nine of the riders were undecided? Any chance to sway the noncommittal ones to our side?" Jackie wasn't sure why she said, "Our side," instead of "your side." It sounded natural somehow.

"I must speak to each secretly at night," Richard mused. "I am sure Johnathan is watching all of us. I do not even know if their barons are allowing the riders to patrol." He frowned. "They may be kept close to the castles in case of an attack, or because they are not trusted." He wandered outside toward the ledge and spied Jackie's dress and short tunic folded at the entrance. He stopped and picked the garments up. "What in the world...? Whose are these?" He broke out in a grin and held the tunic out to her. "Not yours, or do you go in disguise also?"

"Oh, no," Jackie snatched the apparel from his hand, "their, uh—Jaqueline's. She umm... leaves clothes here in case she gets all muddy and dirty collecting wood." She laughed and slapped Richard on the back. "You know how girls are. Always fussing about their appearance."

Richard smirked. "Oh yes. I remember the second time I met her, covered in mud—and she stank to high heaven. The poor girl appeared so embarrassed I thought she would try crawling into a hole and disappear." He glanced around the rest of the entrance. "Say, you don't have anything to eat here, do you? I've had nothing since yesterday."

"Oh." She realized how late it was. She hadn't told anyone where she going when she left, and Victoria would be worried sick. "Jaqueline sneaks me out food. I'll see what I can bring." She surveyed his burnt hands. "Maybe locate salve for your arms, too. You're a mess."

***

Two wagons waited at the front door of the manor house when Jackie arrived home. Workmen scurried in and out of the door, loading boxes. Jackie rushed in and Victoria immediately grabbed her as she directed the men which items to pack. "Jaqueline, where have you been?" She pointed to a picture and snapped her fingers. Workers leaped to take the painting off the wall. "We have been searching for you all morning. Not chasing the fox again, are you. It is a waste of time. If you have not caught him by now, you never will."

"Woods," she mumbled, "and yes, I was hunting the fox. I couldn't sleep. What in the world is happening here? Has Victor ordered the house to be redecorated?" This would be just like the fool. Sell her parent's prized possessions for a pittance and replace it with worthless junk at a high price.

Victor walked down the staircase, directing two laborers who manhandled a plush chair. "Ah, there you are Jaqueline," he exclaimed. "We have your clothes packed. They are in the wagon waiting for you."

"What is this all about?" Jackie repeated, dumbfounded as men passed her by carrying a small end table.

"The baron has offered all the nobility the safety of his castle if they wish it, until this dragonrider thing has been concluded," replied Victor. "I thought it best for the family if we took him up on his offer. I am an important person, you know. These ruffians might well decide to hold me hostage for ransom." He waved a hand to the door. "Go wait in the carriage. We will be leaving in a few minutes."

"I can't go. Who—Who's going to watch the fief? This house? You're not leaving it to the peasants? They'll rob us blind." *I mustn't run away. Not now.*

Victoria glared at her, worry and exasperation flashing in her eyes. "Do not be ridiculous. Allowing a fifteen-year-old girl to remain here by herself? Why, someone will slit your throat during the night, unless they seize you and sell you into slavery. Now be good and sit in the carriage."

"I have my sword, my bow," Jackie replied stoutly. "If you're worried, I'll keep candles and lanterns burning so any strangers passing through will think people are still here—*but I'm not leaving.*"

"*Jaqueline.*"

147

"tut-tut, my dear, the girl has a point," Victor spoke up, stroking his cheek. "The place should not be left unattended, and Jaqueline is right, you never trust servants."

"I'll go armed at all times," Jackie promised. "I'll stay close to the house and only venture out if necessary."

"Well...." Victoria's eyes shifted from Jackie to her husband and back again. "If Victor thinks it is a good idea—" she muttered against her better judgement.

Victor laughed. "I had three casks of wine delivered last night. It would not do at all to leave such a bounty unattended, and I would not wish to bring my poor drink to the castle." He chuckled. "The baron might get offended if I did not indulge in his own drink."

"I'll fetch my bags from the wagon," Jackie shouted as she shot out of the door.

Within an hour the house was vacant, the wagons and carriage rattling down the road to vanish around a bend. Jackie waited another hour to make sure no one returned for some forgotten item. While she waited, she strolled through the house noting Victor forgot his prize rug. She took the time to cook a simple meal and hurried back to Baldhill to fetch Richard.

"The La Montrue's have deserted their home," Jackie told Richard as they hurried through the woods. "The baron has extended sanctuary to the nobility in his castle. The manor is ours if we wish it."

"Events are worse than I feared," Richard rumbled as the entered the kitchen. "He would not make an offer unless he expected more fighting. I...." he stopped and sniffed. "What is that wonderful smell?"

Jackie had made a simple chicken stew with carrots, thickened with barley, and left it on the hearth to stay warm. She grabbed the pot and set it on the table. "Supper," she announced, "but first we must attend to your burns." She hurried to the stillroom and returned with a jar. "Pig's fat and honey," she said. "Put out your arms and hold still."

After they ate, Jackie built up the fire in the hearth. Richard pushed himself back from the table and exclaimed with a contented sigh, joking. "You will make some woman a fine husband one of these days."

"Not for a few years yet, I think," she laughed back.

"I often dream of having a wife and home as this," Richard said, gazing around the neat kitchen and dining hall, "returning after a hard day's labor with supper waiting and a beautiful woman—A fief to call my own."

"That would be nice," Jackie said softly. "Do you think it'll ever happen?"

"Not tonight." Richard slapped his knees with his hands. "Tonight I must speak to the rest of the riders and convince each to rally to our cause."

"I will go with you," Jackie said at once. "Who knows what tricks Johnathan is playing."

"No." Richard shook his head. "This must be done as stealthily as possible. One dragon flying from castle to castle is bad enough. Two would give us away." When he saw the alarm in her face, Richard added, "Do not worry. Now I understand the dangers I will face. Tricks used on me before will not work again, I assure you."

"Well, at least let me go as far as the mine with you. It is growing dark..."

"You need not worry." Richard stood with a deep sigh. "I know my way now and Niohoggr will guide me if I become lost. Get some sleep. We will need your strong arm in the coming days."

Jackie sat up by the fire waiting for his return the rest of the night. As she fell asleep, a sense of uneasiness haunting her dreams.

***

"You're sure no one's here?"

"Yeah. I told yah. I watched 'em takeoff from the road. The whole bunch of the high and mighty ran as if the devil himself was after 'em. Place is deserted since yesterday."

Jackie woke with a start at the sound of voices issuing from the main hall. Her right hand automatically reached for her sword, while the left sought her belt knife.

"Them lords know how to live right," one voice exclaimed in admiration. "See this? Bet'ch it's worth'a fortune. Let's check upstairs. No sleeping on a pallet of grass fer these folks I bet."

Heavy footsteps tromped up the staircase. Jackie silently crept to the door of the main hall and pushed it open a crack.

The front door was wide open. Sunlight streamed in, making a line across the floor. From her vantage point in the kitchen, Jackie could see the staircase leading to the upper stories of the manor house. Curses and scraping of something heavy drifted down to her.

"Let's get this loaded on the wagon and see what else to grab." Feet appeared and then the bodies of two men, a bed between them swept into view.

Why those two.... They're stealing my bed. Jackie drew her sword and knife. "Okay, you two... Hold it right there." She shoved open the door and stalked into the main hall, waving her blades in front of her.

The two men dropped the bed, staring at Jackie in surprise. "Why now, sonny—it ain't what..." one of the burglars started.

"I know exactly what it is." She stepped forward, blade outstretched until the tip of her sword was inches away from the fat bottom of the lower man. "Both of you move—*NOW,* or I'll skewer your rump and set it in the

150

fireplace to roast for supper."

"Well, yah don't hav'ta be that...." the man lashed out with a foot, catching the blade and knocking it upward. He leaped down the remaining steps, drawing his belt knife, while his accomplish scrambled around the bed to join him.

Jackie backed up two steps, bracing herself. "Good, you're both down. Now go." She waved her sword toward the door.

The second burglar drew his belt knife, too, and began circling her. "You aren't gonna hurt no one, are yah, sonny?" he sneered. "Why, I bet that's yah daddy's sword. Mighty heavy, ain't it? I see the tip dropping already."

Jackie lashed out, feet stomping to cause a distraction, and pricked the man in the knee. He howled, dropping his knife and clutching his leg in pain. Before his companion reacted, she recovered and swung her blade in his direction. "Sword's not heavy at all, but yes, the tip did drop," she said with a smirk. She aimed the point of her weapon at the man's groin, making tight circles. "Should I try for two?"

"Ah, no. We're going, sonny," the burglar stuttered, inching to the door. "Sorry for the misunderstanding." He scurried out, his friend limping behind him.

"Good use of the point."

Jackie swung around. Richard was leaning against the doorframe, eyes twinkling in admiration with a smirk painted across his lips. "If it was me, I would have killed those two."

Jackie wiped her blade and slid it back into the scabbard. "Yeah, well, I would have to lug their bodies outside, wouldn't I," she replied. "Besides, they were following Johnathan's plan."

"Huh?" Richard replied puzzled. "I do not see

what stealing has to do with Johnathan."

Jackie checked out the door to confirm the men weren't returning. "Johnathan wants the commoners to have what the rest of us have, right?" She waved to her bed on the staircase. "You see? They're doing what he advocates. Pilfering what they haven't worked for." Her body slumped as if she'd said something distasteful, as the thought of her brother-in-law flashed through her mind. "Johnathan has a point, but he goes around it the wrong way."

Richard stared at her in a new light. "I have told him a dozen times. You see how well he thought of my ideas."

Jackie swung from the door. "They won't be back, and they'll spread the word not to mess with this house. Nice morning's work I'd say." She pushed past him into the kitchen. "C'mon. I began soaking sage last night while I waited for you to return. I'll start water boiling for tea. Tell me what happened while we wait."

Jackie built up the fire, dipped water into a kettle, and set it to boiling, then sat opposite Richard, leaning forward. "Now spill it," she said eagerly, "what did they say? Did you find anyone at all?"

"Yes," Richard replied. He stretched back and crossed his legs. "As I suspected, they were all at their baron's castles. I do not know if their lords fear they would go rogue and were afraid to let the riders out of their sight, or for protection of their lands. All are with us, more or less."

"More or less?" Jackie's eyebrows rose. "What does that mean?"

"Well, one or two were hesitant, suggested we wait on the barons or king to move against the rebels. We are not sure what good it would do without an army to back us up."

152

"Maybe they're right." Jackie found mugs and prepared tea. She set one down before Richard and resumed her seat, hearing the worry and doubt in the rider's voice. "Without the nobles the odds aren't in our favor, are they?"

Richard sipped, scowled at his mug, and replied, "No they are not. I know the barons and I know Johnathan. The lords will not fight unless forced to, and Johnathan will not move against the nobility until he is prepared. If we wait, we all go down in defeat. The way to stop the rebels is before they are ready to strike, but I cannot figure out a way to force the lords to attack with us."

"You told the rest of the riders this?"

"Yes. They know what I meant." Richard gazed into his tea. "At least I hope they understood. We are to meet tomorrow at the island."

"There?" Jackie said in alarm. "Won't Johnathan be watching for a move as this?"

"We have more places to meet, and he knows each site, but if I were not to lead you, you would never find the location. One spot is as good as another. I did not want to name this hold. Yours is our only supply of lambda so far. If Johnathan discovered this location, our cause is doomed before it starts. We meet at first light tomorrow." He stretched and yawned. "I need to sleep. I fear if I do not, I will pass out on the floor, and you will have to carry me to bed as if I were a baby."

"We can't have you curled up down here. If our two friends return you would be the first thing they'd steal, and you are too heavy to carry to the sleeping chambers," Jackie agreed with a slap on his shoulder. She finished her tea in one gulp and stood. "Help me lug the bed back upstairs those rascals were trying to pilfer, and we'll find you a spot to rest."

The upstairs bedrooms were a mess from hasty packing. They maneuvered Jackie's bed into her small room and she found sheets and blankets for Richard. "There, all set," she announced.

Richard sprawled out on the bed, stretching his lean body to make himself comfortable. "Are you going to get more sleep," he asked, unable to keep his eyes open. "You must have been up half the night worrying."

"No, I'm fine," she lied. Even as she turned to the door, she heard his gentle snores. She walked to the kitchen, made herself more tea, and thought.

There must be some way of keeping Johnathan off balance, slow him down until Richard thought of someway of forcing the lords to fight. They couldn't stop him from rousing the peasants. They wouldn't listen to her, nor would the nobles. ten, no, eleven, adding herself, against how many thousands? Jackie shuttered at the thought. But maybe it wouldn't come to this, but back to her original thought. How to slow Johnathan in his preparations to wage war?

In a burst of clarity, she realized what she must do. Jackie stood and stalked out the door to find Belinda.

Chapter Twelve

"Well, look at you two."

The dragons curled up together. Belinda's head rested on Niohoggr's. Their long tails overlapped.

Belinda's eyes opened, gleaming red in the semi-darkness. *"Shhh. He sleeps. He has flown for two days without respite and wonders why the rest of our kind attacked him,"* the thought flowed to Jackie in a soft whisper. Belinda carefully uncurled herself from the sleeping dragon and slid to Jackie. *"He tries to puzzle this out, as do I. Do you have any idea?"*

Jackie paused. She never realized the dragons would wonder why friends one day were enemies the next. She knew dragons were intelligent, but maybe not *human* intelligence. "Their riders have decided to overthrow by force those who rule this land. The people who oppose them, Richard, I, and a few of the dragonriders, disagree with this idea and plan to stop Johnathan and the men who agree with him."

"These are now bad riders and dragons?"

The conversation was reaching a point where Jackie didn't know how to explain, or what Belinda drew from her explanation. She thought deliberately and replied, "Misguided, shall we say? I don't think the dragons know what is happening at all. They obey their riders and are as confused as you and Niohoggr."

Belinda was silent for a short time. She finally replied, *"I understand. You and Richard wish to restore the natural balance of nature to this realm."*

"Uh, not quite," Jackie hedged, "but there is a right way of doing things and a wrong way. The way Johnathan is handling the situation is the wrong way." She didn't know if the dragon understood right from wrong and wanted to add more, but couldn't express herself. Instead, she said, "We're going for a ride."

"To change bad to good?"

"Yeah." Jackie leaped on Belinda's back. "We gotta start somewhere."

Jackie knew she was being stupid. She didn't care. Richard was right; the people loyal to the crown must stop the rebellion before it started, first and foremost the dragonriders, but she saw no one doing it. In this respect, he was as bad as the rest of the nobles.

"Where are we going?" Belinda wanted to know as she spread her wings and took flight.

"The Nico's mines. Straight ahead."

Late morning traffic scurried on the streets of the town as they flew overhead. *I hope no one saw where we came from.* People stopped and pointed at the sky, screamed in fright, and scattered as fast as possible. *No, too eager to grab cover and protect themselves.*

They traveled along the road using its winding turns as a guide as Jackie had long ago with her father. It amazed her she'd lived all her life in Mercia and didn't know the geography of the land. She resolved to locate a map first chance and fix every landmark and town in her mind.

Belinda stirred restlessly beneath her at the delay of traveling the windy path as they arrived at the crossroads leading to the mountains. "Keep going and steady, Belinda," Jackie shouted into the dragon's ear. "Now is where the trip becomes fun."

"I hope so," the dragon complained. *"This is the most boring flight we've taken. I could be at my nice dark mine still asleep."*

A wide section of one mountain showed a gash as if a warrior took a sword to the stone. Off to one side three dragons rested on a flat piece of rock by a wooden building.

A pile of lambda stacked nearby. Workers scampered in and out of a yawning hole in the cut, hauling wheelbarrows of stone.

"A quick buzz over the mine to allow the workers time to escape," Jackie yelled to the dragon, "afterward we blast 'em. Zoom in low, shoot a short stream of flame so they'll know what they're in for and we mean business."

Belinda swooped down, and Jackie screamed to the miners, "All of you, get out of there—*NOW.*"

A brief trickle of fire spouted from Belinda's mouth, tickling the rock over the entrance to the shaft causing the supports to blacken.

The miners stared up as the shadow of the dragon passed overhead. They yelled and scattered. More poured out of the hole in the mountain. Three men sprinted from the building—Riders. They stood frozen, confused, as Belinda flapped upward and banked, circling around for another pass.

"Okay, Let's blast the mine entrance. On my count. One—Two—*Three.*"

The dragon arrowed downward again and released a long stream of fire into the dark hole. The rock surrounding the entrance glowed red; supporting beams burst into flames and disintegrated, and the mountain shook as the shaft collapsed. Belinda shot upward to avoid the dust bellowing from the tunnel.

"Perfect," Jackie gloated in satisfaction as they zipped beyond the cut. "Do you have one good blow in you, or was this it?"

"More than enough," Belinda made a smug reply. The dragon preformed a loop-the-loop, screaming down on the mine again.

"Hit the building. Try to destroy the stack of lambda while you're at it," Jackie urged, while frantically waving at the riders to scatter out of the way.

The men sprinted for their dragons. When they spied Belinda bearing on their position, they ran in all directions, taking cover behind boulders.

Belinda discharged a tide of fury. The building exploded into nothingness while the lambda disappeared, melted away to seep into the rock below.

"This should slow Johnathan up some," Jackie muttered. She checked behind her. "Oh—oh. Time to make tracks, little girl," she said to Belinda. "The sheriff is on the march."

As Belinda flew away, the riders ran out of concealment and dashed to their mounts again. As crows lifted from a carcass, the dragons flapped into the air, slowly chasing Jackie.

"Why are they acting sluggish?" Jackie wondered aloud when the rapid pursuit she expected did not happen.

"I told them not to hurry. I would see everyone later," Belinda replied. Jackie swore she heard the dragon titter. *"They said to have a good flight."*

The three dragons disappeared in the distance. Jackie flew on. Below, she spied a wagon train, nobles fleeing to the safety of their baron's castle carrying their possessions.

"Maybe we should coast above in case Johnathan's riders chance by," Jackie said to Belinda, "but don't fly too close. We don't want to scare the people into a panic."

Belinda went into a leisurely glide, riding the air currents and keeping the wagons in sight as small specks below her. In the distance, a castle appeared in view, the portcullis dropped down, the drawbridge up.

"Looks as if they're preparing for a siege," Jackie muttered. She wondered if the rebel dragonriders had attacked the baron already, or if this was a precaution on his part.

From the courtyard of the castle, a dragon arose, flapping hard and making a direct line for Jackie. When it was within earshot the rider called out," Declare yourself, for or against the king?"

"For the king, James, as you should well know by now," Jackie shouted back. She flew close until the beasts glided wingtip to wingtip. She gestured to the ground. "Land your mount and bring me up to date what is happening in this part of the country."

The two beasts swooped to earth, fluttering to rest behind the last of the wagons. Jackie vaulted off Belinda as James dismounted. "It is good to see you again," he declared. "I had not thought to see you until tomorrow, if at all."

Jackie dusted off her palms and placed her hands on her hips. "If we are to defeat Johnathan, there is no waiting for tomorrow." She pointed a leather bound glove at the receding wagons. "Why aren't you flying guard for your people? Doesn't you baron realize an attack could descend on him at any time? If I'd been one of Johnathan's riders they'd all be dead by now."

The young man frowned and licked his lips with aggravation. "My lord Baron keeps me close to his castle and estates. I have no choice in the matter. I suppose he knows these people might be attacked but..." He shrugged, "what am I to do? He feels he has done enough by offering his subordinates protection at his castle and that is enough. I have orders."

Jackie's stomach contorted into a knot of rage. Her face grew hot. "You and your lord will sit here and do nothing like frogs on a log while Johnathan and his men conquer this kingdom?" She spat on the grass. "Are you a dragonrider or a milk maid? Your baron may be afraid to fight, maybe the king, too, but I thought Richard, you, and the rest derived from finer metal. I see I was wrong." She stalked back to Belinda and mounted. "I've destroyed the mine at Nicos. That'll slow Johnathan and his plans for a time until he opens the shaft again. Decide if you are a man, because I can't stop the rebels forever by myself." She shot the embarrassed rider a look of scorn and said loud enough to Belinda for James to hear, "Let's go and hope he decides to do the right thing before it's too late."

Belinda soared into the air, Jackie still fuming inside. *Maybe that'll put some backbone into him. If I light a fire under these people, we'll stand a chance.*

***

Richard was awake and sitting at the kitchen table drinking a mug of tea when Jackie stalked into the manor house.

Should I tell him what I did? What I think? Why not, what can he do?

Richard looked up as the door banged open. "Jackie, I...."

"I've destroyed the mines at Nicos," Jackie snapped. "Johnathan's source of lambda is cut off for a time. How are we going to defeat him?" She dropped opposite him and stared the rider in the eye.

Richard's mouth opened and snapped shut. He stammered, "I—I—You did what?"

"I attacked, which is what you dragonriders should be doing, now." She banged her fist on the table, "The barons aren't letting our men protect the countryside or the people who live there. First thing first. Tomorrow we set up a kingdom-wide patrol to stop any attacks. Agreed?"

"Well, yes, but the barons..." Richard began. His hand tightened around his mug. "We still have to figure out how to convince the lords..."

Jackie stomped her foot hard enough on the floor to cause Richard to blink in alarm. "To heck with the barons. If we don't start moving there'll be no barons, or

160

king, or lords. This whole kingdom will be a fiefdom of Johnathan's."

Richard winced, a frown creasing his forehead. He studied his hands. "You are right. What do you suggest? I have yet to thrash out any ideas."

"Well," Jackie leaned forward and clenched the edge of the table, "those provinces the rebels hold, what say we make a visit to each, dragons a-blazing. It'll make the people think twice about attacking the nobles."

"Yes, it might work, but the nobles are half the problem," Richard replied thoughtfully. "They treat the peasants as if they were trash, demand whatever they have, and figure out a way of stealing the rest under the guise of law. If we do not solve the noble problem, a rebellion will break out again, if not led by Johnathan, than by someone else, especially if they see what the riders attained even if they used dragons."

"If, if, if," repeated Jackie with a scowl. "One problem at a time." Her fingers tightened on the table until her knuckle shone white. "We can't fight the peasants, the dragonriders, and the nobles all at the same time." She reached across the table and punched him on the arm. "There's only eleven of us, remember?"

Richard was surprised at her vehemence and the change of her attitude right after. He broke out into a laugh, and released a deep groan, his voice filling with regret. "When this is all over you must introduce me formally to your cousin, Jaqueline. I know of no better way than passing the rest of my days, courting her and settling down to a fief in the country with no problems to disturb us."

Jackie drew back, her mouth open. *He thinks of me this way?* "You would wed her?" she replied in a low voice trying to keep the tremble out of her tone.

Richard smiled weakly, stared at the tabletop while drawing small imaginary designs with his fingers, and shook his head. "In truth, I could not say. I have only met her twice," he replied, "but she is fair of face and disposition. If she contains the same qualities as you, intelligence and bravery, she would make a fine wife."

Jackie's face burnt hot. "I don't know how smart or brave I am, but I thank you for saying I am. I think though, I will not convey your remarks to my cousin until this conflict has ended—one way or the other." Jackie struggled to regain her composure. "Let's return to the problems we face now, and set aside the virtues of my cousin for a different time."

Richard gave her a significant look as if telling her the plans she laid out weren't so easy to place into practice. "Yes. What do we do when Johnathan and his men confront us?" he leaned back in his chair and crossed his arms. "And you know they will, if we start attacking the provinces already taken over, not to mention, the peasants if they decide to fight us. What happens next? Do we kill everyone who resists us? We will be no better than those we oppose."

"Afterward?" Jackie scrubbed at her forehead. "I don't want to hurt anyone, if possible. If we hit and run, and do it fast enough," she thought of how startled the dragonriders were at the mine, "we'll be gone before anyone reacts and fight back."

"Might work," Richard mused, "at least it is a starting point."

"Good. Now here's the plan."

***

"Okay, if no has any questions, this is how we'll divide up." Jackie shuffled through the sand in front of the riders who stood by their dragons ready to leave. She picked out four of the boys by eye. "You'll protection the kingdom. Don't pass over the same area twice." The riders nodded. Jackie addressed the rest of the men. "You will descend on the provinces Johnathan holds. Don't stick around, understand? Let the citizens know they're in rebellion, blow a bunch of fire and *leave*; try not to hurt anyone in the process. Johnathan will have riders in the area and we don't want fighting with him at this point."

James spoke up. "What happens if we do meet one of the rebels? We run?"

Mutters of dissent arose from the rest of the men. None wished to appear as cowards.

Before Jackie replied, Richard answered, "Run if you can—fight if you must. We cannot afford to lose any of you. Regardless, use your judgement, but remember; we are not going to win over allies by killing their friends and relatives, or burning down their homes."

One by one, the riders shook hands, mounted, and flew off in separate directions. When they all departed, Richard said, "What are your plans for us?" His lips lifted.

"Try to be everywhere at once as a backup," Jackie replied as she watched the riders vanish into the clouds. "If I knew for certain where Johnathan has made his headquarters, I'd say drop in on him for a surprise." She swung to face him. "Do you think we should patrol separate or together?"

Richard strolled toward Niohoggr. "Together would be better. If one of our men needs help, three against whatever he faces are much better odds." He scratched the beginnings of a beard. "First over to Barnard's cove, I think," he said as he straddled his dragon. "They are part of my baron's fief, but also boarder the South Bay, which revolted against Baron Cambell and declared for Johnathan. If I were he, I would extend my reach along the coast to collect taxes on shipping and protect myself against invasion from the king by sea. This would be an excellent place for him to attack."

"We have Jeffery covering the area?" Jackie liked

Jeffery. He was her baron's rider, but he was young and untried. *A good region to start with.*

"Yes, and from there I think we sweep inland."

The sun was rising. Sweat trickled down Jackie's face, stinging her eyes. *It'll feel good to fly in the air and cool off. Keeping myself bundled up like this is killing me.* Jackie hoisted herself onto Belinda's back. "Let's go."

The ocean was calm. The waves created lines across the surface in an endless pattern of white capped streaks. As they neared the shore, the tangy smell of seaweed and fish assaulted Jackie, and fainter, the acid taint of burning wood. Above the sand dunes, a grey fog drifted into the air from Barnard's Cove.

"Fire."

Jackie nodded to Richard, and the dragons swung in the direction of the smoke. When they reached the shore, three dragons swooped to the sky—two chasing a third.

"That's Jeffery they're chasing," Jackie shouted. She urged Belinda to greater speed. Niohoggr mirrored his wing mate's flight pattern, flying above Jackie as they streaked upward.

Jeffery's dragon was twisting and rolling in a valiant effort to throw the two pursuers off his tail. One of the attackers, lucky or anticipating a move, banked, narrowly missing the escaping rider. The dragon veered back, doggedly hanging onto Jeffrey's rear as he sought to overtake the loyalist.

Jackie intercepted the lead dragon at an angle, a shaft of flame leaping from Belinda to engulf the beast's head. The dragon dove down to escape. Belinda fell into a stoop and sped after.

The other rebel, seeing his companion flee, and the approach of Richard, swung upward to meet the attack of Niohoggr. A blast of fire erupted from both dragons in a cascade of fury as they neared. They passed, each trying desperately to swing in the tightest circle possible for another clash.

The dragon Jackie chased dove close to the earth, flattening out at the last moment to skim across treetops before flying skyward again. Belinda chucked, *"Trying to make me crash into the ground, huh? I dreamed that one up while I was still an egg."* She leveled off and shot upward in pursuit with a savage roar of joy.

A streak zipped by her the other way, and then two more. Jackie watched the three dragons flatten out above the treetops and zigzag away.

"Beware."

Abruptly, Belinda banked right as the enemy dragon shot down on her. Wingtips clipped, sending Belinda into a spin. She recovered with a muted, *"Ouch, that hurt."*

The rebel dragon was not as lucky. Spiraling out of control, the beast tried leveling out at the last moment before shearing off the top of the trees and disappearing within the waving branches of the forest.

"He is dead."

"Who?" Jackie demanded as she strained her eyes searching for signs of the dragon and rider.

"Both. Man and dragon."

"Are you sure?" Jackie scanned the woods again, worry and a churning in her chest spreading through the rest of her body. "The trees are so thick...."

"There is no room to land. I will have to settle on the edge of the forest." Belinda's thoughts were bleak. She paused, midair. *"I see their spirits rise."* She fluttered down on a wide expanse of field abutting the woods. Moments later, two more dragons with riders joined her, Richard and Jeffrey.

"What happened?" Richard demanded, vaulting off Niohoggr. He ran to Jackie, Jeffrey hurrying in his wake. "Where is the rider? Did he escape?"

"No." Jackie waved a hand to the forest. Tears trickled down her cheeks. "Both dragon and rider are dead—in there. We collided and they crashed." A constriction as strong as a vice clamped at Jackie's throat. "I couldn't help it. They...."

A low hum growing into an ear-splitting whine rose from the dragons, who stared at each other as if mesmerized by their mate's gaze. As one, they lifted their heads to the sky and blast after blast of red dragon fire lashed the heavens.

The three dragonriders lowered their heads.

Jackie whispered, *"Our first deaths."*

Chapter Thirteen

They buried the rider. "Mark the grave well, and remember this place," Jackie said to Richard and Jeffery. "When this is all over, his people will wish to return and move the body to a place of honor."

Jeffery replied solemnly. "The bones of his dragon will identify his gravesite." The dragon was too big to bury. Jackie kissed her fingers and placed the tips on the cold side of the beast. "You have nothing to be ashamed of, noble one. You didn't know." She said to the rest, "What of the rider you pursued?"

Richard replied as they trudged their way through the trees, "He escaped. We had best mount our dragons and start on patrol. He will report to Johnathan what has occurred here and the rest will flock to investigate."

Their dragons were where they left them, silently waiting. Richard said to Jeffery, "What were those two doing at Barnard's Cove?"

"As you suspected, they tried to persuade the people to join the rebellion." Jeffery's eyes narrowed. "When I chanced upon the two, they had collected the people in the town's square." His voice took on a hushed tone. "Some of the people were bound hand and foot. I think they planned to execute the village's leaders as an example to the rest of the people." He kicked at a clump of grass." When they saw me flying overhead, the fight started. This is how the building was set on fire." He appeared puzzled. "I do not understand, though. Why their dragons did not flame more at me."

"Probably can't." Jackie remounted Belinda. "With their stock of lambda cut off, the only stone they have is in their dragon's gizzards or have stored in their purse. This won't last long, and when it's gone—it's gone."

After they were airborne, Richard yelled to Jackie,

"I wish to return to my uncle's castle and report what has happened here. This is part of his fief and he will want to know."

Jackie signaled she understood and together they flew inland. The castle rose into sight sitting atop a hill. They swooped low over the parapets to land in the courtyard.

Four-foot long bolts tipped with sharp iron heads flashed up at the dragons. Belinda banked, swerved and shot upward. One of the bolts bounced off her scaly side leaving a long scratch. *"That smarts."*

More of the arrows peppered Niohoggr as he hovered over the courtyard, confused. Soldiers stormed out of concealment, firing more arrows from crossbows. Richard abandoned his attempt to land and his dragon flapped upward, trailed by a hail of bolts, missing him and falling back on the archers.

"What's with those people?" Jackie yelled as she and Richard circled above the castle. More soldiers ran out of the main door, shaking their fists to the sky and aiming weapons. "Don't they recognize you?"

Bewildered, Richard replied, "I thought they did. I don't understand...." He shook his head. "Let us land outside the walls and discover what this is all about."

"Make it well out of shaft range," Jackie advised darkly. She studied the mark on Belinda's side. "The dragons have tough armor, we don't."

The dragons settled to the earth. Richard and Jackie walked forward, arms in the air over their heads in a sign of peace. "It's me, Richard," the rider called out when they were in hearing reach. "Why are you firing on us? Don't shoot."

A tall man stalked to the parapet, the cowl of his furry mantle thrown back, revealing grizzled hair. Even from the distance they stood, Jackie saw the anger in his face. "Go away, traitor. Return and I'll shoot a bolt in your stomach." He raised a loaded crossbow in his hands.

"Baron—Uncle." Richard lowered his hands. "You know I am not one of the traitors. I am loyal to you. I am here to report we have stopped an attack on Barnard's Cove."

The baron lowered his weapon, but replied, "I do not know what game you dragonriders are playing, but I want none of it." He rubbed his nose and continued shrewdly, "Perhaps some infighting among your ranks? Nevertheless, your orders were to remain close to this castle and you disobeyed. Word has arrived to us the riders we thought loyal to the crown have disappeared, too. None of you are trusted. This says the king and so I believe."

"But...."

He shifted his gaze to Jackie. "Is this the reason for your treason, the phantom rider? What falsehoods have you told my nephew and his friends to subvert those who were once loyal to us?"

The stupidity of this man. No wonder Johnathan discovered it was simple to start a rebellion. "We overthrow no one," Jackie shouted back. "We're trying to help, don't you see that?" She dropped her hands and took a step closer, attempting to make him understand the danger they faced. "It does no good to wait until the whole countryside is in turmoil. We are trying to do what should have been done from the start."

The baron was silent as he contemplated what Richard and Jackie said. Finally, he replied, "This is all well and good, and there may be truth in what you say. Nevertheless, this debated should have started before you acted on your own, and now your actions are suspect. I think you will rue the day you decided to take this rash actions on your own, no matter what your motives were."

"But Uncle..." Tears flowed from Richard's eyes

down his cheek, "if you would listen…"

"Do not call me Uncle or Baron," the old man declared, his face turning cold. "Until this crisis is over you are no kin of mine or liegeman. I wash my hands of you." He disappeared from the parapet.

More stern-faced archers took his place. Richard stood numbly staring at the space his uncle once stood, and then swung around; his face still wet and smashed his fist into his palm as he stalked back to Niohoggr. "This is it— we're on our own," he snarled, leaping astride the dragon. "Our families have cast us out, and our once friends have turned against us."

Jackie mounted Belinda. "Maybe it's for the best," she said solemnly. "If we are thrown away this easily, perhaps they were never our companions to begin with. We will make new alliances and family."

A tinge of fear crept into Richard's voice as he said, "Where will we go now, us and the other riders. We have no home."

"We still have the manor," Jackie reminded him. "We will bring the rest of the riders there to stay for now. We must guard the lambda mine anyway. Sooner or later Johnathan would discover its location. It is well we mount a guard." She lifted Belinda into the air. "We will spread the word to the rest where to meet tonight and plan our strategy for tomorrow.

***

The lawn of the house became a roosting ground for dragons that night. Belinda swooped from her mine to investigate the bellowing of her new neighbors, surveying the milling herd with a touch of humor and declared, *"All right for the males, I suppose. I return to my home. I hope they do not make a racket all night."* With this, she took wing and flapped to Baldhill.

Jackie was going crazy. Scrambling about trying

to assign rooms, directing the men where to stow their gear, and the basic logistics of bedding down nine people was something she'd never done before. *What am I going to feed all these men?* she wondered as she dug out blankets and handed as many as possible to the dragonriders who stood in the dining hall gazing at the blank walls and furniture.

Richard noticed the rising panic in her eyes. "Here you," he called to two of the men, "go see what's in the smokehouse. If nothing else, chase down some chickens. There is a barnyard is full of fowl. We have to eat, right?" he pointed to a rider undecided what to do, "Start a fire going in the kitchen fireplace." He searched around—saw James. "You, go fetch water. The rest of you start hauling wood. If you cannot find what you are searching for, ask me—or Jackie." He gave a hearty laugh. "For tonight we bed down in this dining hall, there is ample room, and all of you remember—we are guests in this home. Do not destroy the place." The riders bobbed their heads and scrambled off in all directions.

A weight lifted off Jackie. She muttered, "Thank you," and dropped into a chair with a sigh.

"It's not your responsibility more than anyone else's." Richard sat also and drew his chair closer to hers. "You act as though this is your home, not your cousin's."

"Well, they are my cousins," she replied. "I can imagine what Victoria would say if she saw what a state the place was in." She chuckled.

"Victoria?"

"Victor La Monture's wife, the lady of this house," Jackie hastened to explain. "Jaqueline's sister."

"Oh." An unfathomable expression passed over Richard's face. "I wonder what she is thinking right now?" He said to Jackie, "Do you think your cousin believes badly of me—us, all the dragonriders, as the rest of the nobles do?"

"Knowing Jaqueline," Jackie said, choosing her words with care, "She knows you are trying to do right. She may not understand why, but she is always willing to let someone explain their actions, allowed the chance."

"Good. When next I see her, I will describe everything that has taken place," Richard replied. "I am glad you are here to verify what I say." He slapped his hands together. "After we eat, a watch must be set so Johnathan does not take us by surprise during the night."

Jackie flashed him a quick nod. "Agreed. There are eleven of us. Two men, two hours each? One man keeps his partner awake."

The aroma of roasting meat drifted to Jackie. She glanced over at the kitchen where a rider was turning a side of beef on a spit in the hearth. Jeffery wandered over, balancing trenchers. "Uh, I was going to set the table," he muttered with a faint smirk. "Is there any wine in the house? I found mugs in the stillroom, but nothing to pour in each."

Jackie bolted upright. "Oh, yes. Three barrels in the basement. I'll show you."

"No need, I will find it," Jeffrey replied.

Jackie sat, giggling to herself. *When Victor returns home, he will hang himself.*

***

When Jackie awoke the next morning, she discovered herself in a quandary. She'd spent the night sleeping in the kitchen, bundled in a blanket next to the fireplace. She and Richard took the first watch, after which, she'd stumbled inside the manor house, too tired to climb the steps to her bedroom and curled up in the first empty space she found, falling into a dreamless slumber.

She woke before dawn. At first, she didn't remember where she was, but the men wandering around in various stages of undress and sitting at the kitchen table talking brought back in clarity the events of the day before.

"Well, the sleeper awakes." Richard rose from the table dressed in nothing more than his braies and stood over her. "Go wash the sleep from your face and join us. We make plans for the day."

"Uh, yeah." Jackie stumbled up, unable to keep from staring. She was used to seeing Thomas running around half-naked, even bathed him once when he was a baby, but this…. She glanced at her feet. "I'll be right back. Maybe in the mean time you should put clothes on. It's cold in here even with the fire, and we can't afford to have any of you sick."

"We should all be as you are," Richard joked, scanning her bundled up appearance from head to toe. "You never take your cape or tunic off; in fact, I have never seen you without your cap, either. I suppose you feel you will be assaulted by bad humors if you expose your skin to the air?"

She paused at the door still not looking at him and chuckled, shouting solemnly over her shoulder, "I have never met a humor I couldn't defeat," and bolted out of the kitchen.

Jackie prolonged her toilet as long as possible, keeping careful watch to make sure she wasn't observed, until it became ridiculous to wait any longer. When she returned to the kitchen she was relieved to see the men clothed and in heated discussion around the table. She drew herself a cup of tea and joined the riders.

"…and it was odd. When I first landed, the townspeople shied away, were fearful of me, but after I identified myself as a rider loyal to the crown they completely changed their attitude." James shook his head in utter confusion. "I wonder why they say the town is in rebellion."

"Ayes," arose from the rest of the riders, and "same thing happened to me." Jackie sat and took a long sip of her tea. "What are we talking about?"

Richard spoke up. "Of the ten towns visited yesterday, six were glad to see us, three were ambivalent, and one was hostile, but all and their surrounding territories have been declared in rebellion against the crown. Any thoughts?"

"You're right, it is odd." Jackie stared off into space, thinking. Why would a baron claim an area in revolt if it weren't? Did they attack the magistrates? Refuse to pay their taxes? "How many people does it take to make an insurgency?" she asked at last, looking around. "Everyone? A majority? Or a few who are vocal enough and act in rebellion while the rest remain silent?"

The riders shook their heads. "I do not know," Richard admitted, frowning as he thought over Jackie's question.

"If a hundred men out of a thousand attacked the baron's soldiers, destroyed his court, or ran off the magistrate, the baron would declare an insurrection, right?" Jackie pressed her point. "And if those hundred had a dragonrider or two to back their actions up, the nine hundred would be afraid for their lives to speak out." She nodded to herself. "I'm betting this is what's happening in the provinces. But —" her forehead crinkled as she mulled the possibilities over in her mind, "this makes our job easier and harder."

Jeffery leaned forward, eyes widening. "How?" The rest of the riders waited carefully for Jackie's reply.

She waved a finger in the air. "Easier because we have to eliminate the few instead of the many, but harder because we have no way of knowing who those few are." She leaned back and chuckled, taking a sip of her tea. "I doubt they walk around with signs."

Murmurs of agreement rose from around the table.

"If what you guess is true," Richard hedged, "we have no way of distinguishing who are the ringleaders, and who follow anyone bold enough to take charge."

"There's one way to learn." Jackie drained her mug and pushed herself away from the table. Someone left the side door open and sunlight filtered in from the outside. Dawn was breaking. "I think the rest of us should keep patrolling as we did yesterday." She winked at Richard. "How about you and I sneaking into of these towns, discover what is happening, and who the ringleaders are?"

Richard lips twitched up in agreement. "I think it's a good plan."

The riders exited the kitchen and checked their dragons. Richard and Jackie continued on to Baldhill, reassuring themselves Belinda still guarded their precious horde of lambda. She was not there, but Niohoggr stuck his snout out the mine entrance and blew a short blast of fire in way of greeting.

"Niohoggr says Belinda flew off before the sun rose. She is hunting," Richard answered Jackie's unspoken question, "but will return shorty."

They sat to wait.

***

Jackie and Richard left their dragons concealed in a jumble of boulders with a stream running down a mountainside, and started their hike toward a town. Buildings came into sight between the trees, separated by a large field of grain. Richard asked, "Where do we begin? We cannot go around asking who is a rebel. We would learn, but in the wrong way, I think."

"The best place to pick up gossip is in the tavern," replied Jackie with a smirk, remembering all the news Victor brought from his frequent visits. "If we sit there long enough, we'll hear about everyone in the town and their lineage back a hundred years."

They located the alehouse easily enough in the center of the village, a green branch hanging outside the door indicating it was open for business. As Jackie pushed the door wide, the pungent reek of urine, sawdust, and wood smoke assaulted her nose. Half-a-dozen men sat at tables in the common room, eating and drinking. When Jackie and Richard entered, conversation stopped and all eyes swung their way. After a brief inspection, the talking resumed.

"...they were my 'taters and his pigs were eating 'em," one man declared to another. Both dressed as farmers, relaxing for a few moments from selling their produce in the marketplace, before returning to their fields.

"But he claims yer shoul'a taken better care of yer crops," his friend said reasonably, "that's why yer 'taters were in 'is pigs."

Jackie nodded to a vacant table. She and Richard took seats. The proprietor wandered over, wiping his hands on a soot smudged apron and asked, "What will it be?"

Richard piped up, "Whatever you have that is hot and filling. We haven't eaten all day."

The tavern keeper pursed his lips in thought. "Beef n' barley soup then. Made it last night. Nice and thick; fill you right up." He checked them over. "Money?"

Richard dug into his purse and pulled out a handful of large copper coins. "Here, this should cover everything. Make sure the soup is hot."

The coins disappeared. Seconds later two trenchers of soup slid in front of the two, coarse black bread on top.

Jackie and Richard picked up their spoons and continued to listen to the conversations flowing around the room.

A portly man wearing the red cap of a merchant

called over to the farmers, "Did you bring the dispute to Rufello?"

"Yeah, I did," declared the farmer in disgust. "'E told me to leave 'em alone and not bother 'em." The man wagged his head in sorrow. "Said if'n I ever came to 'em again with stupid arguments 'e'd confiscate me land." The farmer said to his tablemate, "The rider put 'em in charge of justice after 'em and his robbers ran eh judge out of town. I figured couldn't be no worse than the law the nobles put out, but this is justice?"

A fourth man chimed in with, "This is the new law. Dragonrider law, and better get used to it—things like Rufello and his gang in charge making the rules, until the baron makes a move—if he ever does."

Jackie called out to the man who'd spoken last, "I take it this Rufello runs the town? Is he one of the rider's men?"

The tavern grew quiet, speculative glances shot their way from the rest of the patrons. The person Jackie addressed found cause to study his tankard with intent interest.

When the silence grew long, the farmer whose potatoes had disappeared inside the pigs spoke. "Yes and no. Use to be him and his men were seasonal help, picking crops when they came into season," he replied. "Worked for me a couple of times. Lazy, but when the crops gotta be picked, they gotta be picked, right?" He nodded to the men. "But when the dragonriders rebelled and flew in here, he was the first to pledge allegiance—him and his gang. After this..." His shoulders rose and dropped. "Dragonrider ran the baron's soldiers off. Rufello and his men took care of the rest."

"He hiring?" Richard wanted to know.

The farmer shot him a sour expression. "Not if yer honest." He grabbed his goblet and swung away from

Richard.

After this exchange, the tavern grew quiet, suspicious glances flashing their way from the rest of the patrons. One man in the far corner who hadn't said a word stood and stalked out.

"We better get out of here," Richard whispered to Jackie. *"Something tells me we have overstayed our welcome."*

"Right."

Jackie and Richard finished eating quickly. Jackie stood. "Let's go."

They strode to the exit. Before they left five heavily armed men entered, closing the door behind them, and surveying the common room. "Whoa, hold on there, you two," the leader snapped shoving his outstretched hand into Richard's chest as the rider tried to walk past. His companions blocked their escape. "Where ya going to, so fast?" He backed up a step and placed his hand on the hilt of his sword.

"Finished eating," Jackie said simply. She measured the man by eye. "If you'll move out of our way, we'll leave." She tried to step around him.

The tough grabbed her shoulder by the tunic and shoved her against Richard. "Don't be in a hurry, laddie. We want to ask you some questions first."

Richard steadied Jackie and half drew his own sword. "And who are you to be asking questions? If you must know, we are honest folk, passing through. Now, out of the way. We want no trouble."

The leader laughed and pulled his sword. His men did the same. "I'm the one's giving the orders right now. We hear you're asking about Rufello. What's your interest in him?"

"We understood he runs this town," Jackie replied as she tried to keep the tremor of rage out of her voice. "We thought he might have work." Her lips turned down into a bitter line as she studied the man. "But we've changed our minds."

The man scowled. "So working for Rufello isn't good enough fer yer, huh?" He waved his men forward, indicating they should circle Richard and Jackie. "I think we'll take ya in fer questioning, and find out what kinda work yer good for."

Jackie glanced at Richard out of the corner of her eye, who replied with an imperceptible nod. Her body sagged and she replied meekly, "I guess we have no choice—*NOW.*"

Jackie rushed forward, hitting the man in the stomach with her shoulder. He went down with a loud, HUMPH.

Richard drew his blade, swinging wildly at the men as they tried to close on him. He kicked one in the groin while the rest backed up out of sword range.

Jackie made it to the door, yanking it open. The leader reached out, grabbing her ankle. She fell to the floor, twisting and lashed with her foot at his hand while Richard scrambled past. The rider snatched Jackie under her armpits and lifted her erect. "*Run.*"

They stumbled out of the tavern, down the steps, and sprinted along the street. Three more armed soldiers walked around the corner of a building and saw the two running. The three drew their swords and stormed toward Jackie and Richard. "HALT."

Ahead waited freedom. Jackie drew her sword and she and Richard drove into the men with a flurry of swinging blades.

Pain, as sharp as the bite of a rattlesnake coursed through Jackie's shoulder. She ignored it and dispatched the soldier in front of her with a quick thrust to his chest. She heard Richard beside her, grunting and cursing as two men dropped to his feet. She kept running. The heavy breath next to her saying Richard was still on her flank.

Moisture dripped down her side. Her shoulder was numb. *Sweating like a pig—clothes so heavy.* She gasped for air, the muscles in her legs and stomach screaming.

After an eternity, she glanced behind. The town was gone, also their pursuers. Jackie slowed to a walk, stopped, gulping air into her lungs as she bent over.

"You bleed."

Jackie slowed her breathing, palms on thighs. She glanced at her tunic. Red soaked its length from shoulder to hip. Seeing all the blood, her whole side started to ache. "Mustn't stop now," she gasped, straightening up. "Gotta make it back to the dragons before they send a search party after us."

They kept running, Jackie often stumbling as the agony expanded. A pounding started in her temple, spread to her forehead, blinding her with pain and the sting of sweat. By the time they reached the stream half her tunic was soaked in scarlet and she wavered trying to stand erect.

Belinda swung her massive head toward Jackie at their approach and sniffed with concern. *"You are hurt."*

"I'm fine," Jackie insisted weakly. "Richard, help me on Belinda's back. We have to escape."

"Are you sure? We need to stop the bleeding. We can spare a few minutes...."

"NOW." The pain was growing unbearable, multiplied by the cramps in her side from running. Her whole body shook as she tried climbing onto Belinda. She felt her fingers slide off the scaly skin and drop lifeless to her side.

Richard grabbed her before she crashed to the ground, lifting her up in his arms. He draped her over Niohoggr's back, belly down, and she remembered nothing at all.

Chapter Fourteen

S unlight filtered through the window of Jackie's room. She opened her eyes, stretched, tried to sit up. A heavy weight tugged at her right shoulder. It throbbed dully. "Ohhh."

Jackie pushed back the blanket covering her. White cotton bandages encircled her upper body from collarbone to her chest. She was bare from the waist up. "Oh, no." Her left hand groped at her head. The woolen cap was missing, her fingers tangled into her long brown hair falling down her neck onto her back.

The door opened and Richard poked his head in. "Ah, I see you are awake." He stepped into the room and in quiet strides crossed to her bedside. "Feeling better, *Jaqueline?*" He smirked. "You had us worried. You lost a lot of blood. For a few hours we did not know whether you would make it or not."

Jackie glared back and yanked the blanket up to her chin. "I still hurt. Who undressed me? You?" She moved her legs and wasn't able to tell if her trousers were on or off. Either way it didn't matter. Her secret was out. "Does anyone else know?"

Richard sat in a chair beside her bed. He poured a cup of lukewarm sage tea into a wooden mug and held the cup out to her. "Here, this will help ease the hurt. You're still weak, and you need your rest."

She took a sip, keeping her gaze steady on the rider before her. The liquid tasted bitter and she made a face, coughing as the tea burnt her throat going down.

"Drink it all," Richard advised, pushing her hand back when she tried to give the mug. "It is laced with painkiller. You will feel better." He chuckled as Jackie drained the cup, scowling as she finished the contents in two swift gulps. She fell into a fit of choking and Richard held her until she caught her breath.

"Nasty stuff," she muttered. "Who else knows I'm a woman? Everyone I expect, right?"

"Yes, everyone here knows you are a woman." Richard admitted. A smile crossed his lips as Jackie frowned and handed him back the cup. "After we arrived back here, I needed help carrying you into the house," he paused, "stripping you, washing away all the blood and dirt, and bandaging you up." He shook his head as he recalled her condition. "You were a mess." He leveled a shy look at her. "Nevertheless, I know what you are wondering. Only James and I saw your—" he groped for the words, "woman parts, and we were too busy trying to save your life to take much notice."

"Probably," she murmured, recalling the sight of her tunic and the pain before she passed out. She speculated if she should feel insulted, but shrugged it off. Instead, she tried to guess what was going to happen.

"Am I shunned now?"

"Huh? Oh. You mean..." Richard's eyes held steady on her. She didn't know if he was laughing or frowning.

"You know the rules," she snapped. "Girls aren't allowed to ride dragons." She raised her shoulders and gasped. Pain laced through her body. "But I wanted to..."

"No one is stopping..."

Jackie didn't hear him. Her mind delved back into her past. "My brother-in-law, Victor La Montrue, runs the house with an iron hand now my parents are dead. He fired all the servants, makes me do all the work, and is trying to marry me off to get rid of me... and—and..." As she recounted the injustices of her life since Victor took over the head of the household tears threatened to overwhelm her. Jackie fought back the urge to cry and shouted, "I found an egg and hatched it. Belinda's is mine *and no one will take her away from me."* Her movements made the aching worse, the apprehension she felt drained what little strength she possessed. "May I have another drink of the medicine, please?"

Richard poured a mug full. "This is it for now. You are lucky Jeffery studied the healing arts with his mother. She is a midwife. He knew what to do."

Jackie sipped, trying not to stir. The tea tasted terrible. "At least he should have put honey into it," she muttered as she eyed the liquid with distaste. "What now," she asked again, afraid of Richard's answer. "I'm sorry I lied to you. It hurt me to, and I wanted to tell you the truth." For some reason she couldn't stop talking. If she did, everything she'd achieved up to this point would vanish. "You know I proved all of you wrong, don't you?" she argued as she tried to convince Richard what she'd done was right. "The male dragons haven't killed each other in fighting over Belinda. Girls could've ridden dragons all the time, but I suppose no one wants me around anymore."

Richard drew back, surprise written across his face coupled with disbelief. He waited to see if Jackie had anything more to say, and then declared, "Nonsense. If anything, it makes you more awe-inspiring. No one is questioning your ability as a rider, or warrior—certainly not me." He snorted impatiently and waved his hand in her face. "And who would dare try to take Belinda away from you? If anyone attempted, they would have to fight me, Niohoggr, and the rest of the riders."

The coldness building up inside Jackie drained away. Her lips twitched up in gratitude. "Thank you."

"No. *Thank you.*" Richard chuckled softly to himself with a sheepish grin. "The one who should be ashamed is me. The way I talked about your cousin, err, I mean you. Uh..." he stopped talking, his face growing pink. "Will you forgive me," he stammered at last.

Jackie reached out with her good hand, the pain hardly hurting anymore, and patted him on the leg. "Don't worry about it. You didn't say anything wrong." Her eyes twinkled. "Whatever you said I took as a compliment. You are the first man to say how beautiful I am." Richard cringed. Jackie hurried and added, "We will speak more of this when the war is over, okay? Still friends?"

"Yes."

By the end of the first week Jackie felt she was fit enough to fly, or at least slip out of bed and walk around, although her self-appointed physicians declared she was still too weak, not even allowing her to stand and use the chamber pot. She came to believe the men had a secret joy in lifting her and turning their heads away while she relieved herself, although when she accused Richard he denied the thought ever crossed his mind.

By the fourteen day of her convalesce, she declared, "Enough is enough," when James tiptoed into her room carrying a breakfast tray. "My shoulder hurts, not my feet. I can walk downstairs and eat like everyone else." She struggled out of bed, revealing bare legs and torso. "Trousers... Where are my blasted trousers?" she yelled, fumbling for her blanket when she realized what she'd done.

"I—um..." James stared at her naked limbs in horror, glanced away and scanned the room, perplexed, as he tried not to look at her again. "I, er, I will find you some. Wait right here," he stuttered in embarrassment. James dropped the tray on the bed and fled from the room.

"And an undershirt and tunic," Jackie yelled after him.

What irked her more than anything else was how the men acted. As if she were some pampered *girl*, although they all professed they didn't think of her as a weak anything. Now her true sex was known they pussyfooted around as if she'd melt at the slightest indiscretion or word. *The weaker sex, indeed.* Although she laughed when, a few minutes later, James' arm poked in past the doorframe holding the requested garments. "Drop the clothes if you're too much of a coward to walk in here and hand me my trousers in person," she yelled with a smile. The clothes fell to the floor and the hand withdrew.

After she dressed, Jackie stomped downstairs. Richard and James were the only ones present in the kitchen, the rest departed for patrol.

"You two." Jackie glared at the riders. "Let it be known, I am not an invalid, or some mousy little girl who must be treated as though she were a baby who..."

"...but we were..."

"And furthermore, I will not wear frilly gowns, or a veil. I will ride when I choose to ride, and wear my trousers. Do I make myself clear?" She scanned their shocked faces, running out of breath. "Spread the word... Nothing has changed. I'm still Jackie, understood?" When she saw their heads jumping up and down in silent agreement, she added, "Whoever is leaving me flowers on my side table at night is sweet, but they'd better stop, or they'll find oyster shells in their sleeping blankets."

Richard watched the floor, face red, as he tried not to laugh. James said, "Yes, ma'am."

Jackie choked back a mocking laugh and sat when she saw the color on the back of Richard's neck. *I thought as much.* To put the two riders at ease she said, "Nevertheless, one of you please bring me some tea." She touched her bad shoulder with her good hand. "I'm not able hold and pour at the same time yet."

Richard leaped up, relieved to be doing something and scrambled to fetch tea. James ran back upstairs to retrieve the breakfast tray. When the riders settled Jackie at the table, she said, "Now bring me up to date on what's been happening. No one has told me a thing."

"This is because there is not much to tell," Richard admitted, fixing himself a drink and sitting opposite her. He blew on it and gulped noisily. "Johnathan has made no more advances. The barons and king squabble among themselves and do nothing. What towns we have visited still remain in rebel hands, although as we learned," he flashed Jackie a quick smirk, "it is not *all* the people in rebellion, but the few, however we do not have enough forces to..."

"I see," Jackie sighed. "What are we doing about it?"

"What *can* we do?" James said. "Unless we have an army to our backs, or the king rallies his lords and decides to attack, there is nothing which can be done."

"I made a pass over the lambda mine at Nicos," Richard volunteered. "It is still closed, but workers were digging furiously to open it again."

"As soon as the mine is in production Johnathan will be on the march," Jackie cautioned.

"Why doesn't the king or barons move?" James complained slamming his mug down. His voice rose an octave higher as he said, "Are the lords this naïve or stupid they think Johnathan will go away and leave the nobility alone?"

"The problem is a matter of fear," Richard stated with certainly. "The king relies on the barons for troops in a situation as this. The barons wish to keep their soldiers close, in case an attack comes their way. Without additional warriors, the king can do nothing, and individually the barons are too weak to strike a decisive blow against the rebels."

"The king has moved fast enough in the past when the Easmen attack. The lords offered troops," Jackie began, confused. "Maybe the barons debated between themselves, I don't know, but they did supply men. Why won't they do it now?"

"The Easmen raid on the coast and never move far from their ships. The soldiers the king receives are from those barons inland. They have no fear of an attack, but who knows where a dragonrider will strike next?" He shrugged, the anger he felt showing in his tone of voice. "All are afraid."

Jackie ground her teeth in rage. "Right now it's a simple matter of running those bandits out of the towns, but they'd sneak back in, as rats scurry into the corn crib when the cat goes away. There are eleven of us. If we had more men..."

"You should wish for more dragons while you're dreaming," replied Richard, "men are no good without mounts to ride, and we would have our own army and no need for king or lord to act."

It was a muted group of riders, who for the next few weeks, waited for the stalemate to end. Praying the nobles would march against the rebels, and dreading the time Johnathan regained his supply of lambda from the mines again. The loyalists spent the time drawing up plans, discussing options, and discarding the ideas as impractical. The closest they came to a workable tactic was a raid on Nicos, but after Richard and James scouted the area, they saw the rebels kept a heavy guard on the area now and any attempt was suicidal. They barely escaped with their lives when six rebel dragons swooped down on their party in ambush, breathing fire.

When Jackie was able, she remounted Belinda, whose only comment was *"Well, it's about time. I thought I'd have to adopt a different human."* She swung her head away, blowing a short shaft of flame.

"Not on your life," Jackie declared joyfully,

pulling herself onto the dragon's back. Her shoulder still hurt, but she knew the stiffness from disuse would wear off in time. "Let's get you into the air and work off some of this fat you've accumulated." She patted Belinda's sides playfully. "Do you remember how to fly?"

"Humph."

After they were airborne, the beating of wings thudded behind and Richard on Niohoggr flapped up. "Ready to patrol again?" Richard called out.

"Been ready," Jackie yelled back, smiling in delight. Although she still wore boy's clothes, on this occasion, her head was bare, and her long brown hair streamed behind her in the air. She never remembered the feel of the wind in her face, or the smell of the fresh air, as this refreshing. The whole world was new again, colors brighter, and sounds more distinct. A shift by Belinda caused her hair to swarm across her face and she received a mouthful of the stuff. *Better start putting it in braids or keep the cap.* She raked it out of her face with her fingers. *Could'a been worse. Could'a been a bug.*

They swept over the landscape into rebel held territory. Tilled fields, forest, and open grassland appeared. Richard gestured to his right. "Men."

Companies of warriors massed in a semi-military formation in a meadow by a stream, forming the boundary between two providences—one in rebellion.

"See any riders?" Jackie shouted as she surveyed the area.

Richard scanned the sky. "Nothing. The air is clean."

"Let's go and scare those men off," Jackie retorted. She patted Belinda on the neck. "Okay, you know what to do." The two dragons angled down in a swift dive.

The soldiers pointed, shouted, and bolted in all directions as the dragons released fire over their heads.

Two wagons held giant crossbows mounted on wheels, the crews energetically cranking the string back hoping to release a shot. Belinda hit one of the catapults as the men dove for cover and set it afire, while Niohoggr destroyed the cart carrying the other with a burst of fury.

The dragons lifted upward. Richard called out, "Another pass?"

"I don't think so." Except for the two smoking wagons, the meadow was deserted. Through the gaps in the trees, Jackie saw the warriors still running. "They've all scattered." To make sure the rebels didn't regroup at a new location, Jackie and Richard scouted for an additional hour over the area, scattering any small bands of soldiers they saw.

Far above in the sky, flying their way, four specks grew in size, breathing fire.

"Uh—oh. Let's leave," Richard said. "Four against two. Those are not good odds I would willing face."

Jackie suppressed the urge to leap into battle and agreed, grudgingly. "You're right, although I hate to run." She nudged Belinda and the dragon swung about. Jackie glanced back at the dots and shook her fist. *"Next time."*

It was late in the day when they landed at the manor house, the sun streaking red fingers across the sky, and shaping dark shadows over the baron's woods. They were the last to arrive and discovered a disturbed group of riders waiting for the two.

"Hurry," James yelled from the kitchen door, "important news."

Richard and Jackie broke into a run across the lawn. As they entered the kitchen, Jeffery exclaimed, "We have been summoned."

"What?" Jackie looked at the worried men around her sitting at the table and threw her hands on her hips. "We're dragonriders. No one summons us."

Jeffery ran his fingers over his face, embarrassed, and said in a calmer tone, "I expressed myself badly. I meant to say, Johnathan has requested a parley. He wishes to meet with us."

Jackie sat next to Richard and asked eagerly, "How do you know? Tell us what happened."

"I was flying patrol," Jeffery began, trying to remember each detail, although he'd told the story a dozen times already, "and Sedwick approached me. He is the rider from Baron Fairfox barony," he explained for Jackie's benefit. "I thought to offer him battle, instead he signaled with a flag of truce."

"Go on," Richard urged. "What did he say?"

Jeffery said, "Only Johnathan wished to speak with you. He would wait tomorrow morning at the island, bringing one rider with him—you may do the same if you desired, but no more. Sedwick said Johnathan did not want any fighting to break out."

"Did this rider say what Johnathan wanted?" Jackie asked impatiently. "He didn't said parley and disappear."

"That was it," Jeffery replied with a dark frown. "Although Sedwick hinted, and I quote, 'This farce will soon be over'. When I asked what he meant he chuckled and left."

James asked, "Well, what do we do?" The rest of the riders muttered among themselves, quieting when Richard started to answer.

He leaned back and cupped his chin in his hand. "Meet with him, what else?" He regarded each rider with sober eyes waiting to hear disagreement. When none arose he said, "If no one has any objections I will take Jackie with me. After all, she is the one who brought us the lambda. Without the stone, Johnathan would never have attempted this foolish scheme to begin with. She should see it through to the end." He said to Jackie, "If you are willing to accompany me, I mean."

"Of course," she replied. "I didn't intend for all of this to turn out as it has..."

"...of course not..."

"It is not your fault at all..."

"Stupid Johnathan."

"...but I will stand by your side, and try my best to put an end to the rebellion," she concluded. "I hope this is not a trap by Johnathan though," she said trying to think ahead what the rogue dragonrider might be planning.

"Perhaps two of us should fly guard overhead," suggested James. "After all, Johnathan said to bring one more with him. He did not say anything about riders in the sky." The rest of the riders nodded thoughtfully in agreement. "We would be close enough in case Johnathan plans dishonesty, or if his riders show up 'unexpectantly' shall we say."

"I hope he does not plan deceit," Richard replied, tapping his teeth as he thought. "Nevertheless, if he saw the riders he would accuse me of treachery and depart. I wish to hear what he wants to say." He gazed at the men around the table. "It is settled," he said with finality, "but if this is a trap I suggest we place a strong guard here to protect the mine." He chuckled. "After all, we may have given Johnathan ideas."

***

Jackie and Richard set off as the sun made an orange glow in the eastern sky. A grey fog covered the water and they relied on the dragons superior senses to guide them through the mist. Jackie drew her riding cloak tight around her body, the fingers of haze sending chills up her spine, making her shiver in spite of the warmth of Belinda beneath her. Even the dragon complained, *"This isn't good weather to fly in."* She swung her head to glare at Jackie. *"We should wait until the sun is up and burns the wetness off. The mine is nice and dry and..."*

"Oh hush, you," Jackie admonished, flexing her fingers within her riding gloves to keep her hands from going numb. "We're dragonriders. We fly when we must, not when it's convenient."

"Slave driver," Belinda grumbled.

Jackie wondered if the dragons had got lost when at the last second, Belinda neck pointed down and she swooped low, her wings skimming the tips of the waves and landed on the sandy beach. Niohoggr scattered sand with a flap and settled next to her.

"I don't see a thing," stated Jackie as she dismounted squinting upward toward the grove of trees. "Do you think they're here yet?"

Richard peered up and down the beach trying to pierce the gloom. "I cannot tell..."

"Ho."

Two figures emerged from the fog—the tall lanky outline of Johnathan, and a squat rider Jackie didn't know. Johnathan strolled forward with casual confidence and regarded Richard with interest. His gaze shifted to Jackie, taking in her long hair, his eyes widening in amazement. "I see we have made some changes," he boomed in amusement. "Last time I saw you, you were a boy." He threw his head back laughing and said to Richard, "I suppose all this time you have been a duck in disguise?"

His companion sputtered. Even Richard and Jackie felt their lips twitching up. "Not a duck," Richard said at last. "Maybe a mole. I buried myself too long in my own affairs and dreams and never saw what you plotted, even though it was in the light of day. Have you come to your senses? It is not too late to stop this nonsense. If you wish, I will intercede with the king to issue you a pardon."

Johnathan shook his head as if Richard were a bad

boy who'd been caught stealing cookies. "Soon the king will be no more. I will be king and pardon myself if I choose."

Richard shook his head. "This will never happen."

Johnathan chuckled. "Oh, yes it will, and if you join with me it will happen faster. With the power we will hold, who knows," a wild light shone in his eyes, "Medina is only the start. The whole world will be ours for the taking."

Jackie whispered, *"You are mad."*

The stocky rider, Sedwick, hissed, "You say *madness*? You who are a woman, riding a dragon against all that is holy? Flaunting our traditions and the king's will, himself?" He scurried forward *"Blasphemer—lawbreaker. It is you who are mad."*

Jackie clenched her jaws tight. Her fingers automatically reached for the hilt of her sword. Richard placed his hand on her arm. "Let the two speak. This is not the time for fighting."

Johnathan's voice took on a more serious tone. "You are right, I have not traveled here today for combat, but to ask if *you* have changed your mind and wish to throw in your lot with me." He tipped his head sideways and stared at Jackie. "And you. My friend here is wrong, there is no law against a woman riding a dragon, yet still it is forbidden. Nevertheless, join with me and I will allow your indiscretion in this case."

The dragonrider accompanying Johnathan spoke. "It would be simpler to kill this one off," he said, sneering at Jackie. "That way you will not have to start making exceptions."

"Why you...."

Johnathan put his hand up for silence. "Not so fast, Sedwick, she would be better kept. Perhaps you would enjoy her for a plaything, huh?" He leered at Jackie.

Sedwick released a gruff laugh and gazed at Jackie in a new way. "Maybe you are right. She wants to be a man. I will teach her what men do."

Jackie's face went ashen. She ripped out her sword and stepped forward. "You pig. You would not know a *real* man if he rode up on a horse and dealt you ten lashes for the way you think." She waved him toward her. "If you think I do not know what men do, draw your blade and I will show you exactly how a *person* would treat one as you."

Richard reached out and held Jackie back. "No. This is what they want."

Jackie kept her vison on Sedwick. He glanced at Johnathan, who shrugged and nodded. The dragonrider drew his blade. "All right. Let us see what kind of a man you are." He held his sword out and they crossed blades.

Sedwick lunged forward, the tip of his weapon targeting Jackie's heart. She ducked under the blade, swiped at his feet with her sword, and sprang up again, her point aimed at his throat. The young man danced out of the way, jabbed, and recovered as Jackie blocked his thrust.

The rider ran at her again in a bull rush with a flurry of swing blows, meaning to use his weight and height to overwhelm Jackie. She gave ground, backing up step-by-step, parrying each clout with her blade. Jackie riposted, going on the offensive with a lunge of her own.

For a brief moment all that sounded on the beach was the clashing of swords and the grunts of the two as they battled across the sand.

Sedwick leaped close to Jackie, grabbing her sword arm in a vice-like grip. In turn, Jackie held his arm and the two struggled, the young man forcing Jackie down and backward.

Jackie lifted her leg and kneed him in the groin.

Sedwick crumbed, falling to the ground,

screaming in agony as he held himself. Before he recovered, Jackie swung her heavily booted foot and caught him on the point of his chin, sending the rider flipping over onto his back. She drew a deep breath, stood over the fallen man, and placed the point of her sword at his throat.

"We see what a man you are," she said, "and now you know what a *woman* I am." She glanced up for the first time and sought Johnathan's eye. "I will let this one live to show we hold no malice toward you or your riders. I hope this is the end and we reach a peaceful settlement to our dispute."

Richard handed his former friend a sad look. "I think your heart started in the right place, but you're going about it in the wrong way. Drawing all power onto yourself is not the answer, and will lead to more harm than good. This has gone far beyond righting any wrongs done to the common man. You've fallen into tyranny and what you commit is murder. If you wish to know what our reply is for the surrender of my riders and me, you see for yourself." He pointed to Sedwick, who slowly rose, covered in sand, his face still ashen.

Johnathan grimaced at Sedwick who skulked back to his side, limping. He shrugged and said, "That is your choice. I have extended my hand in mercy. Next time we meet I will not be as kind."

"It is war, then," Jackie muttered.

"Yes, it is war."

Chapter Fifteen

"Another province has fallen."

Jackie's riding cloak was seared black, in spots crumbling to ash. She threw off the cape and watched Richard and James bleakly, who regarded her back with dismay from the dining hall table. Empty mugs and trenchers on the table showed their haste in leaving this morning.

"Which one this time?" Dark circles surrounded Richard's eyes, his face haggard. Sitting there in his ragged tunic, he appeared old.

"Lorine." Jackie dropped into a chair. *We are losing. We try, but we're outnumbered.* "This makes four."

"I know how to count," Richard shouted in anger. He balled up both fists and slammed the table in frustration, glaring at his hands as if they betrayed him. He saw the expression on Jackie and James' faces and his temper calmed. "Forgive me. I do not rage at you. I yell at myself. Maybe we should have thrown our lot in with Johnathan, convince him to our way over time. Now it is too late."

Jackie reached out and touched him on his sleeve. "No. We're doing the right thing. You tried to convince Johnathan and he wouldn't listen. I doubt no one will sway him from the path he has chosen." She felt foolish for repeating herself so many times over the preceding days but she said, "You have done everything possible."

"You think our cause is hopeless?" James asked Richard. "We fight for naught?"

"I do not know." He shot Jackie a wan smile and stared at the table. "Perhaps we should flee across the sea. Prince Sevorson would enlist us. He did once, remember?"

"Isn't the expression, ''Tis bolts or shafts to me'?" Jackie speculated in her mind if the Easmen ever made peace with the Fanks. "I wonder…"

The way Jackie said that made Richard glanced up. "You wonder what? I was joking if this is what you mean."

"No." A rising tide of hope swelled in Jackie's stomach. "Remember he said he would come to our aid if asked? If he wasn't trying to be gracious...." her eyes shone. "A thousand Easmen warriors would change the course of the war." She slammed her fist on the table, making the empty mugs jump. "I will go right now, enlist his help. If he has any honor at all he won't deny me." She sprang to her feet, her eyes widening.

"I will go with you," Richard said at once standing also. "In case you are betrayed."

"No, you're needed here. With both of us gone our forces are weakened too much." When Richard started to protest, she pushed him back down and added, "I'll take my bow and shafts also, and leave the Easmen with a present they won't soon forget if they prove hostile. Besides, Belinda is protection enough for me. What will you do that she can't?"

Jackie ran to gather dry rations, noticed not many were left. *This had better work. We're running out of food, running out of room to maneuver. Soon we'll be out of time.*

She hiked up to the cave. "Going for a trip, you up to it?" she said to Belinda.

The dragon showed burns crisscrossing her body, some healed into scars, more still fresh. She lifted her head a foot off the floor of the mine, eyes fluttering open. *"Go away. We flew all day today and fought bad dragons. I'm tired. Tomorrow will be soon enough."*

A sharp pain stuck in Jackie's chest. She'd pushed the beast as hard as she pushed herself and it showed. She steeled herself and painted a smile on her face. "Sleep on the way. This is important. Up and at 'em lazybones."

A sigh ran through Jackie's mind. *"If you insist, but we'd better not meet anymore of those rebels. I'm in no mood."*

Belinda and she flew through the day and into the night, the stars guiding their flight over the ocean to the distant shore. Jackie felt Belinda's labored breathing as her sense of urgency transmitted to the dragon. Short sand dunes backed by ragged cliffs rose into view.

"Swing north," Jackie ordered, "along the coast, I would think."

Underneath the dragon, a village consisting of a few half-timbered buildings leaped into sight. "Izar," Jackie muttered, "too small."

Forest replaced tilled fields, which in turn gave way to more plowed land. A town appeared. Adjacent to the village large longhouses sprang up, surrounded by wicker fencing and trenches. In the center stood the greatest of all dwellings, smoke curling out from holes in the thatched roof.

"Circle the big one," Jackie shouted to Belinda. "If Prince Sevorson is anywhere around here, he's in there."

Warriors ran out of the building, some still pulling on cloths, but clutching swords and spears as the dragon made a slow arc around the area. When the prince himself emerged, Belinda settled down outside the trenches and Jackie dismounted, hoping no arrows would zip in her direction until she talked to Sevorson.

Lining the fence, soldiers peered over, spears protruding, and muted jabber ran up and down the line.

"Prince Sevorson—Come forth. I would have words with you," Jackie shouted. "If you remember, we met once before and I saved your life."

She waited.

The gate swung open and Sevorson emerged, dressed in chainmail and holding a spear at the ready. He strode forward and surveyed Jackie with grim intensity.

"No woman has ever saved me," he bellowed. The prince leveled his spear and jabbed it in the direction of Belinda. "Be gone, before we destroy you and your animal."

"Animal? Humph."

Jackie drew her hair back from her face and watched the prince closely. "You remember me, or have more than one rescued you from the Fank's swords lately?"

Dawning comprehension spread across Sevorson's face and his body relaxed, the tip of his spear falling. "So it is you. I never would have guessed," he rumbled. "Why have you returned? We have made our peace with the Fanks as you asked, and our ships no longer raid the coasts of Mercia."

"I come to claim the help you offered," Jackie stated. She kept her voice calm, not daring to show the desperation she felt inside, "if you are still willing to provide it."

The prince waved her forward. "Enter. We will discuss the matter." He paused and peered over Jackie's shoulder at Belinda who glared back, streams of fire flickering out of her nostrils. "Your animal will cause no harm while you are inside?" he asked.

"If he refers to me as animal again, I'll set his roof on fire."

"She will offer no problems," Jackie replied, "but call my dragon not animal, it offends her. The name is Belinda."

"I am sorry, *Belinda*," the prince said gravely to the dragon with a short bow. "Forgive me. The ways of the dragon folk are strange to us."

Belinda settled down on her haunches with a snort. *"Better. At least this one knows respect. I will take a nap now."* She closed her eyes.

An extended hallway divided the longhouse into three parts. The prince led Jackie up to a great table at the far end. Sevorson sat in an ornate wooden chair with the heads of boars carved into the armrests. He waved to a bench. "Rest. Tell me what you seek."

Jackie explained the war. At the end she concluded, "If Johnathan should succeed in conquering Mercia, I can't predict what he'll do next. It is possible he would even attack you. The rebel hinted as much. On dragons your kingdom is not far away, and many in Mercia would welcome the opportunity to take revenge for years of raiding."

For a long time the prince sat in silence, eyes closed as he thought about what Jackie had said. She thought he'd fallen asleep when he said, "How many men do you require?"

A spark of hope flashed through Jackie. "As many as you have and as soon as they are assembled," she replied quickly. "Johnathan's power grows everyday as he conquers more territory. It may already be too late."

"I will send riders out to marshal troops," replied the prince, standing. "Allow me two days and we will be prepared. Our ships will dock on your shores within a week. Watch for our boats."

"It will do," Jackie breathed, rising also. She clasped Sevorson on his forearm. "Thank you. Let us pray it is enough."

She flew back to Mercia, her sense of need multiplied by the period she'd been away. *Time. I must buy time.* The thought kept ringing in her mind and took on a life of its own, mimicking the wingbeats of Belinda. *Time. Time. Time.*

She speeded over the coast and hurled inland, dashing above the clouds. She passed a forest and a raging battle spread out before her. On the ground, warriors clashed in fierce combat. The faint ringing of steel echoed in the air along with the cursing of men and the screams of the dying.

Below her, dragons whirled and swooped, gouts of fire lashing out engulfing rider and mount alike. Jackie spied James pursued by two dragons in a spiral as he dove to avoid a rush of flame.

Belinda rolled and dove. The rebel riders glanced up at Belinda's screams of rage. Taken by surprise, the two dragons scissored back and forth, unsure of what was happening and trying to throw off possible attack.

Belinda singled one out, tracing the erratic movements as she drew closer, and snatched the rider of the fleeing dragon with her savage claws. Wingtips clipped bushes as she skimmed the earth, dropping the startled rider who tumbled as if he were a deflated ball, to crash in a group of battling soldiers. A torrent of fire from Belinda sent the enemy warriors fleeing before she pulled up hard and charged for the sky, her wings buffering Jackie with every beat.

Jackie clamped her legs hard against the dragon's sides, yanking the bow off her back and released arrows in every direction. Enemy riders dropped.

"Hang tight."

They broke free of the battle flying higher, empty sky all around. Belinda looped, streaking downward, her momentum aided by the force of gravity. Jackie slammed backward as they entered the fray, leveling out to rush at the rest of the dragons as if she were an unstoppable force gone mad. Jackie continued to draw back her bowstring and fire until she realized she'd run out of arrows—and targets.

Below, the loyalist dragons swept the field, flames igniting dry grass as the rebel soldiers retreated in disarray.

"I see our Jackie is back." Richard astride Niohoggr flapped close, a smile of joy spreading across his face, laughter in his voice. "Whether your mission was a success or failure, you have brought gallant fighting back with you," he exclaimed. He raised a fist in salute.

"Wait until I tell you what happened," Jackie retorted. "What else must be done now?"

William surveyed the field of combat. The sky and earth were empty save for loyalists. "Nothing. All have fled. I will assign riders to patrol in the area in case the rebels return and meet you at the manor house." He studied her with concern. "You need a good rest."

Jackie realized how right Richard was. Her tunic was white from salt where Belinda skimmed the ocean searching for fish. She knew without seeing her face it was gaunt from lack of sleep, with eyes red from staring at the glare of the water. The adrenalin rush she'd felt from the battle deserted her. She gasped, bruises she didn't realize she'd received from the buffering of Belinda's wings screamed. Jackie laid her head on the dragon's back and murmured, "Back to the mine, we're finished for the day." Along her mount's scaly side, lines of white from dried salt interspaced with black splotches from dragon fire. *She needs a good rest, too. Will this ever be over, even with the Easmen's help?*

For some reason the manor was dirtier and shabbier than she recalled before she left. As Jackie stumbled through the kitchen and dining hall on her way upstairs to her room all she could think of was how furious Victoria would be when she returned and saw the mess the dragonriders left the place in.

Jackie kicked off her riding boots and fell across her bed, and then she thought nothing at all.

***

The smell of smoky frying ham woke her. Jackie glanced out her window. The sky was black and stars twinkled in the heavens. "Wonder how long I slept?" she

202

muttered to herself as she swung her legs over the side of the bed and wavered to her feet. Her mouth was dry and felt as if some unclean birds roosted there. The bruises she'd forgotten about awoke anew and every muscle in her body screamed in pain as she made her slow way down the stairs into the kitchen.

"The dead wake," Jeffery chirped as he shook a skillet back and forth. The rest of the riders sat around the table, wolfing down food.

"The dead should'a stayed dead," Jackie snapped back with a groan, dropping onto a bench, "but I think even in death I would ache in the afterlife."

She looked at the rest of the riders. All carried burns, scratches, and bruises. She glanced towards Jeffery by the hearth. The young man's tunic shredded up the back and along the sides held together with hasty stitches. He wore a crude patch covering one eye.

"Where's Richard?"

"Out making a pass over Norington," James replied from across the table. "Johnathan masses troops there from the coast. We believe he will attack tomorrow. What of you mission?" The riders stopped eating and watched her steadily. "Any luck?"

Some of the stiffness left her body as she rolled her head on her shoulders, brushing a loose strand of hair out of her face. "Yes, Easmen come. I will go into detail when Richard arrives. I'm still too tired to repeat it twice."

Before the rest bombard her with more questions, she yawned, stretched her arms over her head to their full length, and peered at the frying pan, inhaling the scent of food drifting her way. She realized she'd not eaten a decent meal in a week. Jeffery handed her a trencher of eggs and fried ham. "Thanks. Where'd you get this?" The smokehouse had long since emptied, the chickens eaten. "The peasants haven't paid their taxes, have they?"

Jeffery chuckled. "No. Three days ago, we attacked a rebel supply wagon. We won." He jabbed apiece of ham from the skillet with his belt knife and took a bite. "We eat." He chewed and swallowed, "Hunger is a wonderful thing, makes you fight harder and everything tastes better."

Jacked laughed along with him and began shoveling eggs into her mouth. She swallowed and exclaimed, "We will win for sure then."

The kitchen door banged open and Richard strode in. "Johnathan is bringing more troops up from the south," he announced, "but they will not arrive for two or three days yet," He threw off his riding cloak and dropped onto a bench with a grunt, "Niohoggr and I made sure of that."

"How?" Jackie asked through a spoonful of eggs.

"The bridges they must cross are made of wood." His lips flickered. "Wood burns," a trencher was handed to him, "which means no fighting for a few days." He took a long swig of hot tea and settled back, smacking his lips. "What of the Easmen, are they rallying for our aid?"

"Prince Sevorson pledged as many men as he could raise in two days," Jackie acknowledged. "He should be here within a week, if he keeps his promise."

Richard swung his gaze to those around him, his face a mask of concern. "The timing will be close. The king has marshaled his troops and marches to meet the rebels, but from what I've seen he is sorely outnumbered," Richard's voice dropped lower. "If Johnathan breaks through at Norington his next stop will be the castle of the king. If it falls...." he left the rest of the sentence hanging, but they all knew what this meant.

"Even if His Majesty falls, I will not surrender," Jackie declared, coldly. "I'll take Belinda into the mountains and fight from there. Mercia is my home." She numbered the riders. "If Johnathan wins, tyranny will sweep this land as has not been felt in a hundred years."

Muted "ayes" returned to her, but the riders were unsure, hesitant. Jackie glared at the table and lifted her head, seeing Richard staring back with admiration. He nodded his assent and resumed eating.

The next two days the riders were not idle. Even though the main thrust of Johnathan's attack had not occurred yet, still small actions occurred as the rebel army crept ever closer to the king's castle. Jackie flew from skirmish to skirmish, sometimes scattering scouts or burning bridges, anything to slow the advance down.

The rebel dragonriders were conspicuously absent from these attacks. Jackie thought Johnathan kept his riders in reserve, allowing the men and mounts time to rest for the main battle. The loyalist riders received no repast.

On the second night Richard announced, "Tomorrow the rebels make their attack. I wish you all well." He picked out Jackie and motioned toward the door with his head. "I think we should all get a good night's rest. We have a busy day tomorrow."

The assembly broke up. Richard stepped outside. A few moments later Jackie met him. "You wished to speak to me?" Overhead the stars twinkled. The cool night air caused little puffs of steam to drift from their breaths.

Without saying a word, Richard took her hands in his. He gazed into her eyes. "We may all die tomorrow," he murmured softly, "and I know what you will say, but I wish you would not join us in battle. Escape to the mountains as you said, save yourself and your dragon. Continue the fight another time."

Jackie gave a laugh and wrapped her arms around his neck. "We live together and fight together, or we'll die together, but I thank you for the thought." She kissed him on the lips. "Now as *you* said, it is late, and if I am to go into the afterlife, I don't want to do it with red eyes and yawning." She released him and quickly entered the house before he protested.

In the morning, Jackie brushed her hair with painstaking thoroughness, braided the strands, and dug out her best tunic and riding cloak. She dressed with special care, even going so far as polishing her riding boots to a high sheen. She marched down the steps from her bedroom, and cheers of greeting and admiration rang out for her from the rest of the riders.

"Since you have outfitted yourself for the occasion, I think it's right you lead our formation today," Richard declared.

"I would be proud to," Jackie replied. She stalked to the door. "No sense waiting around here. Let's get this over with. If any of us survive this day, we'll meet at the island when the battle is finished." She closed her mind to the thought of how many would not show up.

They flew in a wedged formation, Jackie at the apex with Richard on her right. As they approached Norington, smoke from cooking fires drifted into the air, mingled with fog rising from the stream separating the two opposing armies. Rebels and loyalists lined up in long rows facing each other.

Far to the rear of the loyalists, the king sat astride his old dragon. Jackie had never seen the king or his mount before. As they closed in, Belinda thought to Jackie, *"The old one has trouble lifting. He is not long for this world."*

Out of the rising sun flew a dark shape—the rebel dragonriders led by Johnathan. *We're outnumbered, two against one.* Jackie angled up Belinda, the rest of the loyalist dragons beating their wings to keep up, hoping to gain the advantage of height on the approaching warriors.

Three of the rebel dragons arched down to attack the king and his forces, while the insurgent troops swept forward splashing through the stream. The balance of the dragons shot upward to engage Jackie's riders.

The enemy formation hit the wedge, shattering it. Individual dogfights broke out as flashes of fire belched back and forth. Two dragons shot Jackie's way, one on either side. Jackie ducked low against Belinda's back as flames engulfed them and the rebels zipped past. Clear sky shone and her dragon looped, spraying fire in every direction.

Jackie lost sight of her company. The world changed to a kaleidoscope of sky and earth as Belinda continued to twirl, evading flames and firing back in fury. Jackie shot arrows at whatever flew close, not sure if she hit anything. Flaming bodies dropped past, friend and foe alike, with screams ringing in her ears.

I wonder if this is what hell feels like? Heat and flames shimmered in the air around Jackie. The uptick of Belinda's wings protected her as fire spilled over the dragon's body.

Belinda's mind shrieked in pain.

It can't be any worse.

Jackie caught a shape flying toward her. Her bow swung, arrow notched. "We must escape." Richard flew beside her.

"NO."

A blackened finger pointed to the earth. "See?"

The king's troops retreated, stumbling over their feet in terror as the rebels sprinted after them with whoops of savage bloodlust. Above, the rebel dragons belched fire down on the fleeing troops, while in the distance the figure of the king and his dragon faded into the distance.

"Where are our men?" Jackie cried, forlorn, searching the sky.

"Dead, fled, or gone to ground when the lifting air of their dragons emptied," Richard screamed back. *"Beware."*

A shadow obliterated the light above Jackie and the screeching of an attacking dragon filled her ears. Niohoggr leaped forward and the vibrations of the two crashing bodies jarred Jackie to the core as the sickening sound of cracking bones ricocheted through the sky.

A dragon fell, the beast spiraling toward the earth with pitiful cries, while the rider clung grimly to his back.

"Let us escape." Richard was alongside her again astride Niohoggr who flapped awkwardly. "The rest of the rebels are returning. We can do no more here."

Jackie threw a glance over her shoulder—five specks winged their way. "He's right," Jackie whispered to Belinda. "It's time to retreat and plan what we must do next." The dragon dropped in next to Niohoggr and they winged their way from the scene of carnage. "Are they chasing us?" Richard asked. His voice was hollow.

"I don't know." Jackie strained, shading her eyes with her palm. "No, I don't think they are," she said at last. "The dragons are heading back north."

Even at their slow pace, they soon reached the ocean. Niohoggr wobbled, his right wing not moving at all. Belinda flew close, supporting him on this side until the island rose in sight. He landed with a crash, front claws and neck shooting sand into the air. Richard catapulted over his head to sprawl next to him. For a second both rider and dragon lay still, then with groans they righted themselves.

Richard staggered to his dragon's side, stroking Niohoggr's head and whispering words of encouragement into his ear. Jackie ran up, sliding to a stop as she scanned the dragon for damage. "What happened? Is he all right?" She gasped, petting Niohoggr also. "Poor baby, it'll be okay."

"Hurt his wing in the collision," Richard muttered back. "I don't know if it's broken or bruised badly." Richard strode to the right wing and tried extending it.

Niohoggr replied with a bellow and bared his teeth. Richard released the member hastily, paused as if listening, and replied, "All right, I won't touch it anymore." He frowned and said to Jackie, "We will have to wait and see how it mends. Dragons recover quickly from injuries as this." He scanned the sky. "I do not see anyone else arriving. I hope Johnathan doesn't decide to search this spot for us. We would be as ripe grain for his harvesting if he does."

"Do you think many of the rest survived?" Jackie asked. An invisible hand clutched at her chest, squeezing.

"I do not know." Richard kept searching the air. It was empty, "but I know one thing for certain."

"What's that?"

"By now the king's castle has fallen. The war is over."

Chapter Sixteen

J ackie's expression mirrored the shock she felt. "NO." She swung away from Richard, stomping to the edge of the water and pivoted on her heels to face the rider. "How can you say this?" she shouted. "You're not there, you don't know." Tears leaked down her cheeks as she spun back to the ocean.

Richard grabbed her by the arm, swung her around. "You saw what happened. No troops stand in Johnathan's way. The king designed his castle to prevent dragons from landing within, but there is nothing to stop the riders from flying above and raining down fire while the rebels storm the walls. If it has not fallen yet, it soon will."

"We flee to the mountains?" The realization of what was happening broke through Jackie's stubbornness. She said softly. "This is the end?"

"I go nowhere until this one is fit to lift." Richard hooked a thumb at Niohoggr, "but I will not fault you if you wish to flee. We could be attacked at any moment."

Jackie didn't waste time debating in her mind whether she should go or not. She knew she would stay until they flew together. "I'll wait, at least until one of our riders show up—if any do, this is. Perhaps we can devise...." Jackie stopped in mid-sentence, her eyes wide as she gazed out to sea. "I've forgotten all about the Easmen," she exclaimed. "If the prince kept his word they are out there somewhere sailing to our shores right now." She raced to Belinda, halted, and said, "Someone must guide the ships here to the island."

"Go," urged Richard. "We will be all right by ourselves for the time you are gone."

Jackie shook her head. "Too much danger. If Johnathan should arrive, you're dead. I'd never forgive myself." Jackie pointed out quickly with a small chuckle, "The Easmen will find us. They've done it before with no problem, if not this island, then the rebel troops."

"This one says if the need arises he is able to fly." Belinda's head swung from Niohoggr to Jackie. *"His wing is sore, nothing else. Our presence isn't needed for protection."*

Richard read the expression on Jackie's face. "You see? Everything is okay. Go." He gestured to the open sea. "We will be fine."

Jackie threw her arms around Richard in a fast hug. "I'll be back as soon as possible," She promised and leaped onto Belinda's back. The dragon trumpeted and Jackie yelled over her shoulder, "Stay safe."

The two sped into the sky. "Straight out," Jackie said as Belinda gained height. "We shouldn't have far to go. If they've sailed at all they must be halfway here by now. Look for the masts on the horizon."

An hour later Jackie spotted the fleet, thirty large longboats sailing with speed in their direction. Foremost in the lead was the flagship, Prince Sevorson standing in the bow like the figurehead of the dragon carved on the bow below him. When he spied Belinda flying under the clouds, he waved his arms over his head in recognition.

"That's the Easmen," Jackie announced. "Land on the water, but not too close to the boats. I don't want to scare anyone or swamp a ship." Belinda settled in front of the flotilla and waited for the ships to arrive. The prince's longboat rowed up alongside the paddling dragon and Sevorson called out, "I have done as I promised. Two thousand of my warriors at you service." He took in the ragged appearance of Jackie and the scorch marks along Belinda's sides and said drily, "I take it you are still in need of our help?"

Jackie broke out in a hysterical laugh. "Oh, yes,

and you have appeared none too soon, but…" She counted ships, "how did you manage to collect so many this fast?"

The prince released a hearty guffaw. "Even though I have forbid raiding in Mercia, still different places are ripe for the plucking by my people if they are bold enough. I was lucky to catch the men before the boats set sail, else none would be available until after the fall harvest. By then the seas would be too rough to navigate on."

Jackie wondered how much payment the prince offered his men to entice all these into a war when raiding would've been safer. She shuttered at the thought of thousands of Easmen warriors seeking loot would do to the countryside, but was afraid to say anything, and it was too late to send the Easmen away. She hoped the warriors were honest thieves and would only steal what the prince offered. She replied, "It is well you gathered this horde, for we will need every warrior we can muster." She swung an arm toward the way she'd flown. "There is an island in this direction. Follow me. I have one companion there, maybe more by now if luck favors us. It is a place to rest for the night while we plan our strategy." Belinda took wing again and started back to Richard.

When she was sure the Easmen sailed in the right direction, Jackie urged Belinda to greater speed until the island lay below. Two dragons rested on the shore beside Niohoggr, James and Jeffery in deep debate with Richard. At Jackie's approach, they glanced up and hurried toward her.

"What news of the Easmen?" James asked, worried. "Do they come or have they forsaken us?" Both Jeffery and Richard crowded close watching her face.

"They sail to this island as we speak," Jackie exclaimed. "Thirty ships, two thousand warriors. They should be here tonight. I left the prince a few hours ago." It was her turn to study the expressions on the two riders.

212

"Any news of the king?"

"The castle has fallen I was told," James replied. "Johnathan has commenced killing all the lords, starting with the barons. I have this from a noble family I met fleeing when I landed to rest my dragon. They were hazy on details, and I am not sure what was conjure, and what was fact. We didn't talk long, both of us afraid of discovery. Nevertheless, one thing was clear, Johnathan vows to eliminate all the nobility until there are none left in this land and start anew with the rule of the common man."

Jackie's worse fears were becoming true. She said softly, "And of course, Johnathan and the riders will lead the common man, huh? We trade hundreds of nobles for twenty." She released a breath of air, a heavy weight pressing down on her. She recovered and said, "Perhaps those you talked to were mistaken. What of the rest of the riders, any news?"

"Captured or killed," replied Jeffery. His eyes clouded over in sorrow. "Two of ours I saw fall to death myself, the dragons unable to save their riders. The rest, when the air holding up the beasts failed, went to earth. Perhaps some fought their way into the forest and are in hiding, but I doubt it. They would not forsake the dragons by choice, nor would their dragons abandon the riders."

"If they were captured, where would the rebels hold them?" Jackie asked.

"I'm unable to say for certain," Jeffery admitted. "I could not linger to rescue any. I had three riders on my tail." He nodded toward his dragon. Deep burn marks showed on his rear. The beast gave Jeffery a mournful look and made a circle in the sand, sniffing at his end to assess the damage.

"I too," put in James. "My dragon used his air and it was hard going to stay aloft at all. One more breath of fire and I would have been one of the captured." He shook

213

his head. "I am afraid they are gone."

"Nonsense." Jackie swung wildly to Richard. "There must be a way to rescue our people. How do we accomplish it?"

"I have thought," Richard replied, rubbing his chin, "with their riders down, the dragons will not move, and even without flame, they are still formidable creatures. The beasts will balk at the forcible taking of their men for any great distance. It is a good chance all are held close to Norington. The city of Berryhill should be the place to keep prisoners. A wall defends the town, but is too far away. The town of Willowood lies nearby. I have been there before. A small fort is located on the outskirts of the village. If they are anywhere in the area, this is where they'll be kept. If we move quickly we *might* be able to rescue some of our men before they are moved."

"Won't Johnathan have a heavy guard on our riders?" James commented, "Both with dragons and with soldiers?"

"The air holding the dragons aloft will regenerate swiftly," Jeffery pointed out, "but the lambda in their gizzards may be gone. If we free the dragons they will still not be much good in an air fight if it comes to this."

"The idea is to rescue, not fight," Jackie argued, "although we could bring lambda with us." She snapped her fingers. "James, go back to the mine and collect all the stone you can carry and return here. You too, Jeffery, and make sure you feed your dragons well with the stone."

The two hurried off. Jackie said to Richard, "How is Niohoggr? Will he fly in the morning?"

Richard glanced at his mount. The dragon raised his right wing, flexing it in a circle. "Niohoggr says he will be fit tomorrow for battle." Richard chuckled at the dragon. Jackie looked questioningly at him. "He seeks revenge for the pain inflicted on him," Richard explained.

"I seek revenge also," Jackie replied soberly. "We will take our vengeance together. Here is what I plan."

***

The Easmen landed during the night. Jackie laid out her strategy for the next day. "Remember," she told the riders, "wait until we have joined battle. When you see the rebel riders leave, this is the time to attack, not before." She chuckled, "and if they don't run to the rescue of the soldiers, do the best you're able."

"There is good cloud cover," Richard replied. "We can hide until we are sure the rebel riders have left."

To Prince Sevorson and his captains she said, "We will have to move fast." She glared sternly. "No stopping for looting or feasting over victories. We keep marching and don't stop. Understood?"

The Easmen warriors nodded, although Jackie saw a few disappointed faces when she said, no looting.

Richard left while it was still dark. Before he flew off, he said to Jackie, "Are you sure you want to go through with this? I do not know the number guarding our men, nor how many will respond to the attack, but either way it will be hazardous for you. Let one of us stay instead."

Jackie wasn't worried about the danger. She wanted her strategy to succeed. "If I thought it was the right choice I would've suggested it," Jackie put her finger to her mouth, "but you and the rest know the area better than I. Your dragons," she chuckled, "are still feeling the effects of yesterday's battle, more than Belinda." She gazed at her dragon, frolicking in the waves, unconcerned with the approaching fight. "We will be fine."

The dragons lifted off. After they'd vanished Jackie said to Prince Sevorson, "It's our turn."

The ships rowed from the island to the mainland. At first light they struck.

The Easmen stormed ashore in a mass of

215

screaming men and flashing spears. The few fishermen and traders preparing to sail fled in terror. Jackie flew overhead, refraining from attack. Civilian causalities weren't what she wanted, and she needed to conserve the lifting air within Belinda for the fighting she knew was about to occur.

As a great tsunami sweeps forward from the ocean, so too did the Easmen, meeting little resistance as they marched through the coastal towns. After an hour, Jackie spied a column of rebel soldiers running their way. She signaled to Sevorson who readied his forces.

The Easmen barely slowed their advance, scattering the rebel troops, which fled in disarray in every direction when they saw the numbers of enemy they faced.

Before long, another rebel army, much larger than the first, marched their way. Five specks appeared in the sky, flapping toward Jackie as they flew guard over the soldiers.

"This is what we've been waiting for," Jackie whispered to Belinda. *"Let's put fear back in their hearts."*

The rebel riders sailed in advance of the soldiers, breathing fire at the earth in an attempt to throw the Easmen into panic. Belinda sped into the middle of the formation releasing her own blaze before soaring skyward. Three of the rebel dragons peeled off from the formation and swept after her while the remaining two riders continued to zero in on the Easmen army.

This will never do. I need everyone to chase me. Jackie patted on Belinda's neck and yelled, "Little girl, let's do it again and catch their attention."

"Watch this," the dragon purred in delight. *"I'll make their tails curl."*

Belinda reached the top of her arc and rolled over to descend again. She pointed like an arrow at the two attacking riders. The three rebels trailed her, swooping down also, intent on reaching their victim, fire lashing close to Belinda's tail.

Belinda zipped between the two dragons, causing the beasts to veer wildly. The three riders behind tried to pull up. They didn't succeed, and collisions erupted along with flames. Wingtips clipped and jaws snapped as the two dragons thought the three riders attacked from behind. In her mind Jackie heard a *"He—He—He,"* as Belinda leveled out and floated upward.

On the ground, the two armies clashed. Prince Sevorson led a charge of his men, driving deep into the middle of the rebel line with ferocious war cries. The two forces seesawed back and forth, but the untrained rebels were no match for the skill and sheer ferocity of the Easmen barbarians.

The rebel line broke. A small portion of their army disappearing as the left flank of the Easmen swept inward and overwhelmed the soldiers. The remaining portion of the rebels tried to reform by falling back. Prince Sevorson's troops engulfed the warriors from behind, a shark swallowing a school of minnows as their retreat transformed into a rout. Individual battles broke out as the fighting disintegrated into slaughter.

Jackie was congratulating herself on the battle when a blast of flame engulfed her. *Am I on fire?* She reached back and heat seared her gloves. *Oh, no. My cloak.* In desperation, she yanked the cover over her head, smoke and flying ash filling her eyes, Belinda's frantic swerves threatened to shake Jackie loose from her perch. She clung on grimly with one hand and managed to remove the cloak with the other, releasing the smoldering cloth behind her.

Belinda whimpered, *"That hurt."*

Jackie muttered, "Tell me about it."

The two riders resumed their attack on the Easmen while the three continued to pursue Jackie. Belinda swept in a circle meaning to draw her attackers back into another collision with their mates, but the rebels were wise to her trick by now. The dragons assaulting the Easmen kept a wide space between themselves, banking out of the way at Belinda's approach.

A blast of fire washed over Jackie. This time she smelt burning hair.

I'm going to die. I wonder if they'll bury me?

An incandescent stream of flame shot past Jackie aimed at the riders tailing her—a flashing shape zoomed by on her right while a second zipped on the left. Niohoggr flashed in her vison and vanished. Jackie twisted in time to see a wall of fire erupt behind her as six loyalist dragons released their combined fury on the rebels. Belinda leaped skyward into the open sky, twisting and looping at the same time, to disgorge a blast of flames of her own as the rebels flew toward her.

Rebels dropped and their dragons soared on, riderless.

The loyalist dragons fell on the two remaining rebels. They scattered, flapping back inland as fast as possible.

"You look terrible." Richard paced her astride Niohoggr. "Have you been hurt?"

Jackie patted the top of her head. Half the hair on the right side was missing. Her back still burnt, and a stitch ran up her side. *"Fine,"* she breathed. "I'm fine."

The rest of the riders grouped around her in a protective globe. She counted noses. Two were missing. "Where are…"

"Dead, lost in yesterday's battle," Richard shouted gravely, "along with their dragons." His jaws tightened as he ground his teeth. "Johnathan shall pay for this too."

Unnamed loss bubbled up within Jackie. She hadn't known the riders well, no more than a smile and nod at meals, but she knew how Richard felt and she mourned with him for their loss.

From the ground a cry resounded. Prince Sevorson waved his arms and beckoned Jackie to alight. Whatever was left of the rebel army disappeared, the remains of the once living scattered across the field of combat in dark lumps.

"Down," Jackie yelled to the riders. "It's time to sketch out our next move."

They landed. Jackie insisted one rider remain aloft to watch for trouble. The rest dismounted and strode to the prince, discussing the battle excitedly among themselves as they walked.

Sevorson wore a large smirk, his tunic ripped in a dozen spots with marred chainmail showing through. They approached and he shouted out a greeting. "Ho. Good fighting. If we receive no more resistance than what I saw this morning, we will have this war finished in a fortnight."

"We took the rebels by surprise today," Richard hurried to remind the rest of the men. "It will not be as easy tomorrow."

"Aye, you are right. What are your thoughts?" The prince gazed at the battlefield. "We cannot sit here and take on all comers, to try is sure to bring disaster."

"Keep moving and hope for the best," Jackie said. "They have lost riders," she waved a hand at the rescued men, "and we gained fighters." She asked the riders, "What of the battle at the king's castle? We've had rumor and conjure of his defeat. Did you hear words while you were captive?"

"Yes, whatever was said is true." One of the men stepped forward. Jackie remembered his name was Albert. "Our guard boasted to us last night. The castle fell with no resistance except for the palace guard, the king and his old dragon dead in the fighting. Johnathan has taken up residence there and proclaimed it his capitol."

"Troops?" Sevorson demanded to know. "Did anyone number the soldiers he has there?"

Albert shook his head. "After the battle of Norington, the army marched on the castle except two riders and a handful of soldiers to guard us." He cupped his chin and closed his eyes, thinking. "Afterward half returned. You fought those men here today. This is the best I can tell you." He pursed his lips. "Perhaps two thousand warriors?"

"Our course is obvious," Jackie said. "Stay together, march on the castle, and defeat Johnathan. We have no choice."

Shocked expression shone on Richard's and Sevorson's faces. "Do think it is wise to attack his stronghold so..." began the prince.

"We will attack."

Richard waved a hand in denial. "But Jackie, Johnathan still has dragons we must face," he protested, "and even if they are defeated, he has his army, too, and we are still outnumbered." He spread his arms wide. "After a battle as that what army will we have left? Not to mention we still have Berryhill in our path. First, we must take this stronghold. We cannot leave it in our rear, or we face decimation between two forces. The city fell first to the rebels at the beginning of the war, and will not be easily taken, and it is walled." Richard shook his head. "It would be better to reconquer Mercia province by province. There'll be resistance, yes, but not as much as if we attack his main force."

Jackie pursed her lips, considering his words, and the idea was tempting until she'd scanned the battlefield. The Easmen warriors symmetrically riffled through the dead's pockets, and packs, collecting everything of value. How was it possible for her and Richard to keep this army in the field except by stripping every hamlet and town bare? They would create more hatred then Johnathan would ever do.

"The longer we wait, the more control Johnathan and his stooges have over the land," She replied, "and where are we to find provisions for this army?" Jackie stared at the rest, waiting for a reply. When none was forthcoming, she said, "We strike while the rebels are still disorganized, or not at all. If we must take Berryhill, we'll have to figure out a way of doing so. It is this or nothing at all."

"Do you have any idea how to take the town, and if we are lucky enough to breach the walls, how to defeat Johnathan? The castle will be an even harder battle to overcome," Richard wondered aloud.

"I don't know, but I'll think of something."

Chapter Seventeen

"They refuse to submit." Sevorson announced in disgust as he stomped back to Jackie, Richard, and his captains. The walled town of Berryhill stood on a mound. The berry bushes and fruit trees it was famous for spread out around the outskirts in a wave on one side. On the other, tilled fields of grain stretched away to the horizon. The first thing the prince ordered was his men to encircle the hill guaranteeing none would escape or reinforcements to enter. Afterward he'd tried negotiating a peaceful surrender of the town to no avail. "Blast those people, send the dragons in and let us be done with this," he groused. The prince jammed his palm over the hilt of his sword, recalling what the townspeople told him when he asked for their submission.

"We could," Richard hazarded, "but it is not a good idea. The dragons would use up their air and be as lambs for slaughter if rebel riders approached."

"To blazes with the dragons." Severson declared loudly. "We haven't seen the enemy in two days, why would they show up now?"

"Which does not mean they will not show up," Richard replied quietly. "Besides, we cannot afford to lose any of our beasts." He gestured to the walls. "Look. They have mounted giant crossbows on the wall capable of hurling four-foot bolts at the dragons. If we are to take the town it must be with troops or not at all."

"And kill off half my men in the process?" The prince laughed. "Johnathan's castle, yes, if we have to. This place?" He swept his hand across the open ground and spat on the grass, "No."

One of Sevorson's captains spoke up. "We must do something, or leave. On our approach, our scouts tell us they saw men on horseback racing away to spread the news

222

of our advance. This new king of yours knows we are approaching and is sure to lead a counter-attack whether he uses his dragons or not. The men grumble. They thought this would be a quick raid with loot in plenty."

"...send in the troops," exclaimed Richard in frustration.

"*Never*. Use your dragons. A few bolts will not..."

"*Stop it—both of you.*"

Both Richard and Sevorson looked to Jackie. "Well? What do you say?" Richard asked.

What do I say? I don't know. They're both right. Jackie glanced at the sky. The sun was setting. "It grows late." She sighed, trying to clear her mind and concentrate on the problem. "Let me think. Perhaps by the morning one of us will reach some solution. Who knows," she tried to sound chipper, "perhaps the leaders of Berryhill will change their minds and surrender once they see we aren't leaving any time soon." Before protests erupted anew, she spun on her heel and walked away toward the town.

Jackie found a grassy spot well out of bow range of the archers and studied the city and surrounding area. The wall was high and strong, towers for archers lined the barrier every thirty yards to create a crossfire against attacking troops. Besides, the Easmen didn't have any siege machines with their armaments. A head-on frontal attack of the place was suicidal. Richard was right also, they must preserve the dragons at all costs. To lose even one now would kill their chances for the assault on the castle later on.

The Easmen complain they want a short war. I know my riders wish to join battle and attack the city. They look to me for answers. How'd I get into the mess? All I wanted to do is be treated equal and ride a dragon!

Above in the darkening sky, flocks of birds flew back to their nests in the city from feeding on the bounty of fruit in the forest. Jackie watched the noisy little creatures slip beneath the eves of the thatched houses she saw over the city wall.

Smart little scavengers. Feast in the woods during the day, scoot to their nice warm homes and children at night. First sign of crises they hide under the eaves of the buildings until the danger is past. Same as the birds at the manor house. Wish I could do that for a change.

As she thought about it, an idea sprang into her mind. At first, the horror of the idea frightened her, but as she weighted the grim choices she faced and the deaths of the people if a solution to their problem wasn't found, she blanked all else from her mind.

For a long time she sat hugging herself, watching white clouds and sapphire skies fade away.

As it grew dark, she sprang up and raced back to the pavilion, she, Richard, and the prince used as their command post. The two men were inside standing around a table rehashing possible plans for an attack that didn't entail the decimation of troops.

"Prince Sevorson, do your men know how to catch birds?" Jackie gasped, out of breath as she threw the tent flap open wide.

"What?" The prince stared at her as if she'd gone mad. "Birds? What birds?"

"Yes, birds." Jackie dropped down on the table, swinging her arms as if casting a net wide.

His brows drew close, but some subtle tone in her voice caused him to pause and consider carefully what she asked. "Of course, why would you wish to know something like this? In their breeding season we net hundreds on the cliffs, also plunder their eggs. Why?"

"Tomorrow morning the birds fly out of the town into the forest to feed," Jackie replied earnestly, watching to see if he understood her reasoning. "When they do, we catch birds. Have your men start constructing nets tonight. We will also need string, and cages to hold the fowl until we've accumulated enough for our purpose. You can do this?"

The prince was still doubtful but replied. "If you wish."

The next morning the Easmen spread their nets among the branches of the trees, and making loud noises, drove huge quantities of fowl into their traps.

"Now what?" Sevorson shouted over the squawking. Feathers flew in all directions as the birds tried to escape their prisons.

"Have you men tie dried grass onto the bird's legs, set it afire and release the creatures," Jackie commanded, "as quick and as many as possible."

"What?" Richard exclaimed in horror as he wondered why Jackie would do this cruel act. "How can that possibly gain...?"

"Do it."

The prince glanced from Jackie to the birds and slowly nodded. He shouted to his captains, "You heard her."

Working in pairs, The Easmen wrapped, lit, and set the birds loose as fast as possible. The terrified fowl fled back to the safety of their nests under the eaves of the houses.

Smoke arose in small puffs from the town as the nests and thatched roofs caught on fire. In a half-an-hour, the whole town burned as the blazes spread. Those structures not falling victim to the birds, nevertheless ignited as flaming embers settled on their exteriors. The screams of trapped people rang out over the walls.

The gates of the city swung open. The townspeople and soldiers stumbled out, many holding white flags of surrender as they tried to escape the inferno inside.

Jackie's face was a frozen mask as she turned to Severson and said, "The town has fallen, Prince. Soon it will burn to the ground. Take what captives as you will. It is time to march on." She spun away with a sharp sob, unable to watch the carnage she'd created any longer.

Easmen warriors passed her by, running forward as she walked into the woods, not even realizing Richard followed next to her in silent companionship.

When she didn't hear the cries of the people or the crackling of the flames any longer, Jackie stopped and stood staring at a fallen log blocking her path.

"It was a good plan," Richard said at last when Jackie didn't move or say anything. "An idea no one else thought of."

Abruptly, Jackie turned on him and glared with eyes wide. She clenched her fists and beat on his chest. "Is this what I must do now, become a destroyer of towns and animals? Murderer of innocent women and children—a monster that lets nothing stand in her way?"

Richard's voice softened and he murmured, "You saved many of our men's lives. More if you count the city's soldiers who would have died in battle. You had no choice."

Jackie swung away with head bowed and studied the log again. She muttered in a hollow voice, "I know."

Chapter Eighteen

"**W**hy won't they fight?"

The dragonriders and their Easmen allies advanced toward the headquarters of Johnathan with minimal resistance. A small force of rebels opposed the loyalists with hit and run attacks, more interested in destroying villages and setting fire to surrounding crops than engaging in full-scale battle. As the allies approached the castle, the insurgent's defense hardened and a standoff between the two forces emerged.

Prince Sevorson's Easmen warriors surrounded Johnathan's citadel. Both sides dug trenches, threw up breastworks, and waited for what would happen next.

Jackie paced outside her pavilion set on a hill overlooking the castle, glaring at the rebel troops bivouacked outside the fortress walls. She repeated, "I don't understand why they won't attack."

Richard shrugged and stood next to her. "For the same reason we do not make a full scale offensive on his forces and stronghold. If we attack—we lose. If Johnathan orders an assault he will win, but at what cost? Losing half of his troops? It is to his advantage to sit and do nothing."

Jackie stared back at him with incomprehension. "How will he win by doing nothing? He's trapped, as is his army. Even his dragons sit and wait." She pointed at the beasts pastured outside the castle walls. "Why doesn't he attack us with those?"

In annoyance at Jackie's lack of understanding, Richard waved a gloved hand at the town in the distance and the Easmen camp along their line. The village sat in ruin, the fields surrounding it burned to the earth. Closer by, The loyalist army bent in a circle, smoke curled up from cooking fires, tents and lean-tos scattered behind the fortifications they'd dug.

He awarded Jackie a hard look. "There are no provisions to be had for thirty miles in any direction. What do we feed the troops?" He said to Prince Sevorson, who watched in mute judgement as the two riders argued, "How long before your rations run out, and the men begin to complain?"

The prince grimaced and shook his head. "Food we have for a short time, small parties of my men have gone foraging and stalked wild game, but you are right." He gave a wry smirk. "I have already heard grumbling. Many thought this raid would be finished by now. They are not use to sitting, doing nothing, and most are farmers during the year. Harvest time approaches and they wish to return to their fields to gather in the crops." He frowned. "Even I wish to go soon. Once the weather turns cold, the ocean becomes choppy. I have no desire to lose my ships to a turbulent sea and gale force winds."

"You understand Johnathan's strategy now," Richard said to Jackie with a sour smirk on his lips. "All he must do is sit and wait. Time is on his side, if nothing happens soon, our army will fall apart. As for the dragons," he gestured to their mounts, "Johnathan's first priority is the same as ours. Preserve his mounts. He knows we have the giant crossbows from Berryhill. He will not risk their death in combat unless forced to."

Jackie faced the castle, rage burning inside her as she scanned the parapet. The solders standing guard stared back, leaning on their weapons, half-asleep or yawning. Some did not even watch the loyalist army, but turned their back on the Easmen, talking to their comrades. Out of frustration, she marched to her tent and kicked the side. She swung around, hands gripped into vises of rage. "If only we could devise a plan of passing the troops without fighting or scaling the walls unseen," she muttered to Richard and Sevorson. "Think. There must be some way."

The look on Prince Sevorson's face told Jackie the ruler ran out of schemes long ago. "It would be easier to contrive a way of sneaking my men close enough to their army to fight." He squatted on his haunches and drew two parallel lines in the dirt. "It is this, right here," he laid his palm on the no man's land between the lines, "stopping us from storming the walls. Between their catapults and the dragons my warriors would never survive the assault." He glared up at Jackie and Richard with his mouth twisting into a bitter line. "I do not mind losing men, but a suicide rush would prove nothing." He said to Richard half in jest, "Perhaps there is a way to mount our men on your dragons and drop our troops on the castle and army from the air? Perhaps huge nets as we used to catch those birds?"

Richard drew back, startled, and began to retort until he saw Sevorson's lips twitching and failed to answer. Jackie threw the prince a stare meant to freeze water. She swung to her pavilion again, decided it had taken enough of a beating, and muttered, "I'm taking a walk. Think, my friends think. I'll be back." She stalked off into the Easmen camp.

The warriors glanced up as she strode along, a few made feeble attempts to engage her in friendly conversation. She ignored the men, trying to concentrate on the problem at hand, Jackie also ignored the comments of, "the girl," and "the woman."

Yeah, this is I. Always "the girl." This is how Victor referred to me. They'll write it on my headstone. "Here rests the girl." She observed a group of Easmen setting fire to a funeral pyre, one of their own who'd died from wounds in battle. *Maybe when it's my time, I should have my burial this way.* She paused to watch the smoke rise and flames leap higher. *I wonder if anyone will remember me when I'm gone?* With a sigh of regret they'd lost another warrior she marched on.

The dragons rested behind the camp in a meadow where they had room to stretch out and relax, or take flight as the mood struck the beasts. Most slept in the sun, some crouched on their haunches, watching the camp and castle beyond with interest. Jackie spied Belinda sprawled on the grass by herself, and sauntered over to her, feeling guilty she'd ignored her friend for the past few days since the siege started.

"Are you finding enough to eat?" Jackie ran her hand over the dragon's scales. The skin hung in folds, the scales ashen.

"We have to search far afield to locate game and fresh water," the dragon complained. She twisted her head under Jackie's hand to receive a scratching behind the ears. *"When do I return to my nice dark mine and quiet forest?"*

"Soon, honey," promised Jackie. She scrubbed her fingernails behind Belinda's ears and stroked the dragon's neck. A low buzz issued from deep within Belinda's chest and Jackie laid her cheek against the warm flesh. She murmured, "I'm sorry I got you and the rest of the dragons into this mess. Are you mad at me?"

Belinda lifted her head. *"Of course not. We, the dragons, honor you above all else. You are the human who brought us the rock, which makes us breath fire. This is our birthright. Long after your passing your name will be remembered by dragon kind."*

Jackie drew breath in a gasped. "Really? I never thought I was this important to anyone." She added to herself with a laugh, *Maybe I should send a message to Johnathan to have me buried under the stones slabs in his chapel when I die. How would this be for "the girl"? The whole kingdom would remember me.*

With a lighter heart and the peace coming from talking with her dragon, Jackie retraced her steps to the pavilion. At the funeral pyre, a much larger crowd gathered saying their last good journeys to their comrade. Jackie paused as heads swung her way.

I am known to these people also. Even if they think of me as a mere woman, they might wish to mourn for my death. On impulse, she stopped, took a knee, and said a silent prayer for the fallen. Appreciative nods drifted her way at the respect she paid to an Easmen she didn't know.

While she prayed, she imagined herself in a wooden casket, carried into the chapel. Candles glowed, the priests swinging thuribles full of incense in every direction, while a multitude crowded the entrance to the castle, waiting to enter the sanctuary to mourn her loss and pay their last respects. In her imagination, wails rose to the ceiling and even Victor was there, gnashing his teeth in regret for the way he'd treated her when she was alive.

Jackie stood, still tracking the smoke of the pyre as it twisted into the sky, inhaling the odor of burning wood and flesh, thinking of death. A strange idea popped into her mind. Snickers rose in her throat, threatening to burst out if she didn't keep her jaws tightly locked.

The laughter erupted into peals of hilarity she was unable to contain any longer. Her chortles flowed over the kneeling men, mounting into roars of merriment until the warriors praying glanced up and looked at her curiously. Frowns of disapproval flashed from man to man, and then concern as tears rolled down her cheeks. One asked, "Are you okay?"

Jackie put out a hand, gasping. "Sorry, but yes." She raised her head to the sky with a bright light shining in her face. "No. I am sick, yes, sick, and fain would I die." She spun and rushed away.

***

The dragonriders huddled around Jackie's tent, ill at ease as they shuffled their feet, raising hands in helplessness as they muttered to their comrades. Richard emerged and hurried to each, whispering urgently into their ears and reentered the pavilion. Prince Sevorson arrived next with a cluster of his men, shooting anxious glances left and right at the men surrounding the tent flap as he disappeared into the entrance. After a long time, he sped out, wringing his hands and collected his captains who stood next to the riders speaking in low voices. The Easmen rushed off, spreading through their camp with loud cries of anguish.

From the parapet of the castle, the rebel warriors watched with interest. Finally, Johnathan himself appeared to see what the ruckus was about. He bent forward, holding the cap of the wall, and surveying the scene with puzzlement.

"What is that caterwauling going on over there?" he asked a warrior standing guard.

"I do not know," the soldier replied, shading his eyes as he peered over the parapet for a better view. "They started the howling at the break of dawn, people rushing in and out from the woman's tent. I have not seen her emerge yet." He hazarded a guess. "A council of war, maybe?"

"If that is a conference, it is the noisiest war council I have ever heard." He drummed his fingers on the parapet, listening to the babble of voices rising from the Easmen. "Keep me informed of any changes," Johnathan ordered at last as he swung back to the steps. "There is definitely something strange happening in their camp."

More men congregated around Jackie's tent. Richard emerged again, this time with his head bowed, walking slowly as he ran his fingers through his hair. The wails of lament rose louder from the Easmen and riders alike, shrill enough for the observing soldiers at the castle's walls to hear.

Curious onlookers from inside the citadel stormed the battlements of the fortress and packed shoulder to shoulder to watch. Inquisitive cries flew down to the soldiers at the breastworks on the ground who replied in ignorance, confused as the spectators on the wall what was happening in the enemy ranks.

The battlements of the castle grew quiet as Richard trudged out of the loyalist camp into the no-man's land between the two armies. He stopped, body slumped as if he carried a heavy weight, and raised a white flag of truce, waving it over his head. "I wish to speak to Johnathan," he yelled. The marks of tears made dirty streaks on his cheeks.

After an eternity of waiting, the portcullis of the fortress lifted and Johnathan emerged from the castle entrance clothed in shiny chainmail. Soldiers leaped to open the gate of the wicker breastworks and he swaggered into the no-man's land, a broad smirk on his face. "So, you have changed your mind and decided to surrender?" he sneered to Richard with his hands resting on his hips. "I am glad you have come to your senses. We have wasted enough time on these games."

"Jackie is dead."

"What?" Johnathan's mouth bent down and his eyes opened wide. "How?"

"A wound sustained in battle," Richard muttered. "It swelled into an infection our surgeons could not correct, no matter how much blood they let out of her. She died this morning."

Johnathan said with sincerity, "I am sorry to hear this, truly I am, but what does it matter to us here and now? We still have this war to conclude."

Richard studied the dust at his feet before replying. "It was her dying wish to be buried under the stones in your chapel," he murmured, not looking up. "I promised I would ask." He raised his eyes and stared Johnathan in the face. "It meant a great deal to her. When she was younger she studied with the nuns in her village and heard tales of how the noble dead reside there."

The rider cleared his throat and threw up his hands, palms out, hardly believing the audacity of Richard's request. "Out of the question," he declared, his voice livid in disbelief. "You must be mad. This is a place of honor for great men. Why would I permit a female to rest there for all eternity? I would defile God if I placed a woman on the same level as men of importance. She opposed me from the start."

"Why?" Richard crossed his arms against his chest and replied with sullen anger, "She is—was—the first, and perhaps only, woman dragonrider. If for no other reason, this would be enough even if she fought against you. Do not truly great leaders honor the bravery of their adversaries? She should be esteemed for her valor and courage."

"You are correct, of course," mused Johnathan, calming, "but…"

Richard's voice took on a sterner tone. "If this is not enough for you, she brought the gift of fire to the dragons and their riders. The dragons themselves revere her for this. Can you, as a dragonrider do less? Ask yourself, if she had not conveyed the knowledge to us, would you be sitting on your throne today? You should be begging me to bury her in your castle." He inhaled and shook his head knowingly. "Your victories are hers. Woman or not, her name will go down in history. In fact, her legend will continue because she *is* a woman."

Johnathan scratched his chin, thinking. "I must admit, you have the right of it, and I have heard mutterings from the woman of my court how the females of this kingdom were treated during the war." He laughed to himself. "Some of my men took, uh, liberties when they should not have. This would go a long way in quieting complains, if I honored one of their kind." He pursed his lips and regarded Richard for a long moment. "I did not think far enough in advance of her deeds, but it is not alone for me to say yea or nay. I must consult with the priests and see what they voice about the orthodoxy of the matter." He swung as if to go, paused, and asked, "When did you wish to bury her?"

Richard gestured to the loyalist camp where the faint sound of banging echoed across the two armies. "We build her casket now. I hoped to lay her to rest tomorrow. The body...." he left the rest of the sentence hanging, both men realizing what would happen to the corpse after a few days in the heat.

Johnathan nodded. "Of course, I understand. Wait here. I will summon the clergy within the hour and tell you what their reply is." He hurried away.

Well inside the allotted time, Johnathan returned with an answer. "Both the priests and I are in agreement." He beamed at Richard. "Jackie shall be given a place of prestige in our small church. In fact, the priests are eager now that I have explained the importance of her deeds."

Richard bowed. "I am sure Jackie would be happy to hear this. You have made her spirit smile."

"Oh, it is nothing," Johnathan replied with serene dignity. "You were correct. Now I am king I must think as a king. The people in my court will act accordingly. The priests pry up the slabs and sanctify the earth as we speak. They feel it is a great honor to have her in the chapel, and who knows," his eyes lit up, thinking about the future, "perhaps one day sainthood is in order. You are right; the gift of fire she furnished me was a miracle in a fashion. Bring her here in the morning." He said in a more serious note, "Now about your surrender..."

"After the burial," snapped Richard, gesturing to the camp where the Easmen and riders lined up watching.

"I must still discuss our submission with my men and allies. Today is a day for grieving." He added bitterly, sagging, "remember though, the gift of the lambda was not given to you, but to all dragonriders. Jackie's legacy is not yours alone to claim."

Johnathan put his hand up. "Of course, of course. We will speak more of this tomorrow after the burial when you and your people have had time to think."

The next morning seventy-five hooded men lined up in a column, an honor guard and pallbearers to escort Jackie's coffin to her grave. They marched in slow cadence, with bowed heads, across the no man's land with the casket between them. The rebel soldiers threw their wicker gate open wide, allowing the column to enter, where a priest wearing his finest robes waited. He proceeded the group into the castle, swing his censer of incense, while behind, the Easmen followed, chanting a funeral dirge. Outside in the loyalist camp, strange howls and cries arose from the dragons, their calls picked up by the rebel mounts. The giant beasts hurled gouts of flame into the sky while Easmen and insurgent soldiers paused in awe at the sight.

Behind the honor guard, both loyalist warriors and rebel troops crowded the corridor to the chapel and entrance to the castle, attempting to have a glimpse of the ceremony about to occur. All wished to recount the tale to those who were not present. More Easmen troops lined the wicker barricade waiting their turn to enter.

Johnathan met the procession at the chapel door and watched in silence as the honor guard and pallbearers pass within. Richard and Prince Sevorson trudged in last.

"Which ones are the riders?" Johnathan whispered to Richard, scanning the cowled honor guard. "I wish your people to sit with my riders. We were friends once. In this time of mourning we should join." He waved to an empty section of pews where his men sat.

"If you do not mind, they will be here in a moment," Richard replied gravely, his face clothed in shadows as he waved to the castle entrance. "They stay to comfort their mounts." From outside the faint squealing of the dragons reverberated off the fortress walls. "I hope you do not mind."

Johnathan scowled and muttered under his breath as he took in the number of people crowding the chapel, but said, "Fine. Let us begin the ceremonies. I hadn't realized this many would attend, and did not wish this to become an all-day affair. We still have much to discuss afterwards."

Richard nodded. "As you wish." He waved to the pallbearers, who trudged forward and set the coffin down before the altar.

The lid of the casket creaked opened.

Jackie leaped up in full battle gear.

"ATTACK."

Chapter Nineteen

Pandemonium erupted.

The honor guard threw off their hooded cloaks, revealing mailed clan Easmen warriors jerking out blades. With savage whoops of joy, they leaped on the seated rebels, taking prisoners, or slaughtering all who resisted. The startled clergy scattered in all directions with wails of fright, while the chorus of young boys Johnathan assembled for the occasion huddled in fear.

"Treachery," Johnathan bellowed. His hand jumped to the hilt of his weapon. Jackie, Richard, and Prince Sevorson leaped on him, Jackie drawing her sword and holding it to his throat, pinning him to the wall before he reacted. "It's over, Johnathan," Jackie yelled in triumph. "You're our prisoner now. For your life, order your soldiers to surrender, or you'll be the first to die."

Johnathan tried to clear his throat, speechless at the rapid turn of events. He looked left and right, saw most of his men captured already, and shouted in a loud voice, "Throw down your arms. The fighting is over." Jackie heard him mutter under his breath, "For now."

Outside the castle, the Easmen warriors, who'd stood patiently to enter the chapel and mingled with the rebel soldiers while waiting, drew swords also and started a massacre of their own. The stunned soldiers, surrounded and confused, surrendered or scrambled over the earthworks, fleeing into the ruined town beyond.

In the meadow, the riders saw the fighting start and leaped onto their dragons. They rose in a flurry of wings, swooping down on the battlements of the castle, breathing fire and spraying incandescent fury on all. Futile bolts flashed upward, silenced as the dragons swung their wrath on the men and weapons. The crews huddled in terror, not daring to expose themselves to the blaze.

Easmen warriors stormed into the castle from outside. Cooks, stewards, and scullery maids hid, the castle guard long since having disappeared when the battling started and the order to surrender given. Within an hour, the last of the resistance ended and the fighting stopped. As the rebel dragonriders stumbled away in chains, Jackie and Richard climbed stairs to the parapet and gazed out over the countryside.

"It is finished," breathed Richard, "like that."

"Uh—uh." Jackie swept her hair out of her face, failing to note the blood coating her fingers. She left a red streak on her forehead. "You are only beginning." She pointed to the town and the lands beyond. "Mercia is ripped apart, the king dead, and many of the barons are killed also. You wished to set up a kinder equal kingdom? Now is your chance. You and your riders. No one in authority is left to oppose you."

"What do you mean, 'You and your riders'? You are part of this from the first." He poked a finger into her chest. *"We* will help establish a fairer kingdom. I need you to make sure I do not set myself up as a tyrant."

"You've known what you wanted from the first. No one has to watch you." Jackie laughed. "All I ever wanted is ride a dragon and be treated as an equal. You do this now. Politics is way beyond me." She thought about Victor and his cronies. "As long as you keep the crazies out and act fair to everyone, you'll do fine. I would be in the way."

Richard looked down on her, complete understanding in his voice as he said, "I will not try and force you into anything you do not wish to do, and I should know better than to attempt such a feat." His eyes clouded over. "This war has proven you are more than equal to any man. Yours was the driving force making this all possible. Every person in Mercia and the kingdom of the Easmen will wish to be you." His voice lowered and he said, "There is still the question of you and me, though. How shall we proceed?"

Jackie fell silent. How did she feel about Richard? They were comrades-in-arms, fought and struggled for months now to achieve this one goal. He said she was the metal behind this victory, but she knew he was as much to be praise as she was. Their lives implacably bound together from now on by the events they'd gone through, no matter what happened in the future. Was this the right time to contemplate love, though, when he had so much more to do? "Let us think about this," she said at last. She took his hands and squeezed the tips lightly, staring up into his face. "You still have your mission to start, and I must return to the fief. I don't know what has transpired with my family, if they're alive or dead, and who knows what's happened to the manor house since I've been gone. We have waited this long, we can wait longer until our paths are clear."

Richard's shoulders sagged. "I suppose I have no choice, now do I?" He clasped her hands in return. "But while I am busy, my every waking thought will be upon you."

Jackie stayed around long enough to bid Prince Sevorson and his men farewell. "If you ever need my help, all you must do is ask," she said with a curtsy as the prince's boat was about to set sail to his homeland. "You and your men have saved our kingdom, and I don't know how we'll ever repay your kindness."

Sevorson extended his spear into the air and returned her curtsy with a deep bow of his own. "You saved my life, and I repaid the favor, but if ever I want a brave warrior, I have no farther to look than you and this country you call Mercia."

Jackie reflected the chest of gold rounds and jewels from Johnathan's treasury the prince took with him might have contributed to the prince's happy leave taking, but she shrugged it off. The Easmen did make the difference in the war and she was grateful.

She left for the manor the day after the Easmen departed. She flew over the town and noted with sadness the buildings were in ruins, the streets deserted. Farther on, she saw the baron's castle burnt to the ground. She steeled her mind and hope her house escaped the carnage.

"Home," warbled Belinda as she landed at the mine entrance. *"Maybe now I will have a good day's rest."* With a flick of her tail, and without a backward glance at Jackie, she disappeared into the dark hole.

"Sleep well," she yelled to the retreating dragon, "I will see you tonight." Still laughing to herself, she made her way off Baldhill. *I'm home, too.* She strolled through the woods in a trance seeing the trees as if in a dream. *No more fighting, battles, or short nights—sleeping in my own bed.* Jackie broke out into a run.

She rounded a bend in the trail and stopped. The manor house stood as it did before she left, but the front door was wide-open, hanging by a hinge. Shutters tightly closed yawned open. She sprinted to the front door and peered in.

Looters, and more than one, I reckon. She grimaced in disgust at the wreckage inside. Furniture was missing, paintings gone, the walls defaced by graffiti. Even Victor's prize rug covering the spot where he sat at the table mysteriously vanished, along with his chair; she supposed both hauled away for sale. Muddy footprints on the bare wooden floor showed where people, and *yes*, even animals wandered in and out.

The kitchen and the rest of the house weren't in much better shape. Dirty trenchers and unwashed pots scattered everywhere. Jackie remembered with guilt, some of the mess was hers and the riders when they used the house as their headquarters. She'd never cleaned up after the last meal with the dragonriders before they'd flown off to war.

The stillroom door laid open a crack. As she swung it wide, a flash of red streaked between her legs and out the kitchen door. Jackie leaped back in surprise, and watched the bushy tail disappear behind the carriage house, not knowing whether to laugh or cry. The mythical Mr. Fox finally made an appearance.

She searched around, found a broom, bucket, lye soap, and scrub brush. *Back home, doing housework. Did I ever leave?* Jackie took off her tunic, rolled up her sleeves, and got busy.

By the evening, she'd cleaned the place enough so it wasn't disgusting. Her bed was gone, nothing remained to eat, but she still had dried provisions in her pack, and her sleeping blanket. Jackie made a small fire in the hearth, fetched water, and concocted a warm mush with crumbled rations. Straw fetched from outside made a passable mattress. She spread a quantity on the floor and wrapped her blanket around her for warmth.

Jackie sat on the floor, huddled close to the fireplace, and ate her supper, savoring each mouthful. *Wonder if I'll ever see Victoria* and *Thomas again?* It grew dark. *They took refuge in the baron's castle, and now it's destroyed in the fighting that ravished the countryside. Everyone scattered to the far reaches of the kingdom, if they're alive at all. Maybe after things settle down, if they never return, I'll ask Richard to help search for my family.*

Richard. Even as the Easmen departed, the remaining lords sought him out, demanding he and the riders bring order out of chaos. She chuckled in spite of herself. Poor guy. He'd bitten off more than his mouth could manage, she felt sure. Jackie doubted she'd see him again for a long while. Her last view of the beleaguered rider was with a wild expression on his face, as two fat barons stood on either side of him demanding he send out the dragonriders to collect their escaped cattle.

The next morning Jackie trucked into town, as much to see the damage first hand, as to learn if any food was available for sale or barter.

The once prosperous shops were deserted, their fronts smashed in. One whole side of the main street showed burnt shells of structures, including the tavern. The few people she saw scurried by, heads down, not saying a word to her. The only building still unmarked was the nunnery, but when Jackie tugged on the doors, she found them tightly bared from the inside. When she pounded she heard movement behind the entrance, but no one answered.

She turned to go and out of the corner of her eye, she caught a head peeking out from an alleyway. "Utta?"

The girl took a few faltering steps into the street, glancing with fear left and right. "Jaqueline?" She peered at Jackie as if she'd become an old woman. "*Jaqueline.*" Utta ran forward and embraced her, sobbing. "I thought you were dead."

Jackie pushed the girl's arms gently away. She smelled like a dead goat. "What happened here?" A layer of muck covered the girl's once clean tunic. "What happened to *you?*"

Utta brushed her filthy hair out of her face and gave a bubbling moan. "The rebel soldiers, they took everything. What they did not carry on their backs, they burned." She started to cry. "They ransacked our house, and when my father tried to stop the men they murdered him. My mother and I tried to run. They—they captured her, and took her away, but I managed to escape."

The grief and horror of what happened reflected in Utta's eyes. More racking sobs shook her while Jackie looked on helplessly, unsure what to say. "Uh, it's okay now, Utta." Jackie reached out and shook the girl by the shoulders to calm her. "What happened to you?"

Utta took a deep breath and said, "I found a pile of manure behind the blacksmith's shop and hid underneath it." She laughed hysterically and glanced down at herself. "No one thinks to look there."

No wonder she stinks.

"Have you seen my sister or brother? They went to the baron's castle for sanctuary."

In reflex Utta glanced toward the burned out hulk of the fortress. "No. After the soldiers attacked here, dragonriders appeared and they stormed the castle. Anyone still alive fled, or the rebels captured whomever they found and led the people away in chains. No one ventured into town, most survivors left and headed into the countryside. Safer." For the first time she laughed. "I would too, if I had some place to go."

"Have you seen Ebba?"

Utta shook her head. "No. When the soldiers stormed through any women they ran across were the first taken," she shivered, "then the men if they were young enough. That's why I've been hiding. In case they return."

"Don't worry, the war's over," Jackie assured her. "Tell everyone there's no need to be frightened any longer."

"Are you sure?" Utta's eyes went wide. "We've heard rumors, but no one knew for certain. A stranger passed through a few weeks ago, talking about infighting among the dragonriders and the rebels were defeated, but..." Utta realized for the first time, she hadn't seen Jackie since the war started. She asked, "Uh, where have you been?"

Should I tell her? Jackie decided Utta would never believe her and she wanted to go anyway. The town held nothing. "I, uh, was hiding in the mine on Baldhill," she said. "This is the first time I've venture out for more than a few feet in weeks." She glanced at the sun. "I'd better head back, too. It's growing late." She turned, hesitated, and asked, "Is anyone selling food?"

Utta laughed sadly. "Food? We eat whatever we hunt running wild. I don't know what will happen when winter arrives."

As the days drifted by, Jackie continued to make repairs on the manor, cleaning and refurbishing what she could. Most of the peasants working her fief had disappeared, their plots of land fallow in the autumn sun. The remaining families were as bereaved of food as she was. She smiled at their excuses, telling each she understood, and declared a tax holiday until everyone's fortunes grew brighter. The one positive spot was those who stayed were planting winter wheat, and possessed the foresight to keep seed and livestock for the spring. They would eat, if they survived the snow.

Belinda proved to be a good hunter and was willing to share her kills on the few occasions when the dragon chose to stalk prey and bring something back to the mine.

The dragon also came in handy when Jackie decided to haul wood to the manor house as she prepared for winter, although at first Belinda refused to cooperate.

"Is there some reason for this?" the dragon asked. She surveyed the fallen log Jackie tried to coax her into lifting. *"I've seen oxen do this. I am not an oxen."*

Jackie exhaled a blast of air in exasperation. "If I had an ox, I'd use an ox. They don't hand me backtalk." The two of them had gone around in circles for an hour over this. Jackie sat on the log, face in hands. "Do you want me to freeze to death?"

"Of course not. You may sleep in the mine with me."

"I DON'T WANT TO SLEEP IN THE MINE. I WANT TO SLEEP IN MY HOUSE." She shot Belinda a murderous look. *"WILL YOU HELP ME OR NOT?"*

"Well, if you're going to be that way about it," huffed the dragon. She grasped the log in her claws. *"I hope you realize this is below my dignity."*

After this Belinda hauled wood until Jackie was satisfied she might be short of food during the cold season, but at least she'd stay warm while starving.

To supplement her larder, Jackie used her bow to good advantage, and even Mr. Fox fell to a well-placed arrow. Jackie tanned the hide, unsure if she should keep the fur, or use it for barter. She finally decided to keep the skin. As Utta said, no one in town had food or anything else to trade, and the times she'd returned to the village, she noticed the dogs roaming the streets vanished also.

On the brighter side, though, no one in authority was around to tell her where she was not allowed to roam, and she freely stalked the baron's land as well as the king's, acquiring a stash of meat for the cold months.

When she wasn't hunting she fished in the lake. Sitting in the shade, waiting to feel a nibble, she thought how Richard would've enjoyed being here on these lonesome afternoons with her. The quiet, red and orange leaves creating a riot of colors on the trees, with a slight breeze, cool enough to build a fire and snuggle. At one point during those long, solitary days, Jackie almost decided to roust out Belinda and rush to him, knowing she was being silly even as the thought crossed her mind.

Late one afternoon she wandered back from the lake, stringer of fish thrown over her shoulder. *Fish stew tonight again—smoke some, brine some.* Winter was in the air and she'd have to throw herself into gathering whatever was available if she was going to eat. *Never planted wheat and barley, but there should be some self-seeded and ripe*

*for harvesting. I'll go out into the fields tomorrow and look,
might pick up some birds while I'm at it.*

Lost in thought, Jackie didn't hear the voices until
she was about to open the kitchen door.

"Do you see this place? An absolute pigsty." The
voice belonged to Victor. "What has the girl been doing
while we were gone?" A short pause followed, then,
"Where is she anyway?"

"I do not know." It was Victoria. She sounded
tired. "Maybe she left when the fighting started. Anyway, it
is too late to start searching for her now. It will be dark
soon. Let us settle ourselves in. I wonder if there is any
edible food in the larder. We have not eaten for two days."

Jackie pushed open the door. Victor and Victoria
stood in the middle of the kitchen. Their clothes were dirty
and ripped, hair unkempt, and the skin on their faces hung
in folds.

Victor swung to the door when she entered. "Well,
it is about time." He glowered at her, drawing the remains
of his cloak tighter around his narrow shoulders. "Where
have you been and what have you done to my house?"

"Happy to see you too," murmured Jackie under
her breath as she dropped her fish on the table. "When the
battles started I left and hid in the mine on Baldhill," she
replied unable to conceal the bitterness in her tone. "After
the fighting finished I returned here. The place was looted,
everything of value stolen by thieves." She said to Victoria,
"How are you doing? I was worried about you when you
didn't return. I saw what happened to the baron's castle and
thought you'd be here." She peered around the room and
into the dining hall fearing the worse. "Where's Thomas?"

"Asleep upstairs." Victoria absently put her hand
to her mouth suppressing a yawn while looking at the
staircase. "We have traveled for days to make our way
here, sleeping on the earth, begging food at every house we

passed." She shuddered, recalling their journey, and glanced around the sparse kitchen and dining hall, stripped of all its finery. "It is good to be home."

Victor was eyeing the fish lying on the table. "And I suppose this will be supper?" he sneered in distaste.

"We have nothing else," replied Jackie, savoring the expression on his face. She took out her belt knife and commenced to sharpen it. "All the animals are gone. What few peasants remaining have less than we do. It's this or go hungry." She shot a glance at her sister, knowing speaking to Victor was useless. "Food is scarce until after the spring planting. We'll be lucky if we don't starve during the winter."

Victoria gasped. Victor exclaimed, "Well, I will have none of it. I am going down to the tavern and buy food fit to eat. I shall bring back enough to last a day or two until I straighten all this out." He stuck his unshaven chin out, and nodded sharply to Victoria and Jackie showing he was taking charge.

"Tavern's gone," Jackie replied, testing the edge of her blade and not bothering to glance up. "Looters or rebel soldiers broke in and stole what they could carry away, and burnt the half the village down, the tavern included."

"What?"

Jackie looked up long enough and took pleasure in watching Victor's face blanch at the news before returning to her blade. "Wouldn't matter anyhow. I told you, there's no food, let alone drink."

"This is intolerable," Victor sputtered as he started pacing across the kitchen floor. "My parent's estate flatten to the ground, now I'm told the village is destroyed, and this place," he glanced around the bare room, "not fit for a dog to live in." He slammed his fist on the table. "First thing in the morning I am sending a message to the king.

He will do something. He must. It is his responsibility."

Jackie raised her eyes from her knife. "The king? The king is dead."

Victor stopped walking and chuckled. "My, you have been out of touch here. The crown was set upon his head a week ago. We heard it from a family who allowed us to sleep in their barn. For all his strange ideas about equality between lords and commoners, calling councils and gathering in the peasants to air their grievances, he is still bringing stability from mayhem." Victor raised a forefinger to his lips and studied Jackie speculatively. "I remember you went visiting with him once to his uncle's castle. I am sure he remembers us, and will provide aid once he knows who I am."

"But you're thinking of Richard..." Jackie stopped short. "Richard is king?"

"Of course, foolish girl. His grandfather, uncles, and father all died in the war. Who else would be crowned king? He was next in line."

"The slaughter was greater than I thought," Jackie mumbled, wiping the blade of her knife slowly and thinking.

"Lucky we were not caught up in it." Victor surveyed his clothes with disdain. "After the baron's castle fell, we escaped into the mountains and pretended to be commoners to avoid detection, but..." he lifted his shoulders in a slight shrug, "...this is all over now." He made a face and pointed mournfully at the table. "Now about those fish...."

Jackie put her sharping stone away and tested the edge again. "As quick as I can," she replied with a sigh.

**

As dawn broke the next day, a flight of dragons visited the manor house.

Thomas ran inside from the water trough as Jackie

finished cleaning the remains of a poor breakfast. *"Jacqueline—Victoria—Victor—Hurry quick!"* The boy jumped from foot to foot in excitement, pointing. "The sky is full of dragons." He took off up the stairs.

"What the...?" Jackie wiped her hands on her apron and peered out the window. Dragonriders astride their mounts landed in a long sweep across the front lawn, first among the squad was Richard on Niohoggr.

From above in the bedroom Victoria yelled, "For heaven's sakes—I'm coming." Thomas dragged Victoria down the staircase while Victor hurried behind, almost trampling his wife in the process. "You are stepping on my heels," she yelled at her husband. "Slow down."

What could he want...? Jackie pushed the hair out of her face and ran outside, meeting Richard halfway to the house as he strode forward. *"Richard."* Jackie skidded to a stop before she collided with the rider.

"Jackie." He picked her up by the waist and spun her around in a circle, placing her on the ground again. "I see you are surviving," he remarked with a slight hint of irony in his voice as he studied the yard and manor with interest.

"I endure," she replied, beaming as she rose on her toes and waved to the rest of the riders. "I understand you do better than this." She gestured to the overgrown lawn where sheep once grazed. "You are king now I am told?"

Richard placed his arm around her shoulder. "Sort of," He admitted, grimacing. "The kingdom had no one to rule it. I was the next in line. In order to accomplish the changes I need to do I took the authority." He swung her around to face him, his lips twitching up into a smile. "It has been easier than I thought though. With many of the peasants dead from the fighting the remaining nobles are more than willing to allow their farmers more privileges, otherwise they have no one to till the land unless they do it themselves."

"This is true," admitted Jackie, thinking of her own workers and the concessions she'd given.

Richard nodded in agreement. "Also the guild masters are eager to open up their crafts to new people. Since they are short of apprentices and we have much rebuilding to do, they actively search the towns for willing youngsters. Everyone I talk to almost begs for the reforms I wished to implement anyway. It is a matter of telling the nobles and guild masters how and when." He face brightened with excitement as he explained the changes he'd begun. "I have started a council of commoners. Each town will elect a representative to advise and help make laws."

"You are accomplishing everything you wished for." Jackie said. "You must be truly happy."

A shadow passed across Richard's face and he shook his head, gazing at her.

Jackie noticed his expression. A flutter ran through her chest, but she didn't know why. "What of Johnathan and the rebel riders?" she asked. "Are they still prisoners or have you executed the whole lot?"

"Banished from the kingdom," Richard replied with a heavy sigh. "Put the entire bunch on a ship and sent the lot to Prince Sevorson. He will keep an eye on our rebels and out of my hair while I repair the damage done by the civil war."

"Exile?" Jackie was stunned. "They took their dragons along? What is to stop Johnathan from returning and starting the war again?"

"Well, they don't have their mounts," admitted Richard with a harsh laugh. "Right now, the dragons sit in my stable, riderless."

"How did you manage…? Didn't the dragons follow their riders? I always thought…."

Richard awarded Jackie a mischievous gaze. "This is usually the case," he admitted, drily, "but Niohoggr talked to the rebel dragons and explain how their riders caused so much destruction."

"But still...."

"One of my reforms is to make nomination for rider open to everyone, not just men," Richard continued. He shoved a finger at Jackie. "You proved women are equal to men, and maybe more, when it comes to the ability, and of course, you destroyed the myth female dragons would cause fighting between the males."

Jackie was confused. "I'm glad you made the change. It was long overdue, but I don't see what this has to do with the dragons?"

"I think," Richard said with a smile, "even though nomination is open to everyone, in the next few years we will be seeing many more women riders. Which means...."

Jackie smiled along with him. "Which means many more female dragons?"

"Correct." Richard snorted in delight. "Once Niohoggr told the rest of the dragons this they decided to stay here."

"What do you know about that," Jackie exclaimed in surprise. She glanced at the rest of the riders. "Your men have no objections to women dragonriders?"

Richard checked behind him at the men milling around. They cluster together, watching him and Jackie while making low comments to their fellow riders. "Actually, they were more than willing to welcome females into our ranks," he said. "After meeting you everyone is hoping they'll meet a Jackie."

"Richard!"

His tone turned serious. "It is true. A man appreciates a woman that understands his work and sympathizes with what he goes through. Who better to do this than a female dragonrider?"

"Your work is well underway. I knew you'd do fine," Jackie said in admiration. "You have started on everything you wished to do."

He gazed into her eyes. "Almost. I still need one more thing."

Jackie scratched her cheek and thought. *What else could he possibly need? He's got everything he asked for and more.* "I don't know what...?"

"I told you, a man desires an understanding woman. I don't want to wait until another Jackie flies along." His voice grew so low Jackie strained to hear him. She leaned forward, staring into his face, her mind fusing with his. "I will need someone at my side that is brave and wise also to help me rule, and you, more than anyone else, sees through all things. Where I falter, you run. I have traveled here to ask you to marry me."

Jackie thought about this over and again on those lonely days after she'd returned to the fief. She admired Richard, her mind returning to him every waking moment as she recalled their adventures together. He wasn't bossy the way Victor was. He wouldn't try to belittle everything she said and did. He allowed her to spread her wings and soar like a dragon, even encouraged her. On occasion, he made her laugh. But did she want to spend the rest of her life with him? She gazed back at Richard and realized this was all she'd imagined her life to be. This was the person she wanted to do all these things with.

"I..."

A blast of fire swept through the sky and the beating of wings echoed across the lawn as Belinda swept in from the mine. She immediately waddled to Niohoggr and entwined her neck with his. *"You should have told me we had company coming,"* the thought drifted to Jackie. *"Why am I the last to be told these things?"*

She giggled. "I didn't know myself," she replied taking Richard's hands in hers, "but they're company no longer." She stared up at Richard. "I do."

Richard embraced her, crushing her body to his as if he'd never let her go. She returned his embrace fiercely as their lips met.

Somewhere in the background Jackie heard the rest of the dragonriders cheering, dragons roared and flames sprouted to the sky, the loudest and brightest those from Belinda and Niohoggr. Jackie broke away from Richard, blushing, as she pushed her hair back in place.

"Uh—hum."

Victor stood behind her and Richard, beaming foolishly, while Victoria and Thomas nervously shuffled their feet next to him. "Your Majesty," he began, "I see there is need of celebration."

A mischievous smirk lit Jackie's face and she drew Richard's head down and whispered in his ear. He beamed back, nodded, and released her. "You are Victor," he boomed, striding forward with his arm outstretched, "Jackie's brother-in-law. She has told me all about you."

Victor puffed out his chest and took Richard's hand, pumping it as if it were the handle of a water pump. "Yes—yes I am. Since her parents passed away I have raised her as if she were my own daughter."

Richard threw his arm around Victor's shoulder and started walking toward the manor house. "Jackie tells me you were a candidate to become a dragonrider?" he asked.

Victor's eyes opened wide and his walk became a swagger. "Oh, yes. I know all about the beasts." He raised his hand in a wave, all smiles and exclaimed, "Why I could even tell you a thing, I imagine," he boasted.

Richard slapped him on the back and exclaimed, "Fine. You're the man I've been searching for. I have an important position for you if you do not mind taking it. I have riderless dragons stabled, plus now Belinda and Niohoggr...."

"Anything, your Majesty," Victor replied importantly. "Training, exercising. Why, you could persuade me to become a dragonrider—your captain, sort-of-speak, if you know what I mean. Teach the young pups what being a dragonrider is all about."

"Well, I have a captain of dragonriders," Richard swung his head and shot Jackie a wink, "but you see, it is this. Those dragons eat a lot, and in their stables they drop big piles, you understand. Now here is what I will need you to do...." He bent close to Victor's ear and talked in a low tone.

Victor blanched.

Jackie couldn't stop giggling as she ran inside to fetch her things.

The End

About the Author:

Army Veteran, graduate of Florida State University, former police officer and plant manager. Native Long Islander now living in Florida was wife, two puppies and SnoopyCat. (and yes, a coffee drinker!)

Acknowledgements:

Summer Solstice, K.C. Sprayberry, and all the other wonderful people at Solstice Publishing.

Social Media Links:

Twitter – https://twitter.com/artyny59
Facebook / Author Page –
https://www.facebook.com/pages/Arthur-Butt-The-Fantasy-SyFi-Author/1528729850734703

www.ingramcontent.com/pod-product-compliance
Lightning Source LLC
Chambersburg PA
CBHW051147030726
47504CB00004B/1086